Igor was ou_____r a lilac
tree, appar_____k green
leaves whic_____ooked a
sombre figure in the black clothes which he habitually
wore, and Mila gave a little shiver as she descended the
steps of the cathedral and went towards him.

He held out his little twig to her and she took it,
puzzled, not at first recognising it, despite the spicy
fragrance of the crushed leaves, until he said in English,
'*Here's rosemary . . .*'

'*That's for remembrance*,' she continued the
quotation automatically. '*Pray, love . . .*' and broke
off suddenly.

Igor waited a moment, and she was conscious that he
was watching her in his heavy-lidded, inscrutable
fashion, and her colour rose. Then he completed the
sentence. '*Remember.*'

Dinah Dean was born in Northamptonshire, but she has lived for most of her life in the Home Counties. She was a teacher until 1979, when she decided to give more time to her writing, and since then has fitted it in 'around local history studies, reading and conversation, well-seasoned with trips abroad, preferably to Scandinavia and Russia.' She lives at Waltham Abbey in Essex, and finds it a very stimulating place for a novelist.

*The River of Time* is Dinah Dean's sixth Masquerade Historical Romance set in Russia and features some of the characters from her earlier books.

She has also written two Masquerade Historical Romances under the pen-name Marjorie May.

# THE RIVER OF TIME

## OF TIME

### DINAH DEAN

**MILLS & BOON LIMITED**
15–16 BROOK'S MEWS
LONDON W1A 1DR

*First published in Great Britain 1985
by Mills & Boon Limited*

© Dinah Dean 1985

*Australian copyright 1985
Philippine copyright 1985*

ISBN 0 263 10814 7

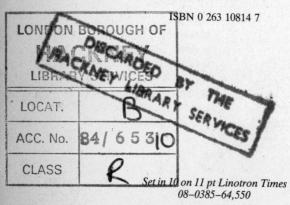

*Set in 10 on 11 pt Linotron Times*
08–0385–64,550

*Photoset by Rowland Phototypesetting Ltd
Bury St Edmunds, Suffolk
Made and printed in Great Britain by
Richard Clay (The Chaucer Press) Ltd
Bungay, Suffolk*

Note for readers who would like to follow Mila's journey on a map.

*Since the Revolution in 1917, many towns and cities in Russia have changed their names:*

| | | |
|---|---|---|
| St Petersburg | is now | Leningrad |
| Tver | is now | Kalinin |
| Ekaterinoslav | is now | Dnepropetrovsk |
| Alexandrovsk | is now | Zaporozhye |

*Similarly, some street names are different:*

*In Leningrad*

| | | |
|---|---|---|
| The Haymarket | is now | Peace Square |
| Horse Guards Boulevard | is now | Profsoyuzov Boulevard |
| Gorokhovaya | is now | Dzerzhinsky Street |

*In Moscow*

| | | |
|---|---|---|
| Tverskaya | is now | Gorky Street |
| Varvarka | is now | Razin Street |
| Prechistensky | is now | Gogolevsky Boulevard |
| Sparrow Hills | is now | Lenin Hills |
| Vozdizhenka Street | is now | Kalinin Prospect |
| Bolshaya Dmitrövka | is now | Pushkin Street |

*For Pat and Ron*

### Note

Some readers may find that the Russian system of naming people takes a bit of getting used to. The principle is that a person's name has three components: the name given at baptism, the father's name and the surname. The two last, furthermore, are modified to show whether the child is male or female. Thus, in this story, the son and daughter of Mikhail Kalinsky are Boris Mikhailovich Kalinsky and Olga Mikhailovna Kalinskaya. In conversation, people are often addressed by their first two names. This applies even to the Tsar, in this case Alexander Pavlovich—Alexander (I), son of Paul.

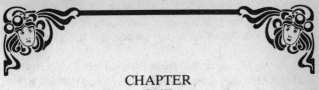

# CHAPTER
# ONE

THE SPRING sun shone on the fashionable centre of St Petersburg, sparkling on the rivers and canals, burnishing the gilded domes and spires and turning the pastel-tinted palaces and churches into sugar-fondant creations for a banquet of giants. That part of the city was quiet, for the Emperor Alexander was abroad, the noble owners of the fine palaces had gone to their country estates for the summer, and the greater part of the Army was exercising itself elsewhere or marching south-westwards to assist the Austrians against their Italian rebels.

In the other city, where the serfs and the barely-free lived in crowded tenements, and particularly around the Haymarket, things were different. There, the sun shone on crumbling brick and peeling plaster, on warped and rotting wood and cracked, dirty windows, and there were many narrow, foul-smelling alleys where it failed to penetrate at all.

Mila de Romarin lived on the corner of such an alley, and was thankful that the one window of her small first-floor room looked out on the wider street, which was occasionally swept, and not on the narrow passage, which stank of rotting vegetables and filthy rags. Even so, she seldom opened her window, for the basement of the building housed one of the innumerable cook-shops of the area, and the smell of rancid fat and boiled cabbage rose from it all day and half the night. In warm weather the room was uncomfortably hot and airless, but opening the window did little to lower the temperature, and whatever air came in brought the smell with it.

It brought noise, too, for these streets were paved with cobbles, not wood-blocks, and this particular street led to the market square, so iron-shod wheels and hooves pounded along it all day as an unending procession of carts passed by, carrying the essential fuel which powered the transport of the capital city of the Russian Empire. Mila sometimes wondered how many horses there were in Petersburg, and could only conclude that there must be at least twice as many as there were people.

On this particular day she was not thinking of horses, and was, for once, hardly aware of the stuffiness of her room, or of the noise which rose from the street or flowed almost unimpeded through the walls between her and her neighbours, a family of constantly crying children on one side and a man with a hacking cough on the other. She could only think of the letter.

It had come early that morning, brought by a liveried footman whose supercilious eyebrows had risen almost as high as his hairline by the time he had made his way from the small town-carriage in which he had arrived, across the crowded footway and up the narrow, creaking stairs, pursued by a shouted injunction from the *dezhurnaya* not to let the Oblomovs' thieving brats rob him as he passed their door. His voice, however, had been correctly expressionless as he enquired, 'Is this the—er—residence of the Countess de Romarin?' in what Mila privately called upper-servants' French.

'It is,' she replied, her own French excellent and almost indistinguishable from that of Paris. She had taken the letter which he proffered with a calm 'Thank you', and shut the door on him, ignoring the gloved hand which, having handed over the letter, from force of habit remained slightly extended. She had no kopeks to spare for tips, and he, for all that he was a serf, probably had more money to his name than she possessed.

For a few moments she felt the little flicker of hope which rose on each of the rare occasions when she received a letter, but the crest on the seal was not her father's, or, indeed, one that she had ever seen before . . . At least . . .

She stared at it for a second, for there was something vaguely familiar about it. It showed a mail-clad arm, rising from a conventional helm-wreath, and flourishing a sabre. Some faint elusive memory was stirred, but she could not place it, so she shrugged, broke the seal and unfolded the stiff paper.

The signature at the foot of the page caught her attention at once: *Varvara Denisovna Charodyeva*. The Christian name and patronymic were unfamiliar, but the surname—the feminine form of Charodyev—aroused a surge of feeling in her which took her by surprise.

It was all so long ago—he must have forgotten her by now—yet she remembered, and felt the same mixture of attraction and bewilderment, the same uncertainty, the same bitter regret. For a few moments she stared unseeingly at the letter, then gave herself a mental shake. It was not such an uncommon name, after all! Very likely this Varvara Charodyeva was not even related to him. She began to read.

Since then, she had gone back to it a dozen times, and almost knew the words by heart. After the usual formalities used by one lady of quality to another, it said:

I venture to address you at the suggestion of my friend Praskova Petrovna Karichneva, who tells me that you are her aunt, and may be able to help me. It is not easy to explain in a letter, so I shall call on you, if I may, at three o'clock this afternoon, and hope that you will do me the honour of receiving me.

It then ended with even greater formality than that with which it had begun, and was signed flourishingly with the name which had first caught Mila's eye.

She hardly knew what to make of it. The address at the top was the Smolny Institute, that most select academy for daughters of the Nobility, and, to judge by the very correct French and careful handwriting, the author was probably one of the pupils. The reference to Praskova Karichneva was most surprising, for she must be the daughter of Mila's brother Pyotr. It seemed quite incredible that she should have any knowledge of Mila's existence, let alone know where she lived, for she could not have been more than five or six years old when Mila's father had disowned her, since when, she had assumed, her name would never have been mentioned by the family.

Presumably, then, her brother must know her present address, for there was surely no one else who could possibly have provided Praska with it. It was heartwarming to think that perhaps her brother, of whom she had been very fond, still cared about her, although he would never go against their father's wishes, of course. Here, also, was a possible confirmation of the suspicion she had treasured for a long time; that it was Pyotr who had applied on her behalf to the War Ministry for the small pension she received ever since her husband had been killed.

A few days earlier, Mila would not have been at home at three in the afternoon, for she supplemented her pension by giving lessons in French and English to the daughters of ambitious shopkeepers. Every ambitious shopkeeper nowadays, though, had his country *dacha* and, aping his betters, sent his wife and daughters to it for the summer, where Mila's pupils forgot what she had taught them during the previous winter.

Not surprisingly, she dreaded the summer months, for she could not afford to leave the city, and, indeed, had nowhere to go. Petersburg could be very hot in July and August, and her room grew well-nigh intolerable as she sat, hour after hour, doing the fine sewing and embroidery which supplied her summer income, until her eyes ached and her fingers were sore, and she could escape for an hour or two to walk by the river or in the Summer Garden, a lonely figure in her plain black clothes.

At half-past two she folded her work and put it away, then tidied up the little room, smoothing the faded cloth which converted her narrow bed into a couch, picking up the odd ends of thread from the stained board floor, and adjusting the window-curtain to cover the dark stain where the rain came in beside the rotting frame. The faint, far-away chimes of the carillon of the Peter-Paul Fortress threaded their way across the city in a brief lull in the grinding of wheels outside, and, almost immediately, there was an emphatic knock at her door. She took one last look round the room, shifted one of her two wooden chairs a fraction, and went to answer it.

Contrary to her expectations, the figure standing in the dingy passage was not a young girl, but a lady in her middle years, dressed in a drab pelisse and bonnet of excellent cut and material, but extreme sobriety. She sailed past Mila into the room, turned, and surveyed her from head to foot through a lorgnette, nodded sharply once, and said, 'Good afternoon. Countess de Romarin.' It was a statement rather than a question.

Mila cautiously admitted to the ownership of title and name, at which the lady gave another sharp nod, and continued, 'I am here on behalf of the Directrice of the Smolny Institute, who wishes to be sure of your suitability for the post for which you are under consideration before Countess Charodyeva is permitted to see you. You are, one understands, a widow?'

'Yes.' Mila swallowed her natural resentment at the high-handed tone and contented herself with the single word, for she was much in need of a 'post' to help her through the pupil-less summer.

'Your husband was, presumably, French?'

'Yes. He escaped from France during the Revolution, and took service in the Imperial Army—the Akhtirsky Hussars. He was killed in the war against Bonaparte.'

Again a sharp nod, as if the interrogator already knew this, and then, 'You are yourself of Russian birth?'

'Yes,' she agreed briefly again, hoping that she was not to be questioned about her family, but the next question came inexorably.

'You are, one understands, estranged from your family? One is informed, you understand, by the young Countess Karichneva, who says you are her aunt.'

'Indeed. She is the daughter of my brother, Pyotr Lev'ich Karichnev.'

'One understands that you support yourself by teaching French to girls of the merchant class.'

'And English,' Mila replied a shade defiantly, for she saw nothing to be ashamed of in teaching the daughters of respectable shopkeepers; after all, her questioner presumably taught at the Smolny, and some of the pupils there were descended from ambitious and successful merchants.

'Your French is excellent.' The comment was made in a dispassionate tone, but Mila felt that it was a compliment and acknowledged it as such with a slight inclination of her head. There was a short silence, and then the lady said decisively, 'Very well. I shall send Countess Charodyeva up, and await her in the carriage. Good day.' With that, she sailed out of the room as she had entered it, and Mila had to hasten to open the door before it impeded her progress.

'I don't know your name . . .' she called after the retreating figure, but the only reply was, 'It is of no consequence', uttered on a note of finality as the unknown reached the stairs and began to descend.

Aware that at least three doors along the passage had opened sufficiently to allow her curious neighbours to peer out and listen, Mila retreated into her room, closed the door and waited, absent-mindedly contemplating her own reflection in the old discoloured cheval mirror which was so useful when she made her own clothes.

She was, as usual, wearing black, relieved by a cream lace collar that she had been given, torn, by one of her pupils, and carefully mended by herself. The frock was discreetly fashionable in the new style with the fitted sleeve and slightly belled skirt, which was easy to copy, particularly now that the waistline had at last descended to its natural position. But the stuff was cheap, and black was not becoming to her, for it made her look a little sallow and her full twenty-eight years. Perhaps she might venture on a coloured fabric next time—one which might flatter her dark hair and eyes a little more.

There was a discreet scratching at the door, and, when she opened it this time, it was to admit a lively-looking young lady of sixteen or so, with shining dark curls peeping from a fashionable flowered and feathered poke-bonnet, which framed a remarkably vivacious face with sparkling brown eyes and a peach-bloom complexion unmarred by a single blemish. The red lips parted in a smile, revealing even white teeth and a charming dimple.

'I hope it wasn't inconvenient for me to call this afternoon?' the vision asked with a wide-eyed expression of concern. 'I'm Varvara Charodyeva, but I hope you'll call me Varya!'

'Ludmilla Levovna de Romarin.' Mila unconsciously smiled in response to the girl's infectiously merry look. 'My friends call me Mila,' she continued, thinking to herself that, in fact, no one had called her that for a very long time.

'Oh, good! I thought it would be Madame de Romarin, but Mila is much more comfortable.' Varya apparently assumed herself to be a friend already. She glanced round her, but showed no sign of surprise or contempt at the shabbiness of the room, merely observing that there were two chairs, then went on, 'May I sit down and tell you all about it? Mam'selle Agathe says you'll "do" very well!' She gave a conspiratorial grin which robbed the condescending verdict of its sting and, at Mila's gesture of invitation, sat down on one of the chairs with a rustle of pale blue silk, waited a moment for her hostess to be seated, then assumed an earnest expression and began in a headlong fashion.

'It's quite a long story, but I'll be as brief as I can. My parents had a dreadful quarrel when I was quite young, and Mamma left Father, taking me with her, and we went to live on one of Mamma's own estates, as far from my father as possible.

'I ought to explain that my father is an officer in the Imperial Navy, and after—afterwards, he was out of Russia for a long time, serving in the Adaratic—no, that's not right! I mean the Adriatic—I nearly always say it wrongly!—and, of course, the Fleet couldn't come home—I expect you remember—because the Turks wouldn't let our men-of-war through the Bosphorus into the Black Sea.

'Anyway, after a few months, I was six and old enough to enter the Smolny, so I did, and Mamma entered a convent to be a nun. When she said goodbye to me, she made me promise I would never have anything to do with my father as long as she was alive.'

Varya broke off, bit her lip, and became very engrossed in smoothing her gloves for a few moments, all the life and sparkle gone from her face.

'I'm sorry,' Mila said gently, feeling she should say something, however inadequate.

'Thank you.' Varya pulled herself together sharply. 'It was not exactly a pleasant experience, to be left suddenly among strangers, knowing that one was unlikely to see either of one's parents ever again.'

'But surely someone was responsible for you?' Mila ventured.

'Oh, yes—my uncle! Father's brother. Unfortunately he's abroad at present, and I'm unable to get in touch with him, or everything would be much simpler!'

'Simpler?' Mila echoed, wondering what was coming next.

'Mamma has died, you see.' Varya's lower lip trembled a little. 'Oh, I'm not broken-hearted or anything, so pray don't be alarmed! I've not seen her or heard from her for ten years, so it was only like hearing that someone one had known long ago had—had gone. It's just that one feels very much alone, you understand. That's why I'm going to see my father. I feel I was robbed of him, and there's so much lost time to be made up.'

'Well, yes. I mean . . . I suppose your promise is terminated . . .' Mila said a little blankly, forced to speak by the expectant gaze of Varya's large brown eyes, but wondering what all this had to do with her.

'Yes, that's what my confessor says. *Madame la Directrice* has agreed that I may go, and she is arranging my papers for the journey, and I'm to see some stuffy old Admiralty-person about it tomorrow, for usually only naval and army people ever go there, you see, so it's not very easy to arrange the journey oneself.' Varya had recovered her spirits.

'No, I suppose not,' Mila replied, thinking vaguely that it shouldn't be very difficult to find a ship sailing to the naval base on Kronstadt. The island could only be thirty *versty* (1 *verst* = 1.06 km) away at the most, out in the Gulf of Finland, and surely most passenger ships called there? Why, one could see it from Peterhof!

'But I can't go alone, of course,' the girl continued. '*Madame la Directrice* says I must have a companion—a chaperon, that is—and a maid. She's quite right, I know, but the difficulty is that we don't have individual maids at the Institute, and I have no female relative to hand—no spinster aunt living conveniently in Petersburg. Indeed, I've no aunts at all, my uncle having disobligingly omitted to get himself married!'

Mila smiled at the girl's mode of expression, and was not particularly surprised when she explained, 'That's why Praska Petrovna suggested you. We thought, you see, that as you're quite . . .' She suddenly looked a little disconcerted, for she had clearly been about to say 'old' and realised, almost too late, that it was not a fortunate choice for anyone approaching thirty.

'Of sufficient age,' Mila supplied gravely, and was thanked with a twinkling smile.

'Yes,' Varya agreed. 'Of sufficient age, without being old and stuffy, or likely to be too infirm for the journey, and not having any—er—children or anything . . . I'm sorry about your being a widow. Praska Petrovna told me there was trouble with your family . . .'

Varya seemed to be a little out of her depth, so Mila rescued her by saying baldly, 'My father wished me to marry a man of his choice, but I ran off with a Hussar officer, who was foreign and therefore ineligible. My father disowned me.' It was not the whole truth, but enough to explain the position.

Discretion, interest, excitement and sympathy struggled for domination in Varya's face, and Mila learned something of the girl's character when sympathy won, and she said, 'How dreadful! Why that's quite inhuman! Didn't he relent even when you were widowed?'

'No,' Mila replied sadly. 'I wrote to tell him, but the letter was returned unopened.' She did not add that there had been a line scrawled on the cover in the hand of her father's major-domo, 'The sender is not known to the person addressed.'

'I hope my father is more reasonable,' Varya said pensively. 'I wrote to him when I heard about Mamma, and in his reply he said that he would look about for a suitable husband for me! I didn't at all like the sound of that, so that's another reason why I wish to see him. I shall certainly not let him marry me off to someone I don't even know! I shall marry for love, as you did!'

Mila gave a wry smile. 'Be careful, my dear! It's easy to be mistaken when you're young and inexperienced.'

For a few moments Varya looked at her consideringly, then her lids dropped demurely over her eyes, and she said primly, 'I shall remember, and be very careful, and not too hurried!' and she gave a little private-looking smile, which jolted Mila's memory painfully.

'You say you have an uncle?' she asked, her voice sounding strained in her own ears. 'What is his name?'

'Igor Grigorovich Charodyev,' Varya replied promptly. 'He looks after the Emperor's collections of *objets d'art* and so on. Do you know him?'

'I—I may have met him, I suppose, but it's all so long ago . . .' Mila replied evasively, conscious of a curious sensation in her throat, a dryness, as if she were afraid . . . 'You say he's abroad?'

'Yes, with the Emperor; and goodness knows when they'll be back! The last letter I had from him said that the Emperor is planning to stay in Austria until the trouble in Italy is over, but now there's trouble in Greece as well, so I suppose they'll be there for an age yet! Well, if you do know Uncle Igor, that's even better, isn't it? I mean . . . that is . . .' Varya's youth showed in her sudden loss of confidence as she reached the point where she had to ask for what she wanted. 'Will you come with me? I know it's a great deal to ask, for it's a long, trying journey, but it's very important that I go, and I'll pay you, of course.'

She named a sum which startled Mila, in a gruff, straightforward manner which robbed the difficult matter of payment of any offensiveness.

'Long and trying?' queried Mila. 'Where is your father, then?'

'At Kherson. It's near the mouth of the Dnepr, almost on the Black Sea coast,' Varya said apologetically. 'It's not far from Odessa,' as if that made it a more desirable destination. 'It's about 1,800 *versty*.' She lowered her voice, for it did sound a prodigious distance. 'But it's only about as far as from here to Vienna, and the Emperor travels there quite often. Uncle Igor has been to Vienna at least five times!'

Mila had a strong feeling that she would prefer not to hear too much about Uncle Igor, and if he was in Vienna now, she hoped he might stay there. She concentrated on the problem of this strange post she had been offered. 'There are one or two practical problems,' she said. 'If I were to go with you to Kherson, how should I return here? Do you intend to go there permanently, or on a visit? Will you wish me to stay there with you, and if so, for how long? You see, I have to think of my future, for I cannot simply go so far away and trust to luck for what will happen after!'

'No, of course not!' Varya agreed. 'I thought to go quite soon, before the weather is too hot, and stay there for the winter, at least. I don't know exactly, for it depends on what happens when I get there. Naturally, my father will undertake to send you safely back here whenever you wish to return; there are always officers travelling to and fro from here to there and back again, you see, and their families too, sometimes. It just happens that there's no officer's wife going at present, because of the trouble in Greece making people afraid there might be another war with Turkey.' There was another private little smile and the oblique look which Mila recalled went with it, but not, as she remembered, with the charming dimple which appeared when Varya smiled. 'Anyway, you may like it there, and find a handsome naval officer . . .'

Mila smiled fleetingly, but her next question must appear very casual, yet was of such importance that it took all her concentration. 'Is there no possibility that your uncle will return in the near future and undertake the journey with you?'

Varya took the question at its face value, and replied, 'No, for he won't be coming back to Russia until the Emperor gives him leave, and that won't be until Alexander Pavlovich himself returns. In any case, I'd still need you, for *Madame la Directrice*, I think, regards all men as hopelessly incompetent to look after anyone properly. Oh, if it's an escort you're worried about— that's why I have to go to the Admiralty, for they've offered to detail an officer to go with us! Please say you'll come with me!'

She turned the full force of her innocent charm on Mila, who hesitated only a moment, weighing her need of money against the inconvenience of a journey from one end of the Russian Empire to the other. It was not, however, the money which tipped the balance, but the possibility of a new life, of going away from these sordid surroundings for a while, and mingling in her own proper class of Society, if only in the capacity of a chaperon.

'Yes,' she said simply. 'I'll go with you.'

Varya sprang up, clapped her hands and cried, 'Oh, capital!' then put one hand over her mouth and made a mischievous face. 'We're not allowed to say that at the Smolny—it's vulgar!' she explained before rushing on. 'I've brought some money with me, which you'll need for clothes and things for the journey—it will be very hot in the South by the time we reach it!' She deposited a handful of gold coins on the table, and rushed on before Mila could say anything. 'And tomorrow I should be most grateful if you would come with me in the morning to see about a maid, and then in the afternoon to the Admiralty about my escort—*Madame la Directrice* says I may invite you to luncheon at the Smolny in between— and then you'll need some time for your shopping and packing, of course, but I shall tell the Admiral that he must find me someone very quickly, for I wish to leave on Monday, and it's already Wednesday . . . Will that be convenient?' with another sudden loss of confidence.

Mila looked at the eager face framed in the pretty bonnet, the wide brown eyes, the expression of mingled hope and doubt, and smiled. 'Yes, perfectly convenient!' she replied, wondering where in Petersburg she could find ready-made travelling clothes and muslin frocks to fit her.

Even that problem was solved, however, for Varya said, 'Oh, I've just remembered—there's a little shop at the back of the Gostinny Dvor—the not-so-fashionable part—where they have frocks and things ready-made. I expect you know it? No? Well, we often go there when we need something new and there isn't time to have it made. I'll take you . . . Can you come now? I'll call there on the way home and introduce you, and then I can leave you there, if that's all right?'

By no stretch of the imagination could the back of the

Gostinny Dvor be said to lie on the route from the Haymarket to the Smolny, but Mila, feeling that she had been picked up by a small whirlwind, found herself, in bonnet and shawl, climbing into the town carriage with Varya and a resigned-looking Mam'selle Agathe and being taken at a brisk trot, by way of the Horse Guards Boulevard, Gorokhovaya and Sadovaya Streets to the narrow street at the back of Rastrelli's beautiful bazaar buildings. There the whirlwind rushed her into one of the shops, introduced her to a smilingly obsequious person in elegant purple who spoke ungrammatical French with a strong Russian accent, and left her with a promise to call for her at ten the next morning.

Mila never did discover the name of the person in purple, whose French may have lacked refinement but whose stock of ready-made garments was worthy of a Parisian establishment, and all at quite reasonable prices. In no time she had produced a serviceable travelling-dress in dark grey, with a matching pelisse, trimmed discreetly with a little frogging in black braid, four muslin day frocks, and two demi-toilette evening gowns in a soft cotton which looked like silk, all in the sober colours suited to Mila's situation in life, well made, and sufficiently fashionable in style, and needing no more than a little stitching to make them fit very well. Mila asked the price with well-counterfeited casualness, and was delighted to find that it left enough of the handful of coins for her to buy nightshifts, and a stout valise from a near-by shop as well.

The person in purple, of course, offered to have the purchases delivered, but Mila had no wish for anyone from the shop to see where she lived, neither did she wish her ever-curious neighbours to see such deliveries being made, and so she said firmly that she would take them with her, and the shop's page-boy was sent to fetch her a *droshky*, in which she rode home somewhat nervously, for she had never travelled in a hired carriage before.

In the morning, Varya arrived promptly at ten, rushing up to Mila's room instead of sending the groom, and remarked in the slightly gruff voice which she used when she found what she had to say a little embarrassing, 'I expect you'll be quite glad to be away from here for a while. It can't be a very pleasant place to live in the summer?'

'Indeed no, and not at any other time, for that matter.' Mila replied. 'But one must suit one's residence to one's purse.'

'I thought my family was quite poor,' Varya confided as they went downstairs. 'At least, we were until quite recently, and then one of Mamma's uncles died and left me his estates; about the same time, Uncle Igor was able to help a gentleman out of a great difficulty while he was abroad, and the man gave him a ticket in someone's national lottery—France, I think—and it won! Of course, once he had some money—quite a lot of money, actually—he could turn it into more, because he knows about Art and things.'

'How fortunate,' Mila said, sounding a trifle stiff, for she preferred not to be reminded of Igor Charodyev; yet, at the same time, it gave her a secret pleasure to think that he had been fortunate in something.

Mam'selle Agathe was again Varya's companion. She greeted Mila with formal courtesy, but said nothing further, leaving Varya to explain that she intended to call on a family friend who would probably be able to provide her with a lady's maid.

'I haven't seen her for some time, and she's really a friend of Uncle Igor's, you understand, but she's a very kind lady. Her name is Tatyana Petrovna Kalinskaya, and she lives in the Gorokhovaya. Actually, it's her brother's house—Count Orlov. I do hope they're not out of town . . .'

Her hope, however, was in vain. When they reached Countess Kalinskaya's residence, a fine house set back from the street behind a fine wrought-iron screen, they were received by Count Orlov's major-domo, Pavel Kuzmich, who informed them apologetically that the Orlovs had gone into the country for the summer.

'Countess Kalinskaya has married again,' he added. 'She's Countess Karacheva now, and she and her husband are travelling abroad somewhere, I believe. Er— may I be of service in any way?'

He had a kind face, and must have observed that the news was a considerable blow to Varya, who explained earnestly that she urgently needed a lady's maid to accompany her on the long journey to Kherson.

'I know Countess Kal—Karacheva employs all her people. I mean, they're not serfs, so I thought perhaps she might be able to lend me someone . . . Oh, dear! Now I don't know what to do!'

Pavel Kuzmich considered for a moment, then said hesitantly, 'There is a girl . . . I think she would welcome an opportunity to travel, as she has personal reasons for wishing to leave Petersburg for a time . . .'

'What reasons?' Mam'selle Agathe's sharp voice enquired.

'A small problem of the heart,' he replied smoothly. 'Nothing to the girl's detriment, I assure you. She's clean, honest, intelligent, and of exemplary character, but a little inexperienced. Presumably, however, the young Countess will not be requiring a maid capable of dressing her *en grande tenue*?'

'Oh, my goodness, no!' Varya exclaimed. 'I'm not even Out yet! No, I just need someone to keep my things in order and sew on buttons and mend torn frills and make my hair tidy—You know! May I see the girl?'

They were in a small salon on the ground floor of the great house, the ladies seated on elegant little chairs, and Pavel standing attentively before them. He excused himself and went just outside the door, where he engaged in a murmured conversation with the footman on duty in the hall, then came back inside and said, 'I have sent for the girl. Her name is Nina.'

There was a wait of a few minutes, during which Varya and Mila looked about the room with interest, for it was charmingly furnished with satinwood chairs and tables, and silk upholstery and curtains in pale apple green to match the painted walls. Mam'selle Agathe apparently considered such behaviour vulgar, for she gazed fixedly at one point on the gleaming parquet floor, causing Pavel to look uneasily for the dirty mark which he thought was attracting her attention, and so failed to notice what her pupil was doing.

There was a discreet scratch at the door, and Pavel admitted a very pretty girl with an oval face and large dark brown eyes. She was wearing a dark red braided *sarafan*, embroidered white blouse and crown-like head-dress in the style of the Moscow region. Her carriage was worthy of a graduate of the Smolny, and she curtsied most gracefully when Pavel presented her. Mam'selle Agathe eyed her with approval, and remarked that Varya might well learn how to comport herself in a less hoydenish fashion by observing her new maid. 'If a servant-girl can carry herself so, a lady should be ashamed to find it difficult,' she said severely.

'Yes, mam'selle,' Varya replied meekly. 'I'm so glad you approve of her, for I think she'll suit me very well.' She explained the situation to Nina, starting in hesitant Russian, for, like most young ladies of her class and upbringing, she spoke and wrote in French, seldom using her native language. But Nina broke in with a charming smile and said, 'Excuse me, Countess, but I understand French,' speaking in that language with a very good accent.

'Oh, excellent!' cried Varya, and went on with her explanation more easily. Nina, it soon appeared, was pleased with the opportunity to leave Petersburg for a few months, but anxious to return afterwards, and Varya gave her the same assurance about that which she had already given Mila.

'Perhaps you and Countess de Romarin can return together,' she said. 'But we'll think about that when the time comes.'

There was a further brief discussion with Pavel about the amount of the girl's wages, for paid servants were so unusual in Russia that the three ladies had no idea of the proper rate. Pavel recommended a sum which was agreeable to both parties, and Varya told her new maid to be ready to leave early on Monday.

'That's one bridge crossed,' she said as they left the Orlov house. 'Next is luncheon.'

Mila had been dubious about lunching at the Smolny, but it proved to be less of an ordeal than she expected, for she and Varya were served in a small private room with an adequate but simple meal—the Smolny's pupils were not pampered—and she caught only fleeting glimpses of the other young ladies. *Madame la Directrice*—an elegant lady of severe aspect—appeared for a few moments to make a gracious remark or two, and departed after telling Varya not to be late for her next appointment.

'Now for the Admiralty-person!' said Varya, hurrying Mila out to the waiting carriage. 'Then all we have to do is go to Kherson!'

# CHAPTER
# TWO

THE 'ADMIRALTY-PERSON' proved to be an elderly captain who had brought up several daughters of his own and quite understood Varya's desire to see her father again after such a long separation. His co-operative attitude was almost an anticlimax after the struggle which Varya and her two companions had undergone to reach him.

To begin with, they arrived at the main door of the Admiralty to be faced by an armed sentry who stared straight through them without moving a muscle, and made no reply to Varya's request for directions until she repeated it for the third time; then he jerked his head sharply sideways a fraction of an inch, indicating the massive doorway which he was guarding, from which Mila deduced that they were meant to go inside and enquire.

'How silly!' commented Varya. 'What's the use of a man guarding a door if he's not allowed to move and stop people entering!'

The vestibule was full of naval officers and sailors, all moving about in a purposeful manner, either carrying papers or talking loudly in twos and threes. Varya selected the only person standing still, who appeared to be a porter, and asked him where they should go.

'Have you come for the launching?' he asked. 'All guests for the launching must show their cards over there.' He nodded vaguely across the hall, which was large enough to use as a parade-ground.

'No, we haven't come for the launching, whatever that is . . .' began Varya, but got no further, for the man started back with a look of amazement and exclaimed, 'You don't know what a launching is?' and proceeded to explain.

When he had finished, Varya tried again, but the man seemed to have no idea where anyone was, except those responsible for the launching (and only the vaguest knowledge of their whereabouts). Eventually Mam'selle Agathe became indignant, tapped a near-by officer on the shoulder with her parasol and demanded assistance for her pupil in tones which were intended to strike terror into the souls of the servile class, but had a lesser effect on the officer, who happened to be a rear-admiral. As he had been educated at the Naval Academy, he responded to the female version of his former tutors in the proper manner and summoned a young lieutenant to conduct the ladies to the right office.

Unfortunately the lieutenant selected was a comparative newcomer to this enormous and complicated building, and after leading them in a hopeful manner along several corridors and up or down two or three staircases, he finally had to knock at a door and ask the way. After that, things progressed more smoothly, apart from the fact that the officer had conducted his charges almost to the extreme north-eastern end of the building, whereas the room in which they were expected was at the extreme south-western end. By the time they reached the right office they were quite half an hour late for Varya's appointment, but the Captain did not seem particularly put out, and was certainly not surprised by the explanation.

'Oh, you're not the first to be lost in this warren,' he said. 'In fact, you're to be congratulated on finding me at all! Why, there are officers wandering about here who entered the building as midshipmen, and have risen to admiral without ever finding their way to the right place in all the years they've been here. Some of them have even been posted as missing, I believe!'

Mam'selle Agathe seemed to find this statement incomprehensible, but Varya and Mila both caught the twinkle in the Captain's eye and laughed appreciatively, and even the Lieutenant, who had entered the room with them, smiled in a constrained fashion.

'Ah!' exclaimed the Captain, taking a closer look at him. 'Korovelsky, isn't it? Don't go away . . . You're concerned in this matter. Could you find your way to Kherson, do you think?'

'Yes, sir,' the Lieutenant replied a trifle tersely. 'I'm under orders to do so.'

'Capital! I thought you were!' The Captain rubbed his hands together, and bustled about finding chairs for everyone. Once they were seated, he went on. 'Now, Countess Charodyeva, I understand that you wish to join your father in Kherson, and to take these ladies with you as your companions.'

'Indeed not!' exclaimed Mam'selle Agathe in great indignation. 'The young lady wishes to go, and Countess de Romarin has undertaken to chaperon her. The other member of the party will be the lady's maid.' She seemed quite ruffled at the thought of being included in the arrangements.

'Ah, yes, I see! You have passports to leave Petersburg and travel to Kherson?' the Captain asked Varya.

She produced the papers, which they had collected from the offices of the Governor of St Petersburg across the road on their way to the Admiralty, and the Captain studied them carefully.

'Oh!' he said, stopping and re-reading one section. 'But this says "by way of Moscow"! The usual route is by way of Kiev.'

'I wish to stop in Moscow for a few days,' Varya said firmly.

The Captain looked at Lieutenant Korovelsky, who said, 'I intend to take the Kiev route.' He sounded a little truculent, possibly because his earlier loss of face made him feel the necessity to re-establish himself as the dominant member of the party if he was to travel with the witnesses of his humiliation.

Varya turned the full force of her charming smile on him. 'My mother died recently in Moscow, and I wish to visit her grave on my way to Kherson, so you see how imperative it is that we go by way of Moscow.'

Lieutenant Korovelsky, to Mila's surprise, was apparently not affected by the girl's charm, for he replied obliquely. 'Then perhaps it would be more convenient for the young lady to travel with another escort.'

'Possibly.' The Captain seemed to consider the suggestion, but continued, 'Unfortunately there does not happen to be another suitable officer going to Kherson at present. There are, of course, other officers,' he added, seeing Korovelsky's look of surprise. 'But the key word is "suitable". One could not send Captain Charodyev's daughter on a long and difficult journey with just anyone, you understand! There will, of course, be certain compensations arising from the undertaking. One could hardly expect ladies to travel by *kibitka*, so you will be provided with a coach from the Imperial coach-house, and a *jäger* to go ahead and make all the arrangements.'

Varya simply looked impressed by these marks of favour, but Mila glanced at Lieutenant Korovelsky with some amusement, knowing that the 'compensations' would certainly appeal to him. The usual mode of travel for an officer on official government business of any sort was in a *kibitka*, a little unsprung cart with two backless, uncushioned benches, one for the driver and one for the passenger, with no form of shelter from the weather or the dust of the roads. The thought of travelling 1,800 *versty* in that bone-shaking, back-breaking fashion was enough to daunt the stoutest heart, and the offer of a coach instead was surely sufficient compensation for being saddled with three females, and a different route for the journey?

The Lieutenant hesitated, and then said, 'If Countess Charodyeva intends staying a few days in Moscow, it will take considerably longer than usual to make the journey, for I suppose the ladies will not wish to go as fast as an officer would normally be expected to travel.'

'Your orders will be amended to take account of that,' the Captain replied smoothly. 'It is more important that you deliver your charges safely at their destination than that you report for duty at the earliest possible date. It occurs to me,' he went on, changing the subject as if he assumed that the question of the Lieutenant escorting the ladies was now settled, 'that I have not yet made you known to the Countess and her companion. Ladies, may I present Lieutenant Count Maxim Efremovich Korovelsky . . .' and, after another glance at the passports, 'Countess Varvara Denisovna Charodyeva and Countess Ludmilla Levovna de Romarin.' He looked at Mam'selle Agathe but, either because she was not directly involved or because he did not know her name, did not include her in the introductions, and she seemed content that it should be so.

Lieutenant Korovelsky perforce stood up and made his bow. He was a well-built, handsome young man in his mid-twenties, with light brown hair and a weather-beaten face which seemed to redden even more when he was subjected to any emotion, and severe-looking grey eyes. Faced with a *fait accompli*, he apparently accepted the situation with good grace, and said, 'I am honoured to be of service to the daughter of a man whose reputation has earned my respect and admiration. I had hoped to set off on Monday.'

'At what hour?' Varya enquired briskly, having acknowledged the compliment to her father with a very regal inclination of the head. 'Would nine o'clock be convenient, or would you prefer to go earlier?'

'Nine o'clock would be perfectly in order,' the Lieutenant replied, sounding disconcerted—he had clearly not expected Varya to be ready by Monday, let alone at an hour when most young ladies were hardly out of bed.

The Captain, meanwhile, had made the necessary amendments to the Lieutenant's orders and passes, and signed those of Varya, Mila and the maid. When he handed them out, Lieutenant Korovelsky made one last effort and said, 'The road's better via Kiev.'

'Surely not!' Varya replied. 'The road from here to Moscow is the best in Russia!'

'That's not saying a great deal!' the Lieutenant riposted. 'And beyond Moscow . . . !' He grimaced expressively.

'I thought we might take ship down the Dnepr from Alexandrovsk.' Varya sounded as if she were offering him a tempting treat, but it failed to lighten the severity of his expression. He was probably thinking of the 800-odd *versty* between Moscow and Alexandrovsk.

By the time the coach from the Imperial coach-house— an elderly vehicle, but in good repair—had made the tour of the city to collect its passengers and their baggage and had reached the Moscow Gate to begin its journey, nine o'clock was, in fact, well past, and it was nearer eleven, but, under the circumstances, this was probably earlier than Maxim Korovelsky had expected. He sat in one of the forward seats, gloomily looking out of the window at where they had come from, with Nina, properly self-effacing, occupying as small a space as possible in the other corner, so that Mila wondered whimsically if the maid would eventually disappear into the worn leather upholstery.

Mila herself sat opposite the girl, with Varya beside her, constantly pressing close to the window to see what they were coming to, rather than what they were actually passing. This was, perhaps, understandable as the passing scene was remarkably monotonous.

For as much as two hours at a time, apparently unending forest—pine, birch and rowan—hemmed in the straight, broad highway, and even the other traffic was a repetitive succession of carts, coaches, *kibitkas* and small herds of cattle on their way to market. The occasional wrought-iron bridge or road surveyor's house was a welcome relief, and the widely separated villages a positive source of near-excitement. These were, of course, all much alike, with a row of wooden cabins lining the highway on either side behind a broad grassy verge on which a selection of goats, cows, chickens, ducks, geese, donkeys and an occasional horse for the most part ignored the passing traffic. Each cabin had carved gable-ends of more or less elaboration, and stood within an intensively cultivated vegetable-patch, but most of them looked dirty and dilapidated. Usually the only building of any note was the village church, its brightly coloured or gilded domes rising above its sordid surroundings towards an almost cloudless sky.

The coach was drawn by a team of four horses, small animals by western standards, but fast-moving and not easily tired. Lieutenant Korovelsky's valet sat on the box with the driver, and the second driver shared the groom's perch at the back. The vehicle, being large, old-fashioned and built for very long journeys, had a sufficiently large basket to take the small trunks and valises of the travellers, so that there was no need for a *britska* to follow with the baggage.

At regular intervals they stopped at a post-house to change horses, the *jäger* having ridden ahead to bespeak the new team. He waited only long enough to see that his charges had arrived and were served immediately with any refreshment they desired, and then rode off on the next stage. At the end of each day he awaited them at the inn which he had selected for their dinner and overnight rest.

On the second day of the journey, between Novgorod and Valdai, the coach developed an irritating habit of shedding parts of itself—once a bolt, then the linch-pin of one wheel, then a longitudinal strip of the iron tyre of another wheel. As a final flourish, the back axle broke. The driver, however, did not seem to find this particularly unusual or distressing, and simply stopped the vehicle to find and refasten the errant articles on the first two occasions. The section of iron tyre he could not replace, so the coach went with a slightly uneven gait for a time, but this was remedied when the axle broke, for it chose to do so within sight of a village which owned both a carpenter and a wheelwright and repairs could be effected quite speedily while the passengers strolled about to visit the church, and then took tea at the local inn.

Until this enforced delay, the atmosphere in the coach had been one of armed neutrality, for whatever Varya or the Lieutenant said, the other seemed bound to disagree—in the most courteous terms, of course. The series of accidents, however, seemed to assist the Lieutenant to become a little more resigned to his fate, and Mila assumed that it was because neither of the ladies had screamed or indulged in hysterics, even when they were severely jolted about by the near-overturning of the vehicle on the last occasion. In fact, even Nina did

little more than gasp with alarm as she was suddenly
flung from her seat to land half on the floor and half on
Mila's lap, and Varya merely said, 'How provoking!'
which was, in the circumstances, an entirely reasonable
remark. Whether this unexpectedly stoic behaviour
allayed some of the Lieutenant's misgivings, or whether
a sudden determined effort by Varya to charm him into
submission over tea at the inn had, to some extent, its
desired effect, was not entirely clear to Mila, who had
tried to remain on good terms with both parties, but
somehow, by the time the coachman was ready to
continue the journey, they were addressing one another
as Varya Denisovna and Maxim Efremovich in a more
amiable and less formal fashion than before.

Perhaps because Mila had been for so long disre-
garded by those few of her own class with whom she had
come into contact, she failed to notice that Maxim had
been glancing in her direction with increasing frequency
during the journey, and she assumed that his attentive-
ness to her during the enforced wait was due to his good
manners, for he enquired at least four times whether she
felt quite well after the shock, and it did not occur to her
that his more amenable attitude towards her charge
might be intended to earn her approval.

The new and, to Mila, welcome détente almost came
to an untimely end in Torzhok, where Varya insisted on
stopping for 'an hour or so' to buy gloves, boots and
slippers from the famous leather-workers of the town,
despite Maxim's terse remark that they were still about
60 *versty* from Tver, where the *jäger* had recommended
they stay for dinner and lodging. The result of the
comment was that Varya took nearer three hours than
two to make her purchases, and they arrived at Tver very
late indeed, the *jäger* having been sufficiently worried
about them to ride back from their next post-house to
see what had become of them.

Even on the Petersburg to Moscow road, which was kept in good condition, the combination of distance and the speed of travel necessary to cover it in a reasonable time was normally expected to lead to six or seven stops for repairs to the coach, but the travellers found that their vehicle, despite its age, was of stouter construction than most, and the little crop of accidents on their second day sufficed for the time being. A delicate harmony prevailed once more within the coach as they dozed, read, or looked out of the windows at the landscape, which was now more open, the trees occurring in bands or clumps rather than solid walls, although villages and signs of cultivation were still widely separated.

About the middle of their fifth afternoon on the road, Varya said, 'That must be Moscow, I suppose, but there seems to be nothing but churches!'

A bend in the road brought the distant city into view for all four occupants, and it did seem as if a forest of domes and towers was rising on the horizon above a low ridge and the haze of dust. But as the road straightened again to point itself more directly at the city, Maxim said prosaically, 'It's only because you can't yet see the lower buildings.'

Varya's expressive face said quite clearly, 'I know that, stupid man!' but she closed her lips firmly and only opened them again to smile at Nina, who was looking very tired, her eyes huge in her wan face, and say encouragingly, 'It won't be much longer now, and then we can all have a good rest for a week or so before we go on.' Maxim reacted to 'a week or so' by opening his mouth to protest, but shut it again, frowning but saying nothing.

They caught a few more glimpses of the fairy-tale towers, their gilded domes glittering in the sun, and then they passed the ugly red brick Petrovsky Palace, where the Emperor customarily stayed before making his state entries into the old capital. After that, the city lost its air of ethereal exoticism as they jolted over ill-paved streets in the dismal suburbs.

At this point, Varya, who had blithely informed the *jäger* that they would all be staying in her family's house in the city, began to show signs of misgivings, and said in her gruff embarrassed manner, 'I say—I do hope you're not both expecting a grand palace! Our house is very old, you know, and not at all modern—my great-grandfather made everyone promise that they'd never alter it because it's a relic of Old Russia.'

'Was it not burned in 1812, then?' Maxim sounded surprised, perhaps not having realised that not all of the inner city had been destroyed in that great fire.

'No, only scorched, although many of the buildings across the street were destroyed. In fact, it's survived *all* the fires since the Time of Troubles, and it's a real old boyar house!'

'I didn't know any still existed!' exclaimed Maxim, looking really interested. 'Whereabouts is it?'

'In the Varvarka. That's why I was christened Varvara,' the girl replied. 'There are just two of them left—ours and the Romanovs', crowded in between three or four churches and an old warehouse. It's the little street that runs between Red Square and the Kitaigorod Wall,' she added for the non-Muscovite's benefit. 'Of course, it's very small and poky, so if any of you don't feel that they would like it, and would rather go to a hotel, you mustn't be afraid to say so—I won't be offended!'

She looked at her companions with such wide-eyed appeal that Mila, who had not wished to admit that she knew the house, resolved to be content with whatever accommodation she was offered in it, only afterwards reflecting that it was hardly proper for her, as Varya's

employee, to do otherwise. Even Maxim was moved to
remark that anything seemed large and luxurious after a
junior officer's cabin in a man-of-war.

As they passed through the line of the demolished city
wall at the Tver Gate, Varya said to Nina, 'You're a
Muscovite, are you not? Is your family here?'

To Mila, Nina's reaction seemed a little odd. She
started, flushed, seemed to shrink even further into her
corner, and said in her soft, pleasant voice, 'I—I think
there is no one here now.' She sounded very nervous,
but since she had hardly spoken on the journey unless
someone had first addressed her, Mila assumed that she
was shy, and perhaps a little apprehensive about her new
duties. She did notice that, as they drove along the
Tverskaya, instead of looking out of the window, the girl
turned her face away from it and even put her hand
against her cheek, as if to shade her eyes.

From the Tverskaya, their route ran directly across
Red Square, round the spectacular bulk of St Basil's and
into the Varvarka, which ran along the edge of a terrace
rising above the wide bank of the Moskva River. That
part of the street which had survived the 1812 fire had
gone down in the world in the long years since it had
been a fashionable place for boyar town-houses, and one
side was now occupied by the smaller of Moscow's two
bazaars, and a number of poor shops and taverns, at
which Varya sighed and said, 'Oh, dear!'

The coach drew up about half-way along the street
before a small two-storey house, which appeared to be
built out over the edge of the terrace, as did most of the
other buildings on the same side. The travellers dismounted and stood on the narrow footway, the ladies
discreetly shaking out their crumpled skirts, while
Maxim looked at the little house with a puzzled expression, obviously wondering how three people, with a
maid, a valet, a *jäger*, two coachmen and a groom could

possibly fit into a building which hardly looked big enough to house the serfs who worked in it.

'Do go in,' said Varya. 'I must just tell the driver how to get to our coach-house.'

An elderly footman had already opened the door and was bowing expectantly, so Mila led the way inside. As the vestibule was very small and half-full of a token representation of house-serfs waiting to greet Varya, she turned without thinking to her right and went down the stairs, for the greater part of the house was built against the side of the terrace, with all the main floors below the street and the garden and stables at the bottom.

'Now, how did you know that?' Maxim asked, following Mila down the stairs. But before she could think of an answer other than the truth, which she would rather not have admitted, Varya came running down after them in a manner which would not have met with approval at the Smolny, and said, 'Shall I go in front and show you the way? It's all a little dark and peculiar until you know the house.'

She slipped past them and led the way down to the bottom of the third flight, then opened a door into a room which, although small by Petersburg standards, was pleasantly furnished as a parlour, with long windows opening on to the garden.

The man who was sitting by the window looked up as they entered, put down his book on the occasional table at his elbow and rose unhurriedly to his feet, saying in a mildly ironic tone—all too evocatively familiar to Mila, 'Well, Varya! Did you have an enjoyable journey?'

'Uncle Igor!' exclaimed Varya, impulsively dropping her bonnet and reticule and running to embrace him with enthusiasm, which he bore with an air of mild resignation. 'What on earth are you doing here? I thought you were in Austria! Why aren't you with the

Emperor? How glad I am to see you again! Do you know about poor Mamma?'

'I was,' Igor Charodyev replied succinctly. 'Again, I was, but he's come home—arrived in Petersburg two days ago, I should think. He gave me leave for three months, and yes, I know. I heard while we were still abroad, and I've come here to sort out her affairs. I assume that you didn't receive my letter before you left Petersburg. Now, will you not make me known to your companions?'

Maxim had entered the room and stood just inside the door, patiently waiting for someone to take notice of him, but Mila, the moment she heard Igor's voice, had stepped back and was trembling with shock outside where, as the windows were overshadowed by a large tree and the hall was quite dim, she could hardly be seen in her dark clothes.

'Oh, I'm so sorry!' Varya exclaimed, turning to her guests. 'This is my uncle, Count Igor Grigorovich Charodyev—Lieutenant Count Maxim Efremovich Korovelsky.'

'I take it that the Admiralty dragooned you, so to speak, into escorting my niece to Kherson,' Igor said sympathetically, stepping forward to shake Maxim's hand. 'Pray accept my condolences! Varya, surely *Madame la Directrice* hasn't allowed you to travel unchaperoned?'

'Of course not! Mila, where are you?' Varya exclaimed. 'Do come and meet my uncle.' She peered past Maxim into the dark hall to see what had become of her chaperon.

Mila, feeling as if she was about to face a firing-squad, slowly entered the room and came face to face with Igor, who had moved forward to meet her.

He had not changed very much. In fact, he seemed just as she remembered him—a slimly-built man of a little above average height, who looked taller because he held himself well, with a lean face and a long, thin-lipped mouth, rather apt to twist in an ironic little smile. She tried to avoid his eyes, for she had always found their dark watchfulness unnerving. She noticed that there was a thread or two of silver in his dark hair, which was brushed smooth in spite of a natural inclination to curl, and then she was plunged into further confusion by hearing him say,

'Ludmilla Levovna and I are already acquainted.'

'Are you?' exclaimed Varya. 'Why, Mila! You didn't say that you knew Uncle Igor!'

'I—I wasn't sure if—if he was the Count Charodyev I—I once knew,' Mila stammered lamely, thinking that the statement sounded quite ridiculous.

Igor took her reluctantly extended hand, raised it to his lips and kissed it in a fashion which was rather too long and leisurely for propriety, keeping his eyes on her face meanwhile, but she was too embarrassed by the unexpected encounter to meet his gaze, and looked anywhere but at him, her heart fluttering uncomfortably and appearing to rise into her throat in a suffocating manner. He then continued to hold her hand until she drew it out of his grasp rather sharply, remembering that he had often done that in the past, and then clenched it on the handle of her reticule.

'I had thought you settled in France these past seven years,' he said smoothly, providing cover for her confusion without removing attention from her, which, she thought a trifle bitterly, was typical of his ever-ambivalent attitude towards her in the past.

'I have never been to France,' she replied baldly.

'Did—er—your husband decide to settle in Russia after the Bourbon Restoration, then?' There was a tiny nuance in the way he said 'your husband' which would have been unnoticeable to Varya and Maxim.

'Étienne was killed at Dresden,' she said, keeping to plain statements.

'Dresden? The battle . . . ? In '13?' For once, Igor's air of unruffled calm deserted him. 'I didn't know!' The last words were spoken in a quiet but agitated manner, as if to himself, and his face, usually so unreadable, showed signs of shock. 'I had no idea . . . ! Eight years . . . !' His voice had sunk to a whisper by now, and only Mila heard the last phrases, but Maxim, sensing than an awkward situation had arisen, took command, and said in a reasonable manner,

'Well, there were so many killed . . . I remember, the casualty lists seemed interminable, and I know I missed seeing the names of men I knew. I'm sure Mila Levovna won't hold it against anyone that he didn't happen to notice—er—Count de Romarin's.'

He was obviously a little put off his stride by not knowing the rank of Mila's husband, but she was grateful to him for the intervention, and Varya, who was not imperceptive, seized her chance and said, 'I'm sure you must both wish to change your clothes after such a journey. Shall we go to our rooms?'

Without waiting for a reply she went out of the door, calling for Grisha Semyonovich, who was apparently the major-domo, as that elderly, benign-looking person arrived and conducted the travellers back up the stairs to their rooms, which, he assured them, were quite ready for them.

Mila's bedroom was small and sombre, with only one small window, and that shrouded with heavy brocade curtains. The walls appeared to be covered with embossed leather, and the furniture was heavy, dark and crudely made. Varya, who had come into the room with her, bit her lip and looked anxious.

'I'm sorry,' she said. 'I'd forgotten how dark and poky everything is. I've not been here since I was little, and it seemed bigger then. This truly is the best room, I'm afraid.'

'It's very interesting,' Mila replied, quite truthfully. 'Now we're all westernised, we forget how our ancestors lived! It's quite all right, my dear, so don't worry. I shall be perfectly comfortable here.'

Varya hesitated for a moment, and then said in her gruff voice, 'Are you very miffed about running into Uncle Igor? I'd no idea he'd be here, honestly.'

'Of course not. Why should I be—put out?' Mila remembered that she should make some attempt to correct the girl's use of colloquialisms. 'I was just surprised to find that he's—someone I once knew, that's all.' It sounded hollow in her ears, but Varya appeared satisfied and went off to her own room.

This was next door, with a narrow slip between which had probably been a powder-closet in the previous century, but what it might have been before that was uncertain. It had a door into each bedroom, but none to the passage outside, and no window. At present it was simply furnished and provided a bedroom for Nina, who scurried to and fro unpacking both Varya's and Mila's clothes, shaking out their frocks and gowns and tidying away the rest of their things. Then she went away in search of a flat-iron so that she could smooth muslin frocks for each of the ladies to wear for dinner.

Mila had, of course, brought her small icon with her, and, before she took off her dusty travelling-dress and washed herself, she unwrapped it and set it on the shelf provided for it in the corner. Then she stood before it to offer a silent, confused and desperate prayer for help in getting through the time she must spend in the company of Igor Charodyev, adding a practical plea that Varya might decide to spend only the shortest time in Moscow before continuing the journey.

Even as she was praying, however, she was conscious

of a breathless sense of anticipation, which was far from unpleasurable, at the thought that she would be seeing him again in a few minutes, and that he had recognised and remembered her. When she sat down to consider this surprising realisation, she discovered that, masked by the shock of meeting him so unexpectedly, there had been a sudden little spasm of joy somewhere deep inside her. She could only suppose that it had been due to his willingness to acknowledge their former acquaintance. After her family's total rejection of her, she had hardly expected that Igor, of all people, would not take the same attitude. After all, he had good enough reason . . .

Her thoughts were interrupted by the return of Nina with a freshly-ironed muslin frock and a message that dinner would be served in twenty minutes. The girl looked anxious on seeing that she had not even started to wash or change her clothes, so Mila, guessing the reason, said kindly, 'It was good of you to unpack for me, but you are Varvara Denisovna's maid, and must concentrate your energies on her. I can quite well look after myself, thank you.' At this, Nina smiled gratefully, curtsied, and hurried away.

It was a relief to take off the clothes she had worn every day and most nights ever since they left Petersburg, to wash in the warm, scented water, and put on fresh linen and the new dark green sprig-muslin, which, for all its sober colour and plain style, was prettier than anything Mila had worn for a very long time. Then she brushed her hair until it shone, and coaxed it to fall in ringlets from the comb (which looked like tortoiseshell, but was only painted metal) with which she had caught it up on the crown of her head.

After a careful inspection in the very old and dim mirror, she decided that she looked reasonably well, bit her lips and pinched her cheeks to bring a little colour to her pale face, and set off in search of the rest of the party.

A venerable footman at the bottom of the stairs directed her back to the same parlour to which they had come on arrival, which was apparently the drawing-room of this little house, and there she entered just in time to hear Igor Grigorovich say to his niece, 'I assume you intend to go on to Kherson to visit your father? I think I might as well come with you.'

# CHAPTER
# THREE

'OH, WILL you really?' Varya was obviously delighted. 'How capital!'

'Young ladies in Society do *not* say "capital",' Igor replied blightingly, 'as your chaperon has no doubt informed you at frequent intervals already. When do you propose to leave Moscow?'

'I thought we might stay two or three weeks . . .' Varya began blithely, but her uncle interrupted before she could unfold her plans for those weeks.

'Maxim Efremovich has a ship, and possibly a war, waiting for him, and his captain will not be particularly pleased to be kept waiting while he squires you about the sights of Moscow! We shall visit the convent tomorrow, as no doubt you wish to see where your mother is buried, and I shall take you to the Armoury on the following day, purely for educational reasons and because one doesn't start a journey on a Sunday. We shall leave for Kherson the day after.'

'But Uncle Igor . . . !' Varya began to protest.

'But Uncle Igor nothing,' he replied tersely. 'Grisha Semyonovich is endeavouring to tell us that dinner is served. You may go in with Maxim Efremovich, if he can bear any more of your company.'

Varya gave her uncle a look which sparkled with amusement, for she clearly knew that there was a certain amount of humour mixed with his severity, then smiled beguilingly at Maxim, who offered his arm, and they went out together to the dining-room, which was next door.

Igor turned to Mila with a sardonic look and said quietly, 'There are only two possible combinations of partners among two men and two females, and no doubt you would have preferred the other. However . . .' He crooked his arm, and Mila had perforce to put her hand on it, suddenly conscious that her long white gloves were darned, and that her hand was not very steady, and they followed the others in silence.

Over dinner, Maxim said thoughtfully, 'I'm very glad, sir, that you've decided to accompany us, but it presents certain problems of—er—accommodation.' He paused, as if Igor intimidated him to some extent.

'There's no need to call me "sir",' Igor told him in a kindly way. 'I'm only your captain's brother, you know, and unlikely to have any influence on your fate—he never listens to anything I tell him! I shall travel in your elephantine vehicle with you and the ladies, and we'll take my somewhat smaller coach for the maids and the valets.'

'But, Uncle Igor . . .' Varya ventured, her mouth unfortunately occupied by some of the excellent roast chicken with which they had been served.

'Young ladies,' Igor observed severely, 'do not speak with their mouths full, nor presume to criticise their elders' arrangements!'

Mila said boldly, 'I think that Varya Denisovna was about to point out that her maid, Nina, is young and pretty, and it is hardly suitable for her to travel alone with two menservants.'

'Have you no maid, then?' Igor enquired.

Mila replied 'No' without explanation.

Although Igor's eyebrows rose slightly, he said only, 'In that case we'll take one of the women from here. She can chaperon Nina, and act as Mila's maid as well.'

Although she was grateful for the thought, Mila hardly managed to say 'Thank you,' for she was so surprised by the rapidity with which he had moved from the formal 'Ludmilla Levovna' to the familiar 'Mila'.

'What a good idea!' exclaimed Varya, still unsuppressed. 'But, Uncle, can you really spare the time to come with us? I mean, I'd be delighted if you did, but I'm sure Mila and Maxim Efremovich will take good care of me, and you've no need to worry about my travelling so far!'

'I've not seen my brother for several years,' Igor replied. 'I've three months' leave from the Emperor's bibelots and knick-knacks, and I feel that a breath of sea air and a few weeks in a sub-tropical climate might stave off the symptoms of advancing age a little. In any case, my dear niece, I doubt if anyone can "take good care of you" as you put it, once you have the bit between your teeth. You're a self-willed kitten.'

It was apparently tacitly accepted the next morning that Maxim would not be accompanying Varya and Igor to the convent, but Mila assumed that her own presence would be required and put on her pelisse and bonnet ready to go. When, however, she went up to the entrance vestibule (which still seemed a very odd thing to do) Igor said quietly to her, 'Don't feel obliged to come if you'd rather not. Varya hardly remembers her mother and is not likely to be overcome with emotion. No doubt you will be glad of the opportunity to visit your family while you're here.'

Mila's immediate reaction to this suggestion was to assume that it was a cruel jibe, and she turned on him in a hurt fury and said in a quiet but extremely cold voice, 'If that was meant to settle some part of your score against me, it was unworthy of you!'

'What do you mean?' Igor asked blankly.

'You must know very well that my father disowned me—don't you?' Mila had a sudden doubt, for even in the dimly-lit vestibule, she could see that he looked puzzled.

'I know he threatened to do so when . . . at the time, but I thought . . . Surely by now . . . ? My dear girl! I'm sorry! I really didn't know!'

Varya arrived at that moment, carrying a small posy of flowers and dressed in plain white, which made her look very young and vulnerable. She said soberly, 'I'm sorry to have kept you waiting, but I didn't quite know what would be the right thing to wear. Is this suitable, do you think? Nina suggested it.'

'Perfectly,' Mila replied, feeling guilty that she had not realised that the girl might need advice, and be glad of her company. To tell the truth, she had spent a sleepless night remembering a great many things she would rather have forgotten, and consequently was not thinking at all clearly this morning.

The New Convent of the Virgin was some distance away, and they went in Igor's small town carriage with the hoods down so that they could see more of the parts of the city through which they were passing.

'I was surprised to find that it was the New Maiden Convent that Mamma had entered,' said Varya pensively as they left the Varvarka and crossed Red Square. She used the more popular name of the convent, which was, in fact, very old and famous, having been 'new' in the time of the father of Ivan IV, better known as 'the Terrible'. 'I thought only members of the great families were admitted there.'

'It has tended to attract the redundant wives and sisters of Tsars and boyars, but your mother's family is of sufficient standing to ensure a place there, even if she did marry a mere Ukrainian.'

'Will you be able to come in with me?' Varya asked nervously.

'I have permission to do so,' he assured her. This seemed to comfort the girl, and she brightened up and began to take an interest in her surroundings, exclaiming in surprise as she realised that the carriage was about to pass through the Spassky Gate into the Kremlin.

'I suppose Bonaparte tried to blow all this up?' Varya gestured generally at the bizarre towers on the crimson walls, the elegant eighteenth-century façades, the colourful oriental-looking *kokoshnik* gables and the myriad gilded domes around them.

'Not personally,' replied her uncle. 'Nevertheless, his men did a great deal of damage, and, as you can see', pointing to the scaffolding which shrouded the Great Bell Tower, 'it's not all repaired even yet. Incidentally, remind me tomorrow to show you the biggest bell in the world.'

'Is it in the tower?' asked Varya, twisting round to look back and up at the campanile soaring above them.

'No, in the ground! When it was first cast, it hung in its own little belfry, but the timbers were burned in the great fire of 1701, and it fell and broke. The Empress Anna had it recast in a pit just beyond the bell-tower, but it cracked while it was still in the pit, and it's still there, waiting for someone to decide what to do with it.'

'Why did it crack?' Mila heard herself ask with the same interest in novelties which Varya was showing.

'Some idiot poured water on it while it was hot!' Igor replied. 'These are the cathedrals where the Tsars are crowned, married and buried—one for each ceremony. At least, they were buried here, but since Peter's time, they've almost all preferred to lie in Petersburg.'

Mila found the easy way in which he rattled on, answering Varya's questions in a humorous, interesting manner, quite surprising. She had expected him to be less patient with the girl, who was at that trying stage of expecting the privileges of a young lady and those of a child, both at the same time. She wondered if perhaps the cold, sardonic, rather acid-tongued man she remembered was not entirely a true portrait of him, or perhaps he had changed. After all, it was twelve years since she had last met him, and much might have happened to him in that time, as it had to herself.

Their route was taking them along the Prechistensky, past the houses of the boyar families, the old nobility. Mila was saddened to see that most of them had been burned in the 1812 fire, and the replacements mostly seemed poor and insignificant compared with the fine palaces of Petersburg. At one point she half-turned to look away across the street, but found herself compelled to glance back out of the corner of her eyes to see her old home, which looked much the same as it had on the night she had slipped away from it to meet Étienne, except that there were reddened patches of scorching on some of its creamy stone, which were inadequately covered with whitewash. The thought occurred to her that she was behaving just as Nina had done the previous day in the Tverskaya, and she wondered what it was that the servant had been reluctant to see.

'It's a miracle it survived,' Igor remarked. 'Everything else round it went, but I suppose the gardens and its stone construction saved it.'

Varya looked puzzled and was going to ask what he was talking about, but she encountered a look from him which made her keep quiet. She glanced sidelong at Mila, who also said nothing, for there was one question which she desperately wished to ask but hardly dared put it to him.

'Your parents are both quite well, I believe,' Igor observed dispassionately. 'I've not seen them since . . .

for a very long time, but I've an old aunt in the city who sends me a three-volume novel of news every few weeks, and tells me the latest tiding of everyone I ever knew, and a great many I don't know at all.'

Mila was staring at him in blank astonishment, wondering how he had known what it was that she so much wished to ask, and what had happened to make him so kind and considerate. Then she gave herself a mental shake and told herself that she was imagining that he was being more than ordinarily courteous to her because she wanted to believe that he cared something for her—which was ridiculous, for he had every reason to dislike and despise her.

The New Convent of the Virgin occupied a large area within a great loop of the Moskva River, and looked from the outside more like a fortress than a convent; indeed, it had served both purposes at the time it was built, when Muscovy was still surrounded by enemies, and likely to be attacked from either east or west. A high brick wall with watch-towers surrounded it, and there were only two gates, one on the northern side and one on the southern, each with a small church built in the wall beside it. The drums and gilded domes of several more churches showed above the wall, which, for all its height, was dwarfed by a tall campanile of red brick and white stone.

The visitors left their carriage outside, and an elderly nun asked their business through a little shutter in the great northern gate before she opened the wicket. They passed through a tunnel-like gateway to an open courtyard and a splendid view of the main church, the great sixteenth-century cathedral of Our Lady of Smolensk.

The nuns' cemetery was tucked away in a corner, and a novice was summoned by the gate-keeper to show them the way. She did not speak at all except to murmur a blessing as she left them by the grave they had come to see.

It was simply a mound of dusty soil, already sprouting grass, with a small wooden Orthodox cross set at the head of it, with Varya's mother's name in religion burned into it in small letters. Varya looked at it for a few moments, then knelt to lay her flowers carefully on the middle of the mound, and crossed herself three times. Then she stood up and said gruffly, 'Well, I hope she's found more forgiveness than she was prepared to grant to other people! You know, I don't really feel anything very much. I suppose I should, but she died for me ten years ago. I think I should now like to go and pray in one of the churches for a little while, if you don't mind.'

There were five churches to choose from, and Varya hesitated in front of the largest, the cathedral, for a moment, then made up her mind and went in, Mila and her uncle following, and all three bought candles at the door.

In the light of the hundreds of candles already burning, the interior seemed to glow with gold and soft colours. The walls were covered with age-darkened frescoes, right up to the top of the interiors of the domes. The soaring iconostasis was elaborately carved and heavily gilded, and even the font which stood before it was enamelled blue, with golden flowers and leaves writhing in Baroque profusion on its sides. Varya went to the north side, where, at the end of the iconostasis, she found an icon of the Holy Mother and Child, before which she lit and placed her candle, and stood with her head bowed to pray.

Mila and Igor lit their own candles and placed them in other stands, by some sort of tacit agreement leaving Varya alone. Mila said her own prayers before the great icon of Our Lady of Smolensk and was completely absorbed in them for some time. When she had finished, she looked about her and saw that Varya was still praying, but of Igor there was no sign at all. So, after another look at Varya to see if she seemed all right, she crossed herself once more and quietly left the building.

Igor was outside, sitting on a wooden bench under a lilac tree, apparently contemplating a little twig of dark green leaves which he was twirling between his fingers. He looked a sombre figure in the black clothes which he habitually wore, and Mila gave a little shiver as she descended the steps of the cathedral and went towards him.

'She seems to be taking it very well,' he remarked conversationally as he stood up and gestured to her to sit on the bench.

'Yes,' she replied, sitting down somewhat primly at a suitable distance from him, with her feet placed neatly together and her hands clasped on her reticule in her lap. He resumed his seat and half-turned towards her, one arm stretched along the back-rest so that his hand was actually behind her, but, as she was sitting upright and not leaning back, not touching her.

'As she says, she can hardly remember her mother. She told me that she was only six when they parted.'

'I can remember people and things from when I was six,' Igor replied. He held out his little twig to Mila, who took it, puzzled, and did not at first recognise it, despite the spicy fragrance of the crushed leaves, until he said in English, '*Here's rosemary . . .*'

'*That's for remembrance*,' she continued the quotation automatically, in the same language. '*Pray, love . . .*' and broke off suddenly.

Igor waited a moment, and she was conscious that he was watching her in his heavy-lidded, inscrutable fashion, and her colour rose. Then he completed the sentence, '"*Remember*." I thought you would still recall your Shakespeare—you were fond of quoting him, I recall.'

'Childish vanity,' she said dismissively. 'I didn't understand most of it. What would you have me re-member?' she added bitterly, twisting the twig between her fingers and breaking it.

Before he could reply, Varya came hurrying out of the cathedral and ran lightly down the steps to join them.

'Don't get up!' she said, plumping herself down by her uncle, who moved closer to Mila to make room. 'Before we leave here, I want you to answer me one question, and I won't be fobbed off with any tale of knowing when I'm older, or it not being suitable for me to know!'

'I see,' Igor replied equably. 'And what if I don't know?'

Varya looked at him, disconcerted, then said, 'Well, I'm quite sure you do, so that won't wash! What did my father do that was so dreadful and unforgiveable?'

Igor replied promptly, in a matter-of-fact tone, 'He spent one night in bed with another female.'

'Oh,' said Varya, apparently nonplussed. 'Is that all? Just *one* night?'

'Yes.'

'And for that, Mamma went into a convent, and forbade me to have anything to do with him?'

'Yes.'

'I must say that seems rather drastic!' Varya both looked and sounded perplexed. 'I mean—if he'd made a habit of it, or it was several different females . . . You're sure that's all?'

'Quite sure,' Igor confirmed. 'I thought myself, at the time, that she was being a mite unreasonable, but men see these things differently, or so they say.'

'Who say?'

'They.' He made a vague gesture. 'You know, the

great anonymous. They who are always saying things.'

'But didn't you tell her she was being silly?'

'Yes, of course, but she was not prepared to discuss the matter. She said that I, being a man, couldn't possibly understand.'

Varya leaned forward to look past him at Mila, and appealed to her. 'What do you think, Mila? You're a female, and you've been married . . . Would you have left your husband for . . . for that?'

Mila looked down at the broken rosemary and crushed it still further between her hands.

'It depends,' she said, trying to find an impersonal answer, for a personal one might betray too much to the man at her side. 'No, I shouldn't think so. I mean—if one loves someone, one can forgive a great deal . . .' She tossed the rosemary away with a sharp movement, as though it had stung her, but the evocative scent was still there on her gloves.

'Was that your question, then?' Igor enquired of Varya.

'Yes . . . But why was I never told before?'

'You didn't ask,' he replied crisply. 'How do you feel, now? Would you like to go home, or shall we drive about a little, and perhaps take luncheon in a place I know in the Sparrow Hills?'

'That would be very pleasant,' Varya said. 'And it would be proper, wouldn't it? I mean, it's not as if we've been to a funeral, and it wouldn't be a restaurant, would it?'

'Perfectly proper,' Igor said judicially. 'If your chaperon agrees, that is?' he went on, looking enquiringly at Mila.

'Oh, yes. Quite proper,' she replied, and went silently with uncle and niece as they returned to the carriage, Igor giving the gate-keeper a handful of coins 'for the poor' as they went out. Neither seemed to notice how

quiet she was, and she sat in the carriage, staring unseeingly out of the window, and wondering if it was true
that one could forgive one's husband even *that*, if one
loved him.

She was recalled to her surroundings by Varya's
interested exclamation as they turned on to the
Dorogomilov Bridge to cross the river, and Igor told her
that this was the road by which Bonaparte had entered
Moscow, and here he had waited for the boyars to arrive
to submit the city to him, not understanding that there
was no one left but the convicts and the fire-raisers.

Mila began to feel more cheerful as they turned off the
Mozhaisk road, after pausing briefly at the police post
where Igor showed an unusual-looking passport which
caused the police to wave them through with much
bowing and saluting. As they began to climb into the
wooded Sparrow Hills, they stopped for a while to look
over the city, which was looking like an illustration for a
fairytale as it glittered in the June sunshine. Then they
found the little rustic inn that Igor had mentioned,
where they were served with a remarkably good
luncheon.

During the afternoon they took a walk in the hills, and
then drove home by a circuitous route to see how the
city had changed in the areas which had been burned and
rebuilt since either of the ladies had last been in
Moscow. They stopped in the Arbat to eat ice-cream
confections in one of the most fashionable restaurants in
the city. Mila was doubtful about the propriety of this,
for ladies did not customarily enter public restaurants,
but Igor bespoke a small private room overlooking the
bustle of Vozdvizhenka Street, which was far more
crowded with people than any street in Petersburg,
although, unlike most Moscow streets, it was almost as
wide as the new capital's thoroughfares.

Later they returned to the carriage to drive back to

Red Square, skirting round the northern point of the Kremlin, because Varya wished to do some shopping in the Moscow Gostinny Dvor.

This was far more like an Oriental bazaar than its Petersburg counterpart, and most of its wares came from the south and east of the country. It was far older and dirtier, too, and Mila drew her skirts in and tried as much as possible to avoid contact with the itinerant pedlars who pushed their way through the shoppers, crying their wares in all the languages of the Empire.

Varya enjoyed herself very much, but Mila felt uncomfortably aware of Igor close beside her, apparently watching his niece bargaining for shawls and white kid gloves, which, although not quite large enough for Varya's hands, were too good a bargain to miss. (She later gave the whole dozen pairs to Mila, whom they did fit, with a gruff little speech of thanks for coming with her.) He seemed to take no notice of Mila, yet she was so acutely aware of him that her body felt his every movement, however slight, as if there were a galvanic current passing between them. She thought miserably that the journey before them would be unbearable if her nerves were to be stretched like this all the time, if she was to be constantly aware of his nearness, expectant of some biting remark, and forced to listen to Varya bickering with Maxim at the same time.

Igor watched his niece at work with that private little smile twisting his lips, but he did not interfere, or volunteer any advice or remark, until Varya, emerging triumphant with her gloves, surveyed the groom's burden and said she thought that was all.

'Have you bankrupted yourself, then?' Igor asked with apparent anxiety, and seemed relieved when his niece replied. 'Certainly not!' in self-righteous tones, adding hopefully, 'It will be time for dinner soon, will it not?'

Maxim Efremovich was already at the house when they returned, and told them over dinner that he had taken their passports, which he had commandeered at the start of their journey, to the Governor's office to be stamped with permission to continue their journey.

'I couldn't do anything about yours, sir, because I didn't have it, of course,' he said to Igor. 'But I thought it would save time if the others were done.'

'Very sensible.' Igor replied kindly. 'I have an Imperial courier's pass, which allows me to travel where I please without bothering with stamps and permits. Don't call me "sir", for goodness' sake—it makes me feel positively ancient!'

After dinner he took Maxim out to the English Club in Strastnoy Boulevard, the most exclusive club for the nobility in Moscow, and the Lieutenant was obviously pleased to be invited. The ladies remained at home, seeing to all the little feminine tasks, such as hair-washing, which seem to take so much longer for a female than for a man.

When Mila went to her room, she found a plump, smiling middle-aged woman there, who informed her a trifle apprehensively that she was to be Mila's maid and go with her to Kherson—news which Mila received with a mixture of pleasure and annoyance, for, whereas it was pleasant to have a maid again, she would have liked some say in the choice of person for the position.

Also, of course, there was the embarrassment of knowing that her wardrobe was very limited and, although the money which Varya had given her had been enough for outer garments, her body-linen and smaller things such as stockings, shoes and gloves were all well worn and carefully darned. She decided to make the reason for this clear, and said with a touch of bravado, 'I must warn you that my circumstances have not been good for some considerable time, and many of my things are not as I would wish them to be, because I have been unable to afford the services of a maid.'

The woman, whose name was Marfa, did not seem at all distressed by this news, and, in fact, was discreetly enthusiastic about the neatness of the darning, saying she wished she could do it half as well, when Mila showed her what clothes she had and how she liked them to be packed. While she was doing this, she also collected together her few pairs of gloves, all old and much mended, and decided to throw them away as she now had the dozen new pairs which Varya had given her.

When she picked up the pair she had worn that day, they still carried the scent of rosemary, and she stood for a few moments twisting them between her hands and wondering what Igor had meant. Perhaps it had only been the association—they had been talking about Varya not remembering her mother, and he had happened to be holding a sprig of rosemary, so it was natural for the quotation to spring to mind, if one happened to know it. But why had he been holding the rosemary? Where had he picked it? She could not recall seeing a rosemary bush anywhere about. Since he had been sitting under a lilac, he would more likely have been holding a spray of those flowers.

Marfa, meanwhile, who had gone to fetch water for the hair-washing, now returned with two footmen in tow with several large pitchers, and Mila temporarily forgot the problem in the pleasure of having ample warm water to do what was normally for her a cold and unpleasant chore.

The gentlemen seemed none the worse next morning for their evening's entertainment, and, after going to service in the near-by church of St Varvara (for it was Sunday), Igor took his three travelling-companions on a

visit to the Kremlin, using his privileged position in the
Emperor's service to gain entrance on a day when it was
closed to the public.

They saw the crowns of Russia, which were, of course,
quite magnificent, from the oldest, the golden Cap of
Monomakh with its sable border, by way of the curious
part-cap, part-crown of the first Romanov Tsar to the
diamond-encrusted closed crown of the Empress Anna.
To Varya's disappointment, the crowns of Catherine
the Great and Alexander were not on show, but she
was compensated by the presence of the coronation
gowns of the four Empresses—Peter the Great's wife,
Catherine I, his niece Anna, his daughter Elizaveta
and Catherine the Great, the present Emperor's
grandmother.

Maxim was more interested in the display of weapons
in the Armoury, but he left them with surprising alacrity
to assist Mila to ascend a small flight of stairs as if he felt
she might be too delicate to tackle them unaided, and
she, turning to protest politely that she could manage
very well, was surprised to see Igor watching them with a
curious, almost sneering, expression on his face, which
made her feel unaccountably near to tears.

There was far more to be seen than could comfortably
be fitted into one visit, but Varya darted about, trying to
catch at least a glimpse of everything and asking a great
many questions, which Igor answered patiently. Mila
followed behind, closely attended by Maxim, who would
keep asking if she were tired until she found herself
growing irritable, and wished profoundly that Igor
would change his mind about accompanying them to
Kherson, for she did not feel that she could bear to be for
so long in his company if she was going to be so much on
edge all the time.

She really was tired by the time they left the Kremlin,
and Varya was a trifle out of temper when her plea for a

few more days in Moscow was refused by her uncle, who was adamant that they must delay Maxim no longer.

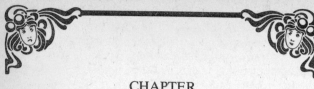

# CHAPTER
# FOUR

IT HAD always seemed extraordinary to Mila that the
weather in Moscow could change with such dramatic
suddenness. She could remember many occasions in her
childhood when she had visited some high tower or
similar viewing-point in the city and looked out over the
domes and crosses of the myriad churches to the rolling
plain and forest which stretched to the ever-hazy horizon
and seen them all basking under a cloudless sky, just as
she had seen them the day before from the Sparrow
Hills; yet, by the time she reached home, a dark mass of
cloud would have come up from the edge of the world
and in all probability it would have poured with rain
within the hour, only to clear again in another couple of
hours, the sky returning to a crystal clarity as if the idea
of rain had never occurred to it.

She was, therefore, not particularly surprised to
emerge from the Armoury to find the atmosphere decidedly sultry, with an angry-looking blackness just
showing behind the furthest visible buildings across the
river, and was only thankful that the rain seemed in no
great hurry to arrive and the clouds had advanced only
by a fractional amount by the time they reached home.

Indeed, they were moving so slowly for once that the
sky was still not wholly covered when they sat down to
dinner, and even when they rose from the table and
retired to the small drawing-room, no rain had yet
fallen, but there was an occasional flash of sheet light-

ning and a distant mutter of thunder. There was not a breath of air to stir the leaves in the garden, and, although there should have been quite three hours of daylight remaining, the candles had been lit and the glazed doors into the garden were standing wide open in the forlorn hope of dissipating the heat they generated.

'Hm!' remarked Igor, looking out at the lowering sky. 'I meant to suggest an early night, as we should start out before ten in the morning, but it's obviously pointless to attempt to sleep until the storm is over.' He gave a resigned little sigh, picked up his book from the table by the window and, retiring to a chair by a girandole, started to read.

Varya and Maxim had somehow become engaged in a slightly acrimonious conversation about chess during dinner, the Lieutenant contending that a female mind was not sufficiently logical to enable its owner to be a good chess-player, and Varya, naturally, disagreeing. She now rummaged in a cupboard and found a chess-set which lacked only one pawn, easily replaced by a silver thimble which she produced, rather surprisingly, from her reticule, and the two young people proceeded to demonstrate their opposed views by engaging in a most engrossing game.

Mila selected a volume of French verse from the small bookcase and tried to concentrate on it, but her attention kept wandering across the room to the enigmatic black-clad figure of Igor, who seemed oblivious of everything; her head ached a little, no doubt because of the impending storm. Despite her light muslin frock she felt uncomfortably hot, and the candles seemed to be raising the temperature and robbing the room of air. Presently she put down her book and slipped out into the garden.

In the eventful twelve years since she had last visited this house, she had forgotten that the garden was larger than it appeared. The part visible from the drawing-room was a small square, hemmed in between the house and the neighbouring church, one wall of which rose like an extension of the cliff of the terrace which formed the third side. There were no windows in it, only two alcoves, one of which contained a statue, and the other, which was some six feet wide, a wooden bench, on which she recalled sitting with Igor one afternoon long ago, miserably self-conscious, responding in monosyllables to his attempts at conversation. In the eerie, leaden half-light, she could barely make out the whereabouts of the site of that uncomfortable memory, but she instinctively turned away from it to her left, and rediscovered the part which she had forgotten.

The garden continued beyond the walls of the house and opened out behind it in a strip some fifteen or so feet deep across the whole width of the site, bounded by a waist-high wall topped by an ornamental railing, through which was a view over the roofs of the single-storeyed buildings on the lower ground to the river beyond. To her right she could see the towers of the river-wall of the Kremlin, and the Moskva Bridge, across which they would drive tomorrow at the start of their journey south.

'An interesting view, don't you think?' Igor's voice suddenly said behind her.

She started, and turned, and he came like a dark shadow to stand at her side, his face illuminated for a fleeting moment by a flash of lightning, which left her with an impression of a satanic mask.

'Did I startle you?' he asked. 'I'm sorry. I've acquired the habit of moving quietly because Alexander Pavlovich dislikes heavy-footed folk about him, but I didn't mean to creep up on you.'

'I was engrossed in the view,' Mila replied. 'I'd forgotten that the garden extended round here.'

'I saw you leave the room, and decided to follow you

after a discreet interval, as I wanted a word in private. It's difficult to evade my niece, I find.'

'Oh, but you've left her alone with . . .' Mila began, remembering her duties as a chaperon, and turned to go back to the house. Igor caught her arm and stopped her, however, saying, 'They're playing chess and will come to no harm—either of them. I wish to talk with you.'

Mila reluctantly submitted and waited, wondering what he had to say to her, and, after a slight pause, he went on, 'I've been out of Russia this past year, gadding about Europe with my Imperial master, and I'm amazed to find that Varya seems to have grown up in my absence. She was still a child when I last saw her, but now she seems a somewhat self-willed young lady. May I ask you to be fairly strict in your control of her?'

'I'll try,' Mila replied. 'But it's a little difficult. You see . . . if I'm too assertive, she may well simply dismiss me and leave me stranded somewhere between here and Kherson.'

'Dismiss you?' Igor sounded puzzled. 'I assumed that she was travelling with you at the request of the *Directrice* of the Smolny. I understand that it is quite usual for her to seek out a lady who is travelling to the destination of whichever of her charges is in need of a chaperon, with a request to that lady to take the pupil under her charge. Am I to understand that Varya is *employing* you?'

'Yes,' Mila replied simply. 'Apparently there were no ladies going to Kherson, particularly by way of Moscow. Varya is a friend of my niece, who suggested that she ask me to go with her for payment. As I need the money, I agreed to do so.' Her voice had taken on a defiant note during this speech despite her efforts to sound matter-of-fact, and she felt that she had said more than she intended.

The silence which followed was broken by a long

rumble of thunder, much closer now, for the storm appeared to have made up its mind to attack in earnest. As it died away, Igor said, 'Did your husband not . . . I mean, were his estates entailed, or . . . ?'

He seemed for once to be at a loss for words, and, having failed to finish two sentences in succession, did not embark on a third, but simply stood looking at Mila in the half-light.

'There were no estates,' she replied flatly. 'Neither was there any money. Étienne left nothing. Someone— my brother, I think—was able to arrange for a small pension for me, as he was killed while serving in a Russian regiment. In the winter I earn money to supplement it by teaching English and French, but the summer is difficult. I've no particular wish to go to Kherson, especially with rumours of war with the Ottomans, but Varya offered me a considerable sum—by my standards—and the promise of the means of returning to Petersburg afterwards. I'll do my best to chaperon her properly, of course, but you understand that it may not be easy.'

There was another silence, and then Igor said, 'Are your children . . . ?'

'I have none.'

Again a silence, then, 'Where have you been since . . . since you lost him? In Petersburg?' His normally, dry, ironic tone was missing, and he sounded sharply incisive.

'Yes. I have a room in one of the streets off the Haymarket.'

'The Haymarket!' he echoed incredulously, for it was one of the poorer districts of the capital. 'You've been there since '13? Eight years?'

Mila replied, 'Yes,' although in fact she had lived there for almost twelve years, but to say so would entail some embarrassing explanations. Her voice sounded strained, and he obviously noticed, even in that one word, for he said, 'No doubt you consider it to be none of my business. I was just startled to find that you've been so near all these years—just half-an-hour's stroll across the city—while ever since Bonaparte was beaten, I'd thought of you settled on a fine estate somewhere in France, rich and contented . . . Why on earth didn't you let me know what had happened? I could have helped you!'

Mila stared at him incredulously, wishing she could see his face more clearly, although she had never been able to read his expressions, but the storm was now so close that it was almost as dark as night in the garden, overshadowed as it was by high walls.

'How could I?' she whispered. 'After what I did . . .'

A vivid flash of lightning lit up the scene, followed immediately by a sharp clap of thunder overhead. Mila gave a jump, and Igor, after the most momentary of hesitations, put his arm about her shoulders and drew her close to him.

'Don't be afraid,' he said. 'You'll not be struck by a thunderbolt for it—not after all this time!' The hand on her shoulder moved in what felt almost like a caress. 'Nevertheless, we're about to be rained upon . . .' As the first heavy drops fell, he propelled her into shelter, not in the house, but into that remembered alcove in the wall below the church, just in time to avoid the heavy downpour as the heavens opened.

Mila sat down on the bench with a gasp, for she seemed to have forgotten to breathe in the dash across the garden.

'No need to be afraid,' Igor observed, looking with apparent interest at the rain. 'The storm's already passed over us. See, the lightning's further away already, and the interval between it and the thunder is longer. One thing one can say in favour of Moscow is

that storms here never last as long as they do in Petersburg. I suppose they're in a hurry to get away from the
place. Now, as I was about to say . . .'

He sat down beside Mila, who instinctively shrank
away a little, but there was a sufficient distance between
them for it to be probable that he did not notice.

'I'm not, I hope, one for bearing grudges. I can make
allowances for the fact that you were very young at the
time of your elopement; too young, probably, to understand how much you were hurting others, and your
Étienne was, as I remember, tall, well-built, excessively
handsome, full of charm, and given to declaiming sen-
timental verse in that extravagant fashion which no
doubt appeals to romantic young females. He was a
remarkably fine figure in that Hussar uniform, and his
sad history—driven from his native land in childhood
by the violence of Revolution and so forth—very
appealing!'

The sardonic note in his voice had increased to a point
where Mila felt that he was actually sneering at her, and
she turned on him with a desperate fury born of a feeling
which she hardly understood, for it was not anger at that
part of his sarcasm which was directed at Étienne,
despite her words.

'How dare you make fun of a man who is in no position
to defend himself!' she exclaimed, her voice shaking.
'Yes, he was handsome and romantic, which you were
not, and he was kind, which you were not! He listened to
me, which you never did! Whatever I tried to say to you
or my father was always brushed aside, treated as the
foolish chatter of a child! Do you wonder that I preferred
Étienne to you?'

Igor was silent for a moment, as though surprised, and
then he said quietly, 'No, Mila, I don't wonder in the
least! I thought you were a child, so I suppose I treated
you as one, and I never seemed to succeed in persuading

you to say anything to me that I might have listened to! Do you realise that you hardly ever spoke to me? The whole thing was ridiculous, of course—you were far too young for your father to be marrying you off to anyone! He should have let you have a couple of Seasons to find your feet and enjoy yourself, and no doubt you'd have fallen in and out of love a few times and ended up with a husband he would have approved. He should never have tried to bully you into marrying me.'

'Oh, you say that now!' Mila replied, almost resenting his reasonableness. 'You took a different attitude at the time!'

'I was almost as young and foolish as you!' Igor replied with irritating calm. 'I was barely twenty, and very much in love.'

'In love!' Mila repeated blankly. 'You were in love?' She felt as if she had received a physical blow, for she had never dreamed that the cool, ironic, unemotional Igor had ever had any such feelings.

'Certainly!' he replied as if he were admitting to a slight fondness for cats or dogs. 'It wasn't entirely your fortune which attracted me, Mila. You complain that I paid no attention to your wishes, but you cannot have paid much attention to mine if you failed to realise that! Perhaps I should have abandoned my usual caution and behaved more extravagantly! Do you think this might have been more effective?' And, before Mila could realise what was happening, he suddenly seized her in a crushing embrace, his mouth seeking and finding hers in a kiss which was so hard and demanding that she was quite unable to resist. It was as if her whole body had turned to a boneless jelly, and there was nothing in the world but the hungry pressure of his lips on hers, his tongue probing, his arms pressing her closer, closer, until she could hardly breathe, let alone resist him.

For a few moments, Mila was stunned, then began to

be afraid, but gradually the nature of the kiss seemed to change subtly, and it became somehow less angry and more passionate, less hard, yet more demanding, and she felt something deep within her begin to respond to it . . . ,

He let her go as abruptly as he had seized her, leaving her limp and gasping, and continued, breathing a little unevenly, but otherwise as calmly as ever, 'Perhaps if I'd done that—God knows I wanted to often enough—at least it might have made you take notice of me! However . . . it's all over and done with long ago. The River of Time flows on and our past mistakes are irretrievable, so all we can do is to try to avoid making the same ones in the future! Now Varya is looking out somewhat anxiously for us, and no doubt she and your nautical admirer are not on speaking terms again. Tomorrow, I'll have a tedious time of it if she's sulking at him, he's mooning over you and you're glaring at me, while I attempt to maintain my usual philosophical detachment from life's little discomforts! What a pity that the young are not born old and wise!'

He was, however, wrong, for the chess match appeared, by some miracle, to have come to a conclusion satisfactory to both parties, and Maxim bade the reassembled company 'Good night' in quite affable tones before taking himself off to bed. Mila and Varya were about to do the same, but Igor requested his niece to spare him five minutes, so Mila went up alone.

She found Marfa sorting out her clothes and packing some of them in the valise, but she abandoned this in order to fetch hot water while Mila undressed, and then insisted on brushing her new mistress's hair, chattering away all the time about whatever came into her head. Mila, who desperately wanted to be alone and quiet so that she could think, listened perforce.

'That Nina's an odd one,' Marfa remarked *à propos* of

nothing which had preceded the statement. 'Such a quiet, well-mannered girl! Why, you'd quite think she was a lady, not a servant, though she's free, you know—not a serf. She gets wages! Makes her a good cut above the rest of us, but she don't put on airs about it! Odd, though. You'd think a young, pretty girl like that'd want to go out and look at the shops and see the sights, but she's only stirred out of the house once, to go to church, and even then only to St Maxim's next door, not to St Varvara's with the rest of us! I offered to go with her this afternoon to visit her parents—she comes from Moscow, you know—well, you would, of course, because of her dress—but she said she didn't think any of them are here—her family, I mean. Well, that's a funny thing, isn't it, not even to go and enquire? I asked if she knows where they live—whose household they're in, I mean—and she said the Kalinskys' in the Tverskaya, but she herself doesn't belong—work for the Kalinskys, apparently.'

'No,' replied Mila absently. 'She really works for Count Orlov. Oh, but Count Orlov's sister's married name is Kalinskaya! Was, I mean, for I've heard that she's married again.'

As she was speaking, Mila remembered how Nina had turned away from the coach window as they were driving along the Tverskaya, but thought to herself that the girl might have good reasons for not wishing to contact her family. After all, she was not under suspicion of having done anything wrong.

'She was very highly recommended,' she said aloud.

'Oh, I'm sure she was, for she's as neat and conscientious as a woman twice her age!' Marfa replied wholeheartedly. 'Will there be anything else, madame?'

Mila replied gravely that there was nothing else, repressing a smile at Marfa's uncharacteristic use of the Petersburg-frenchified 'madame' instead of the customary 'Ludmilla Levovna'—no doubt under Nina's influence—and politely exchanged blessings with her before she curtsied and went out.

Now, at last, she was alone and could think! But no—there was a tap at the other door, which led through Nina's little closet to Varya's room, and Varya herself came in, swathed in an elaborate silk and lace confection of a wrapper which made Mila's eyebrows rise of their own accord.

'I know,' Varya said unrepentantly, twirling round to show it off. 'Nina says it's more suitable for an actress than a young lady, but it's so pretty!'

'*Nina* said?' Mila exclaimed.

'Yes. Oh, she's such a Godsend! You can't imagine! She knows what are the proper things to wear for every occasion, and how to make a frock look as if it came from Paris instead of the Smolny's seamstresses! Now, I won't stay above a minute, but I just had to come and tell you what Uncle Igor said!'

'Don't you think that he would have asked me to stay if he meant me to know what he said to you?' Mila protested gently.

'Oh, he said I could tell you! He thought it would come better from me than from him, you see. He says I shouldn't be employing you as a chaperon, because it puts you in a difficult situation if you have to reprimand me, which I suppose is quite true, though it hadn't occurred to me, for we get along so famously. But if Uncle Igor says so, it's bound to be right, you know!'

Mila, with an odd, sinking, hollow feeling inside her, interrupted the flow to ask, 'Am I to be dismissed, then?'

'Oh, no! Certainly not! He says you're capital—I mean, an excellent choice—but my father's going to employ you instead, so you can be as horrid to me as you wish without any embarrassment! Uncle Igor says the terms will be the same, if you're agreeable, only he'll undertake to escort you back to Petersburg himself. Is that all right?'

'Oh! Yes, of course,' Mila replied, telling herself that the suddenly different feeling inside her must be due to relief that not only was she not to lose the opportunity to earn a goodly sum of money and travel to the South, but that her return to Petersburg afterwards was now doubly assured.

'Cap—excellent!' cried Varya, giving another twirl to set her frills and lace and ribbons aflutter, and then, as she reached the door, assumed a becoming gravity to wish her chaperon a peaceful and blessed night.

And so, finally, Mila was alone and could try to sort out the jumbled thoughts and emotions inside her head and heart. She went through the conversation with Igor in the garden, trying to recall every word and shade of meaning in what he had said, but it was difficult, for the tumult of feelings aroused in her by that extraordinary kiss had left her numb with shock. She had repeatedly to touch her lips so that the tender, bruised feel of them could reassure her that she had not imagined the whole incident.

Could it really be true that Igor, the cool, aloof, ironic, detached Igor, had actually loved her? Had he really longed to kiss her, all those years ago, as he had actually done tonight? For the first time since her elopement she tried to think objectively about him, to try to find her way past the fears and prejudices of herself at sixteen and make some attempt to see the real man behind the armour . . . the armour!

With something of a shock, she realised that the word fitted! Of course—Igor at twenty had been poor, and no doubt self-conscious about it, for he was a proud man. He had been equally conscious of the contrast between himself and Étienne—that much was obvious from his bitter remarks about him. What was it he had singled out for mention? Étienne was tall, Igor only a little above average height—Étienne was handsome, Igor—well, not by any means ugly, yet with that sardonic, heavy-lidded look to his face. It was true that Étienne's French-ness had added to his attractions, whereas Igor, who was Ukrainian, belonged to a nation despised by the majority of Great Russians. No wonder he had felt at a disadvantage, and, being so young, had reacted by appearing cold and haughty!

'How I must have hurt him!' she thought. 'No wonder he's so bitter. I suppose that's what he meant by giving me the rosemary—to remind me of how I treated him. If he did but know the truth about Étienne and me, he'd have revenge enough! How could I have been such a fool, such a silly, empty-headed, selfish girl? He loved me then, and now he says it's all over and done with, too late, too late!' And she put her face in her hands and wept bitterly, as she had certainly not done on hearing of Étienne's death.

Eventually, she calmed herself and went to bed, resolving not to waste her time in vain regrets, although she could not stop herself from including in her prayers a forlorn plea for a second chance. She slept badly, but went down to breakfast next morning with a calm face and replied to Igor's 'Good morning' with an unforced smile for once.

To Igor's expressed amazement, the intending travellers had not only broken their fast and spent the customary few minutes sitting together in silent prayer with the servants, but were actually in the coach and rumbling back along the Varvarka towards Red Square as the Kremlin clock started the chorus of chimes across the city as all the clocks in Moscow struck half-past nine, fully half an hour before his most sanguine expectations. His own smaller coach followed with the maids and the valets, and two extra grooms as well as two drivers, an

addition which he seemed to think necessary, but
whether for show or for protection was not clear.

After threading its way through the jumble of old
buildings at the lower end of Red Square, the coaches
crossed the Moskva Bridge and set off down the straight
but narrow southbound Ordinka, whose name was a
reminder that it had once led to the land of the Golden
Horde of the Tartars.

As the elder of the ladies in the party, Mila had
naturally taken her place in the coach first, and was in
the right-hand corner facing forward, with Varya beside
her. She had not known whether to be pleased or sorry
that Igor had installed himself opposite, for it was likely
that the seats which they occupied at the start of the
journey would remain theirs for the whole of it, and the
prospect of travelling for days on end, facing Igor for
hour after hour, was both pleasant and daunting. There
was, however, nothing she could do about it, and at
present he seemed more interested in looking out of the
window than in anyone or anything inside the coach.

There was a shelf full of books high up under the roof
of the vehicle. She had noticed it earlier and had wondered what it was for, and now she knew—Igor must
have had the two dozen or so volumes put there. They
were held securely in place by a bar set a few inches
above the base of the shelf, so that they would not
bombard the occupants during rough patches of road.
Maxim had already taken down one of the books and
had become immersed in it. Varya was looking out of the
window and commenting at intervals on buildings which
caught her attention, saying two or three times in the
next half-hour, 'It's so unlike Petersburg!', or variations
on the same theme.

Igor bore with this patiently, but eventually said, 'The
building which we are now passing on this side is exactly
like a dozen in Petersburg. Nevertheless, Moscow is not

Petersburg, and we do not need constant reminders that the old capital does not resemble the new, or vice versa.'

'Yes, Uncle, I'm sorry,' Varya replied with such demureness that all three of her companions looked at her most suspiciously. Nevertheless she ceased to harp on the subject, and said very little until they reached the Serpukhov Gate, when she commented that it looked very odd standing there now that the city wall on either side of it had been pulled down.

'I suppose they'll pull the gates down as well, eventually,' Mila replied. 'There doesn't seem much point in having a gate in a wall which no longer exists.'

'Ah, but it comforts the police to have it,' Igor said with a barely-discernible gleam in his eyes. 'They can check passports at it, and close it when they wish to keep everyone either in or out of the city, as they do in Petersburg.'

He spoke with such gravity that both Varya and Maxim were tricked into beginning to point out the illogicality of the argument, and Maxim had even said that the two gates in Petersburg were purely decorative and uncloseable before either of them realised that he was joking. Mila was quite pleased with herself for having seen and recognised the glint of humour in his eyes, and felt that she had made progress in the difficult matter of reading his face.

Before long they passed the outer barrier, where Igor's courier's pass caused much saluting and fussy waving on of the coaches, and then they were out of the city at last, picking up speed as the horses were sprung to a canter and then a gallop, for the road was in good repair.

The *jäger* had gone on ahead to the first relay station, where he waited long enough to see the fresh horses brought out while the passengers got down and walked about to stretch their legs and were served with tea, and then he set off again, saying that he would order luncheon at Melikhovo.

One of the practical advantages of having an Imperial *jäger*, particularly now that his authority was reinforced by Igor's privileged position and considerable wealth, was that the best horses available were provided for the two coaches as a matter of course, and if only two teams were ready, Igor's party were given them, while lesser mortals, even if they had arrived first, had to wait. It was grossly unfair, but no one expected otherwise and so there were no complaints. Indeed, even the favoured travellers thought nothing about it, apart from Mila, who had long suffered from lack of privilege and had some sympathy for anxious-looking gentlemen, and exhausted mothers with tired and fractious children, who were obliged to wait, perhaps for hours, until another team was available.

'There seems to be a shortage of relays,' Igor commented after their third change, where they had left seven vehicles waiting for teams. 'Is everyone fleeing south for some reason? The French haven't invaded again, have they?'

'It's the war with Turkey,' Maxim explained. 'I mean, if there's going to be one. There must be any number of officers recalled to their ships. Army officers too, I expect,' he added in a dubious tone, which sounded as if he did not consider that the Army would have much to contribute to the hostilities.

'There won't be a war,' Igor said briefly.

'But, Uncle—haven't you heard? The poor Greeks have revolted, and there've been the most dreadful massacres and things all over the Ottoman Empire!' Varya exclaimed. 'They say the Sultan *murdered* the Patriarch of Constantinople on Easter Day, and insulted our ambassador! There's sure to be a war!'

'Yes, I did hear about it. Regrettable, but I doubt if

Alexander Pavlovich will go to war over it, especially with the Ottomans.'

'What will he do, then?' asked Maxim, looking puzzled.

'He will pursue "a wise and masterly inactivity",' Igor replied, the quotation being in English, which, although correct, sounded odd in an otherwise French sentence. 'As he usually does. If you do nothing for long enough, the problem disappears of its own accord. Haven't you noticed?'

'He didn't do nothing about Bonaparte,' Maxim protested loyally.

'Ah, but I only said "usually",' Igor riposted. 'Bonaparte was a different matter. He did, in fact, go away of his own accord in 1812, if you recall, but he had an unpleasant habit of recurring, like a decimal. Varya, you look puzzled! Do they not teach you arithmetic in that admirable Institution for the Daughters of the Nobility?'

'Not very much,' Varya replied frankly. 'I know what decimals are, though. They always go in tens.'

'Like councils in Venice,' Mila got in while Igor was apparently still thinking about it. He gave her one of his unfathomable looks and then smiled with open and genuine amusement, which made him look quite handsome, and Mila felt a small triumph that at last she had managed to meet him on his own ground.

'To be serious,' Igor turned to Maxim. 'Alexander Pavlovich has very publicly undertaken to devote his life to the preservation of peace through the Holy Alliance. Whatever he may think of the Sublime Porte, he's in a difficult position. He's twice in the past two years condemned people who rise against their legitimate rulers—in Spain and in Piedmont—so he can hardly perform a *volte-face* and support the Greeks! If he does, the rest of Europe will say that he engineered the revolt as an excuse to go to war with Turkey to take more territory

from them, and force the Sublime Porte to allow Russian
men-of-war to go through the Bosphorus.'

'Oh,' said Maxim thoughtfully. 'I hadn't realised all
that, sir. I'd only considered the religious side of it, and
the insult to the ambassador. Yes, I see what you mean.'

Igor's lean face assumed a kindly and indulgent expression for a moment, as though to parody his apparent
elder-statesman status in Maxim's estimation, and then
he lightened the conversation by wondering aloud what
they were likely to be served for luncheon.

In the event, the meal was hardly worth discussing, as
it was only *solyanka* (fish and cabbage soup), shashlik
(which Maxim said had not been lamb for a very long
time) and some slices of a very dry and tasteless cake.
Varya made a good meal (considering the circumstances), but the others only picked at the food, and
made up for it in the coach by eating some fresh bread
and goat-milk cheese which Igor had providently bought
at a shop near the inn.

Mila had hoped that they might stop for the night at
Serpukhov, but it was less than eighty *versty* from Moscow and, with so long a journey before them, it was
obviously sensible to make the stages as long as they
could bear, so they only changed horses and took a
short rest there before pressing on to Tula, nearly as far
again.

Varya was the first to remark on the smoky atmosphere as they approached the town in the dusk, although
she asked the others if they thought the place might be
on fire, not realising the real cause.

'The air smells smoky, and I can see a great cloud of
smoke and fire in the sky ahead of us!'

'Iron-foundries,' Igor replied succinctly.

'Tula is where the cannon for our ships are made,'
Maxim said in the patient tones of one explaining something to a child. 'Here are the manufactories where all

kinds of iron and steel articles are made, and this produces a great deal of smoke.'

'Oh, it's *that* Tula!' Varya replied, apparently to her uncle's remark, as she seemed to ignore Maxim's contribution.

'Is there another Tula somewhere, then?' Igor asked innocently, and his niece clenched a fist and waved it at him in an unladylike fashion, which moved Mila to tap it with one finger and shake her head.

'He's very provoking at times!' Varya offered by way of an excuse, but she clasped her hands meekly in her lap and donned her demure expression as they slowly crossed the bridge over the River Upa behind a marching column of soldiers, and entered the town.

## CHAPTER
## FIVE

THE INN which the *jäger* had selected for their night's lodging was a superior establishment which no doubt would be calling itself a hotel before long. The landlord clearly supported the local industry, for there were two very large unicorn howitzers set one on each side of the door, which sported an elaborate cast-iron porch with a large lantern suspended over it on a wrought-iron bracket, and illuminated cast-iron window-boxes on the sills of all the upstairs windows.

Inside, the travellers were welcomed by the innkeeper in person, with the *jäger* close behind him, and then ushered into a private parlour where they were invited to sit on some cast-iron chairs at a cast-iron table, all painted bright green, which would have looked more at home in a winter garden. The samovar, naturally, was locally made, for Tula was as famous for its samovars as for its cannon, but the meal, as Varya remarked in halting Russian to the innkeeper (who hovered solicitously while his distinguished guests were being served) was, to her relief, not cast-iron but very edible. He took this as a compliment and presented them with a very passable bottle of Crimean wine, 'on the house'.

After dinner, all four members of the party elected to go straight to bed, for the atmosphere of the town did not encourage anyone to take a stroll outside. Mila found that her room was comfortably furnished with a large iron bedstead and an elaborate iron toilet-table, with, suprisingly, a pottery jug and basin.

Marfa, who was waiting for her, informed her that she had inspected the bed for bugs and found no sign of any, and had bounced on it and thought it quite good, but it was impossible to open the window unless she wished everything to be covered with smuts.

'Not that you'd want to, being as night air's so dangerous, but that Nina thought the rooms smelled stuffy and wanted to open them to let in some air. "Air!" says I. "Smoke, more like!" It's worse than Moscow in midwinter here, for smoke!'

'Have you somewhere to sleep?' Mila asked. 'And have you had a meal?'

'Our supper's waiting for us down in the kitchen,' the maid replied. 'Smells good, too! And for sleeping—well, it's a fine place! No stretching out on the floor with a score of others here! Nina and me, we've got a room to ourselves, up on the top floor, with a bed each and our own wash-stand! The gentlemen's men have got another like it, and the grooms and drivers have a big room over the stables, with a bed each as well. Treating us like gentry, they are!'

There was a very discreet scratch at the door—so discreet, in fact, that the scratcher had to try again less discreetly before either Mila or Marfa heard him. It was Yevgeny, Igor's valet (who had been a Frenchman called Eugène until 1812, when he somehow contrived to be left behind when his Emperor retreated).

'Good evening, Countess,' he murmured. 'Igor Grigorovich wishes to enquire whether your accommodations are satisfactory, and if there is anything you would wish.'

'Please convey my thanks to Igor Grigorovich and tell him that my room is most satisfactory, and I have everything I need, thank you,' Mila replied with equal formality. She received a solemn little bow of acknowledgment and a murmured, 'Goodnight, Countess,' before he withdrew.

'He's always like that,' Marfa commented. 'Never half-way human, except the iron's too hot or the water too cold, and then he swears something terrible! The hot water's really hot here, by the way.'

Mila suppressed a smile at the contrast between Igor's valet and her own (temporary) maid, thanked Marfa, and said she needed nothing more, so they exchanged blessings, and the maid disappeared in pursuit of her much-anticipated supper.

When Marfa had gone, Mila, who agreed with Nina about the room's stuffiness, opened the sash window at the top to let in a little of the dangerous night air, but the soot-laden atmosphere outside rushed in with such a strong smell of acrid smoke that she pushed the sash up again so hastily that it jammed a few inches short of the closed position, and she could not move it.

A few moments later there was a tap at the door, and Mila, who had let down her hair and was brushing it, went with a little sigh of impatience to see who it was, fully expecting to find Maxim's valet come on a similar errand to Yevgeny's. She was startled to find Igor standing in the dimly-lit passage.

'I've been thinking,' he said without any preliminaries, 'that perhaps I should make some sort of apology for my behaviour. I'll not pretend that I'm sorry, so no doubt you'd think my apology insincere and not accept it, but convention demands that I at least offer it.'

Mila was, to say the least, taken aback, and it was a few moments before she could manage to reply.

'I don't see,' she said stiffly, 'that there's any point in apologising if you don't mean it!'

'Precisely!' Igor agreed with a hint of a crooked smile. 'I'm sincerely sorry if I frightened or hurt you, but when one has nurtured a certain ambition for twelve years, one doesn't feel inclined to be sorry one has achieved it! Is your room quite comfortable?'

'You sent Yevgeny to ask that,' Mila remarked absently, grappling with the possible implications of his speech.

'I know, but the fellow turns everything into such a formal statement that he might as well be a government minister for all the information he imparts! Have you everything you need?'

'Yes, thank you,' Mila replied, wishing, at a deeper level than he meant, that her answer might have been true. 'Oh, no!' she exclaimed, suddenly remembering. 'The window! I foolishly opened it, and now I can't shut it again!'

Igor looked at her, his eyebrows quirking a little. 'You opened a window? In Tula? Good heavens! May I close it for you?'

'Please,' Mila murmured, feeling foolish, and stood aside to let him enter the room.

He opened the door as wide as it would go, and made sure it would not swing shut before entering with an elaborate regard for the proprieties, then crossed in an unhurried fashion to the window, picking up a candle-stick from the dressing-table in passing and holding it so that he could see what was causing the window to stick.

'Ah, you attacked it too violently!' he remarked, put down the candle, eased the window down a foot or so by gently wriggling it until it was straight, then pushed it to the top and fastened the catch.

As he turned away, he caught sight of the chair near the window and contemplated it for a moment, much to Mila's chagrin, for her folded and much-mended under-clothes were lying on it.

'You'll need to shake the cinders off those before you put them on,' he remarked, moving back across the room to the door, where Mila was still standing, and stopped very close to her.

'Th-thank you,' she stammered, very conscious that she was wearing only her night-shift and her wrapper.

'For what?'

'Shutting the window.'

'Is there anything else you would like me to do while I'm here?'

There was no particular inflection in his voice, and he was undoubtedly only referring to such matters as closing recalcitrant windows, but a number of rather shocking thoughts raced through Mila's mind, causing her cheeks to burn as she replied, 'No, thank you.'

'Ah.' Igor seemed neither relieved nor surprised by her reply. 'Incidentally, don't encourage young Maxim too much. I know he's only a year or so younger than you, but these sailors lead a sheltered life with only the elements with which to contend. An unsuccessful love affair at this stage in his career could have unfortunate results if he's serious, and, if he's not, which is probable at his emotional age, he's quite likely to hurt the object of his fleeting affections through sheer inexperience!'

'I think he finds Varya more irritating than attractive!' Mila retorted. 'It's not for me to encourage or discourage him. I shall have no say in her marriage arrangements!'

'I wasn't aware that widows wear their weeds as blindfolds,' he replied obscurely. 'Don't you think it time to look about you, *Milushka*?' And, with that, he lifted one long tress of her hair to his lips, bowed slightly, and left her standing in the doorway of her room, puzzling over his meaning and startled by the unexpected endearment.

In the morning she rose early, not so much from inclination as because the noise from a near-by foundry made further sleep impossible, for it sounded as though a dozen giants were making horseshoes of commensurate size. She put on her pelisse and bonnet and went out of the inn, intending to take a walk, but the smoke and smell and the rain of smuts soon sent her back inside again, where she encountered Igor in the narrow hall.

'Fiendish, don't you think?' he enquired. 'Did you succeed in sleeping?'

'Quite well, thank you, until the noise started.'

Igor gave her one of his oblique looks, and remarked, 'One would think we had nothing more important to discuss. Shall we embark on the weather, or save that enthralling topic until after we have eaten?'

'Neither, I think,' Mila replied in a similar vein. 'Because of the smoke, it's quite impossible to see what the weather may be doing.'

Igor's mouth twitched, and he bowed her into the parlour where they found Varya fortifying herself with ham, cheese and black bread. Maxim shortly followed them in, and said, 'The coachmen are making a fuss about the back axle again, but I can see nothing wrong with it.'

'Is that the one we broke near Valdai?' Varya asked. 'Because, if so, it should be all right because they put on a new one, didn't they?'

'Perhaps we might obtain a cast-iron one here,' Igor suggested with apparent seriousness, at which Maxim was diverted into respectfully pointing out that cast iron was generally too brittle for such use and would probably break more easily than wood. He thus failed to correct Varya's assumption, for the axle had not been replaced, but only repaired by having a new piece spliced into the longer part of the original axle, and Maxim had not done more than bend down to peer under the back of the vehicle at it, for his dark uniform was not designed for crawling under a coach in a dusty coach-house. As a result, disaster struck only some fifteen or so *versty* from Tula.

The smoky atmosphere and sooty leaves and grass were soon left behind after they had passed through the town gate, and they were presently rolling through some fine woodland, with large, broad-leaved trees predominating. A brick wall, marking the boundary of an estate, could be seen along one side of the road, with even finer trees rising above it. A white stone gateway, shaped like a small Doric temple had just come into view when the coach hit a particularly rough stretch of road. The off-side wheel struck a rocky outcrop which protruded through the surface—there was a rending crash—and once more the coach collapsed at the back, jerking both the forward passengers out of their seats. Maxim landed heavily on top of Varya, who gave a muffled squeak of alarm, and Igor, who was more agile, somehow managed to divert himself on to the seat between the two ladies, his beaver hat suffering in the process.

There was a brief silence, and then Igor said in a sharp tone, 'Is anyone hurt? Mila, are you all right?'

'Yes, thank you. Are you?'

'You're sure? No bruises or blows on the head?'

'No, none at all! But you—you were thrown out of your seat . . .'

'And landed on my hat,' he said ruefully. 'Varya, are you in one piece?'

'I'm squashed,' Varya's muffled voice said from under Maxim. 'And I think Maxim is unconscious. He's not moving.'

In the meantime the second coach had come up behind them and stopped, and a rescue party of grooms, valets and maids arrived, Marfa praying at the top of her voice to as many saints as she could recollect, and Nina begging her to be quiet as the men wrestled to open the doors. The one on the right seemed to be jammed, but one groom and Maxim's valet got the other open, and unceremoniously hauled the Lieutenant out and laid him on the grass at the roadside. Yevgeny, meanwhile, had gone to the rescue of the driver, whose nose was bleeding, while the second driver cut the harness and quietened the horses.

'He's not dead, is he?' Varya asked anxiously as she was helped out on to the road, and then ran over to where Maxim was being examined by his valet. The man replied in a doubtful tone that he thought not, at which Marfa burst into tears. Nina crossed herself and ran back to the second coach, returning with one of the water-bottles which were part of its equipment.

'Sensible girl!' said Igor, who was looking out of the door and saw what she was carrying. He climbed out gingerly and moved back from the coach to see if it was likely to overturn, but it was sitting quite firmly on the road, looking like a large animal squatting on its haunches.

Mila stood up and moved over to the open door, steadying herself against the back of the seat on which she had been sitting, for the floor now rose at an angle. Igor came forward to meet her, and lifted her down, a hand on either side of her waist, and kept them there while he looked down into her face, for he was a few inches taller than she, and said, 'Here's a fine to-do! Are you about to throw a fit of hysterics?'

'Certainly not!' she replied indignantly.

To her confusion, he bent his head and swiftly kissed her cheek, his hands tightening momentarily on her waist, and then he released her and was already going over to the little group round Maxim, who was now sitting up, one hand to his head, enquiring plaintively if someone would please tell him what had happened.

'You were wrong about the axle,' Igor told him, a little unkindly.

There was a pounding of feet, and half a dozen men came running from the Doric temple, led (by several yards) by a lithe, fast-moving man with the most startling hair Mila had ever seen, for it was bright red-gold. He arrived beside Igor not even out of breath, and had already enquired if anyone was injured by the time his companions, a sturdy-looking group of peasants, had caught up with him.

'We were felling a tree when we heard the crash,' he said when he had been reassured that no one was seriously hurt. 'We dropped our tools and ran.'

This was not strictly true, for one of his companions was carrying an axe, and another a coil of rope. They stood together at a respectful distance for a few moments, and then the red-headed man (who was clearly their owner, even if he was in his shirt-sleeves, with a smear of green lichen across the shirt to show that he had not merely been watching the tree-felling) turned his head and uttered a few laconic orders in Russian. These sent one of them running back to the gate and the others to helping the grooms and the drivers, except for one, who was occupied in directing passing traffic round the broken-down coach, for a number of vehicles and a column of soldiers were trying to get past.

Igor had been studying the man with a look of mild amusement on his face, and he now said, 'I don't imagine there's another man in Russia with hair like that! You must be Vassily Karachev!'

'Yes, and at your service!' Count Karachev made an elegantly simple bow, which Mila thought the perfect example of that movement, which so many men performed clumsily or over-elaborately. She felt sure that he must be an expert fencer, for his every movement was so smooth and graceful, and there was something of the spring and flexibility of a foil in his tall, slim body.

'Igor Grigorovich Charodyev.' Igor introduced himself

with a bow which looked positively stiff after the other's. 'The fellow holding his head is Lieutenant Maxim Efremovich Korovelsky.'

Maxim attempted to bow while still sitting down, and put his hand to his head again with a grimace, at which Vassily snapped his fingers and called 'Yura! Doctor!'

The man addressed gave a military salute and ran back to the gate, where he was almost knocked down by a troika of horses drawing an open carriage, driven by the first man who had gone back through the gate. Fortunately he dodged in time, and disappeared through the opening as soon as the carriage had cleared it.

Igor, meanwhile, had presented Vassily to his niece and Mila, and Varya, who had been looking thoughtful, suddenly asked, 'Are you the Count Karachev who's married Tatya Petrovna?'

'I have that good fortune!' he replied, his green eyes twinkling.

'Oh,' said Varya flatly, and looked at her uncle, whose face had no expression at all as far as Mila could see.

'You know my wife, then?' Vassily enquired. There was something about the way he said 'my wife' which made Mila feel a pang of envy.

'Well, yes, I suppose I do,' Varya replied. 'I mean— she invited me to visit her sometimes when I was a child, but I haven't seen her for a long time. She had a bad accident, didn't she? I haven't seen her since then, for I think she stopped going to Petersburg after it.'

'Yes. She was crippled,' Vassily replied. 'She'll be delighted to see you, now you've grown into such a lovely young lady. You know her too, perhaps?' he turned to her uncle.

'I . . .' began Igor, but Varya replied on his behalf, 'He most certainly does! He was one of Tatya's Beaux!'

'Oh, heavens!' Vassily cried in mock alarm. 'Not another of them? My wife must have had more suitors than Penelope! You won't challenge me, will you?' he asked Igor with apparent anxiety.

'Not today,' Igor replied gravely. 'I don't challenge people on Tuesdays. Does your estate by any chance run to a carpenter?'

'Yes, and a wheelwright.' Vassily glanced at the near-side rear wheel of the coach, which had broken a felloe. 'We'll have it repaired by the time you're ready to go on, but I don't think Maxim Efremovich should travel for a few days. He looks to me a mite concussed, but we'll know better when the doctor arrives.'

'You own a doctor?' Varya asked in awed amazement.

'No, but I have one staying with me.' He glanced back and saw that the carriage had turned itself round and was waiting near by. 'Shall we go up to the house, and leave my fellows to sort things out here? Maxim Efremovich's valet can keep an eye on him until the doctor has said if he's fit to be moved.'

'What if he isn't?' Varya asked.

'Why, we'll build a hospital round him,' Vassily replied reassuringly. 'Now, if you'd like to enter the carriage, your other coach can follow us . . .'

Mila looked round and saw with some surprise that the two maids had already returned to their coach, although Marfa was leaning out of the window as if she did not wish to miss anything; Yevgeny went over to join them. The two ladies were handed into his carriage by Vassily, who then excused himself for a moment and went with Igor to give some instructions to his men about getting the damaged coach off the Emperor's highway, 'And it's a pity he doesn't keep it in better repair,' Mila heard him comment.

'I'm so glad I shall see Tatya Petrovna again!' Varya confided quietly. 'She's the loveliest of ladies! I did hope so much that Uncle Igor might marry her, and I'm sure

he stood as good a chance as anyone, but the Emperor
took him off abroad, and she had the accident while he
was gone. Then he seemed to be so busy with the
Emperor's pictures and pots and things that I don't think
he ever managed to visit her above half a dozen times—
she was living near Ryazan then. I heard that she was
back in Petersburg last summer, but Uncle Igor had
gone to Warsaw ahead of the Emperor to see about
some jewels someone wanted to sell, and he's been in
Austria ever since. I've never heard of this Vassily
Karachev before—I'm sure he was never one of Tatya's
Beaux—and with that hair, someone was bound to
mention if he was about! There was a *Vladimir*
Karachev—perhaps he's a relation. He's an army
officer—very tall and dark and serious.'

'You seem to know a great deal at the Smolny of what
is happening in Society!' Mila commented. 'I suppose
the elder sisters of your fellow-pupils keep you informed?'

'Well, it's not a convent, you know—at least, our part
of it isn't—the actual convent was closed and the buildings turned into a widows' home simply ages ago—and
we are allowed to go out sometimes! Oh, I did enjoy
visiting Tatya Petrovna! Uncle Igor used to ask her help
over choosing my special-occasion frocks, and she was
always so kind and—well—she was a sister and a mother
and an aunt, all at once! I do wish Uncle Igor had
married her!'

Mila looked sympathetically at the girl, touched by
the sad tone in her voice when she spoke of 'a sister and a
mother and an aunt', for poor Varya had not had any of
those relations in her lonely childhood. At the same
time, however, she was conscious of a very tense sensation in her own chest, and her eyes would keep filling
with moisture, however hard she blinked them. She
concluded that she must be suffering from shock after

the accident, although that peculiarly hollow, breathless sensation seemed to increase every time Varya spoke of Igor marrying this unknown Tatya Petrovna.

'Did you say she was a widow?' she asked with a curiously stiff jaw.

'Yes. Her husband was a General Kalinsky, and he was killed or something only a few weeks after they were married. At Austerlitz, I think. There were all these young men in Society in Petersburg who used to flock round her during the Season, and someone nicknamed them Tatya's Beaux—they were quite proud of the title! And then she didn't marry any of them! How strange! I've never even seen anyone with red hair before—have you?'

'We're very rare in Russia,' said Vassily, who had come over to the carriage with Igor, unnoticed by its occupants. 'I had a Scottish grandmother on my mother's side, and she had red hair, which is not uncommon in Scotland. My mother and I inherited it, but my brother Volodya is as black as a crow, like my father.'

'Oh, is he the army officer?' Varya was not one whit abashed that he had overheard her remark. 'I thought he might be some sort of relative!'

'Colonel of the Volkhovskys,' Vassily confirmed, ushering Igor into the carriage ahead of him and giving the driver the office to move on as he took his own seat. 'My grandfather was in the Foreign Ministry, and was particularly impressed by Greek architecture,' he commented as they passed through the Doric temple, and the carriage began to roll along a gravelled drive, Igor's coach following behind. 'As you'll see when we reach the house.'

After ten minutes or so, the drive gave a twist between the thickly-growing trees and emerged from them to reveal a surprising view. Across an expanse of garden, there stood a most remarkable house. The central block

looked for all the world like the Parthenon, but rows of
windows peered uncomfortably between the pillars of
the colonnade, and a gilded Russian dome perched
awkwardly on its roof. Two lower L-shaped wings
sprouted from its sides, coming forward to embrace a
terrace, and there appeared, from the forest of chim-
neys, to be a similar wing at the back on the right, but not
on the left.

'He was also patriotic,' Vassily said sadly. 'Hence the
dome. I'm building a fourth wing at the back, to keep my
books in, although we don't really need any more
rooms. It's just that the house isn't symmetrical with
only three wings.'

It was difficult for his guests to find any comment
which would not be either insulting or a downright lie,
but Mila tried a nervous, 'It's a very—er—interesting
concept. Er—who was the architect?'

'My grandfather,' Vassily said gloomily. 'He may
have been a good diplomat, but . . .' He shrugged, and
then laughed at the expressions on their faces. 'Actually,
I think he meant it as a joke. He was always amused by
the way people reacted at their first sight of it!'

The carriage swept up a ramp on to the terrace and
drew up before the colonnade; behind it a careful scru-
tiny could discern a large pair of entrance doors, which
yawned cavernously. Igor's coach passed the end of the
ramp and continued round the back of the house with
the servants.

'Welcome to Ash Glade!' said Vassily, vaulting over
the side of the carriage and landing lightly on the steps
before a footman could run to open the carriage door.

His guests descended in a more orthodox fashion and
entered the vast entrance hall, where they were greeted
with the traditional bread and salt, and then Vassily
ushered them along the wide corridor of one of the wings
and into a room furnished in pretty pale colours, where a

dark-haired lady was reclining on a day-bed, reading a book.

She looked up and smiled as they entered, laying her book on the table at her side, and Mila felt an almost violent return of that curious sensation of breathlessness which she had experienced in the carriage. She hardly heard the introductions which Vassily made, for she was frankly staring at his wife.

If her first husband had died at Austerlitz in 1805, she must now be thirty-two or three at least, which was about the same age as Igor, but she was still remarkably beautiful. The accident which had crippled her had left its mark on her face in the form of a certain tenseness about the mouth, but her complexion was still petal-smooth, and her glossy black hair had only a few silver threads. She had large, dark-lashed grey eyes and a most charming smile, but her chief beauty lay in the tranquillity of her face.

'Why, Igor! I've not seen you for such an age!' she exclaimed, holding out both hands to him, and when he bent over her to kiss her cheek, Mila caught her breath with a gasp, and knew the peculiar sensation for what it was.

Oh, the dreadful irony of it! Igor said that he had loved her all those years ago, and now she had discovered, at last, that she loved him, only to find that he was now in love with Tatya Petrovna, whom everyone seemed to consider the perfect paragon of her sex—so beautiful, so kind, so—so everything that Mila could never hope to be! And if her own love was now hopeless, how much more hopeless for poor Igor, for his lady was clearly for ever unattainable! Every word, every glance she exchanged with her husband, even their unconscious awareness of one another, showed that here were husband and wife so deeply in love that to see them together must be a torment for Igor.

'And this is my little Varya, grown into a regular beauty!' Tatya continued. 'What a delightful surprise! I'm so glad to see you, and to make your acquaintance!' The last five words were addressed to Mila, who had simultaneously decided to dislike her and been immensely attracted to her, and was consequently reduced to mumbling something inane and flushing awkwardly.

Vassily drew up chairs before the footman whose duty it was had a chance to make any move, and when they were all seated and tea had been bespoken, Igor explained how they came to be passing Ash Glade. Vassily told Tatya about the accident, with much graphic detail, until even the participants in it felt that they had been involved in a theatrical performance staged for the set purpose of entertaining Tatya Petrovna.

Mila had not dared to look at Igor all this time, but when Vassily's tale was interrupted by the arrival of the tea equipage, she stole a glance in his direction and found that he was looking at Tatya with a smile on his lips, his normally shuttered face showing a pleasurable animation. She bit her lip and reminded herself that she already knew that she had met him again too late.

'Oh!' Varya suddenly exclaimed. 'Tatya, I must tell you! I've borrowed one of your maids—I do hope you don't mind!'

'Of course not!' Tatya replied warmly. '*Madame la Directrice* would certainly not have let you travel without one. Did Pavel Kuzmich find you someone suitable?'

Varya explained how she and Mila had gone to Tatya's brother's house, but found the family away, and how Pavel had helped her.

'And he suggested such a cap–splendid girl, and so well trained! He said she'd had "a misfortune of the heart", and would welcome a chance to leave Petersburg for a time, and he arranged everything! I'm so pleased with her and shall be very sorry to part with her, but I've promised she shall be sent back to Petersburg after we get to Kherson.'

'How odd.' Tatya looked puzzled. 'Pavel said nothing about anyone having a problem of that sort in his last report. And why didn't he send her to Ryazan if she wished to leave Petersburg? Still, it's lucky for you that he didn't, and I'm pleased that she's proving satisfactory. Who is she, by the way?'

'Her name is Nina.'

Tatya's face went quite blank, and she said in a thoroughly mystified tone, 'Nina? But there's no one called Nina in the Petersburg house. Are you sure?'

'Well, she answers to Nina, and I'm sure she would have said if that wasn't her name!' Varya replied.

'Perhaps Pavel Kuzmich is running an employment agency for ladies' maids?' Vassily suggested.

'Or perhaps he buys serfs on the quiet and hires them out at vast profit,' Igor added, not to be outdone.

'Pavel Kuzmich is very honest,' Tatya said reprovingly. 'He wouldn't do anything underhand. I'm sure there's been a mistake over the girl's name, and she didn't like to say anything. The mystery will be solved as soon as I see her, in any case.'

The door opened at that point, and a foxy-faced little man in rather formal dark clothes came in. He looked, in fact, as though he were dressed for a morning call in town, in contrast to Vassily, who was very informal in wide Cossack-style trousers tucked into soft boots, and an open-necked shirt which still bore the marks of his tree-felling activities.

'Patient's slightly concussed,' the new arrival announced. 'Nothing to worry about. Couple of days' quiet and rest'll soon put him right.'

'Dr Valentin Alexeievich Kusminsky.' Vassily rose to his feet and made the round of introductions. 'Valentin is staying with us for a few months, as Tatya is . . .'

'With child,' the doctor finished for him, obviously having no patience with polite euphemisms. 'Though why they asked me to take charge, I can't imagine! I'm an army surgeon, not a man-midwife, and she's as healthy as a horse—doesn't need a doctor at all! The damage from the accident's only to the lower part of the limb, and doesn't affect her condition in the slightest!'

'You know very well that you're thoroughly enjoying yourself!' Vassily informed him with a grin. 'He's set up a clinic on the estate, and is training two young fellows to do some simple dispensing and so forth, and he has half a dozen women learning to nurse the sick and deliver babies properly. I've no doubt he'll stay here until he's ninety, if we let him!'

'Would you like some tea?' Tatya asked the doctor, and there was a flurry of making fresh tea and passing cups and dishes about until everyone had been served again.

The doctor handed Mila a cup and dish and then sat down beside her, giving her a frankly admiring look and a friendly grin as he did so. She found this comforting, for she had been convinced that every man who found himself in the presence of Tatya Petrovna would be incapable of noticing any other female.

'Will it be safe to move Maxim Efremovich to an inn?' Igor enquired when everyone had settled down again. 'I suppose we had better return to Tula, unless you can recommend a good inn near here?'

'You'll certainly not go to an inn unless you wish to offend us quite mortally!' Tatya protested. 'There's plenty of space here, now that Vasya has stopped spreading his books about in every room, and you know you're all welcome. Besides, your coach has to be repaired before you can go anywhere, and that will take a day or two, I'm sure.'

The travellers accepted the invitation with relief, for

they had no wish to return to smoky Tula, and it was unlikely that a country inn would provide anything but the most primitive accommodation.

'What about the *jäger*?' Varya asked. 'The poor man will be waiting at the next posting-house, wondering whatever's become of us!'

'I'll send someone to fetch him,' Vassily replied, and went out of the room. A lively conversation started between Tatya, Varya and Igor, full of reminiscences about shared experiences and enquiries about old acquaintances. Valentin Kusminsky listened with every appearance of interest, and occasionally joined in when a military person was mentioned. Mila sat quietly, looking from Igor to Tatya and back again, and thinking wretchedly that she should hardly be surprised that, having been apparently rejected by her twelve years ago, Igor should have recovered from the love which he had admitted he once felt for her and fallen in love with someone so attractive as Tatya.

'Oh, the irony of it!' she thought 'To have found him again after all these years, to discover that he actually loved me, and now it's too late—he's forgotten me, and loves someone else—and even that can bring him nothing but more unhappiness, for she's married to another man!'

As if to underline her thoughts, Tatya, who had been recalling a journey she once made to Kiev with Igor and someone called Galina, said, 'You know, Igor, I fully expected that you'd offer for Galina, for you seemed to get along famously together, yet you let her escape, and she was snapped up by Gennadi Zhadnov! Now I think about it, there were quite half a dozen times when I thought I was about to be invited to your wedding and yet here you are, still a bachelor! Don't tell me that you couldn't find a female in all Russia who would condescend to marry a Ukrainian!'

Mila, who would never have dared to joke about something which she knew was a sensitive area for Igor, realised that Tatya, of course, knew just how to make a laughing reference to it which would make Igor smile, as he did now.

'The girl I love married Another!' he replied with a mock-theatrical air, and it was difficult to tell how much of the regret in his voice was real. Mila knew it was entirely real, and that he was referring to Tatya, for he was looking at her as he spoke, and he had used the present tense.

At that moment Vassily returned, wearing a clean shirt, and said that a groom had just set out to find the *jäger*, and that Maxim had been brought safely to the house and put to bed, protesting that there was nothing wrong with him but a slight headache, at which Valentin said briskly that he would go and give the young man a sedative to keep him quiet.

'Otherwise he'll be getting up and trying to prove he's in perfect health! I know these young officers—always determined to show how brave and strong they are, and I've no doubt the naval ones are even worse than the military variety, having less opportunity to show off to the ladies, being at sea so much.' Which speech carried him out through the door, and the last few words floated back to his audience from the corridor.

'My brother knew him in the Army, back in 1812,' Tatya explained. 'He saved Lev's arm from being amputated, and when my leg was crushed, Lev remembered him and asked him to come and see to it. He saved that, too, although he wasn't able to mend it, of course. He's always grumbling, but he's the kindest and gentlest of surgeons, and everyone thinks the world of him! Your friend is in very good hands.'

'I wondered why you had an army surgeon to—er—to look after you,' said Igor. 'That explains it.'

'Which reminds me—there's something else needs explaining,' said Vassily. 'I've sent for Varya's maid, so that we can solve the mystery of the Nina who isn't supposed to exist! She should be here by now. I wonder what's keeping her.'

As if in answer to his speculation, the door opened and the footman on duty in the corridor said in the wooden tones of a well-trained servant, 'The young person is here, Vassily Sergeivich. She says there must be some mistake, and you can't mean her to come to the salon.'

'That doesn't sound like one of my servants!' exclaimed Tatya. 'I'm sure no one in my employ ever made such a statement! Pray send her in, Mischa!'

As the footman went out, Nina entered the room with a slight jerk, giving the impression that someone had pushed her through the doorway. She looked agitated, and stood in a very hangdog fashion, her fingers fidgeting with the braid trimming of her *sarafan*, her head bent, and her eyes apparently on her feet.

There was a stunned silence in the room for a moment, and then Vassily, rising to his feet, exclaimed, 'Olga! What on earth are you doing dressed like that?'

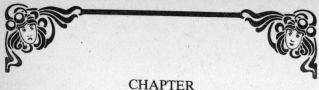

# CHAPTER
## SIX

THE ERSTWHILE Nina gave a little sob, and said, 'Mamma wouldn't let me marry Vladimir, so I ran away!' and then dissolved into silent tears, all the more poignant because she simply stood there and let them brim over the lids of her great dark eyes and run down her cheeks.

'Now, stop that before you ruin the carpet!' said Vassily firmly. 'Come and sit down and tell us all about it.' He put an avuncular arm round the girl's shoulders and led her to a chair, turned her round, and pushed her gently down into it. Tatya fished a vinaigrette from her reticule and held it out, and he took it and waved it under Olga's nose. She coughed once or twice as the aromatic spirit made her catch her breath, then stopped crying, wiped her eyes briskly with a minute handkerchief, and spoke quite lucidly.

'You know Vladimir wrote to Mamma last summer, while I was in Petersburg. She didn't answer for weeks— not until after your wedding, when you'd gone abroad, and then it was only to call me back to Moscow, because she said she was ill.'

'Just a moment,' Vassily said as she paused for breath. 'This is Olga Mikhailovna Kalinskaya. She's Tatya's first husband's niece, and is betrothed to my brother Volodya—Vladimir, that is.'

'That's just the trouble,' Olga said sadly. 'Mamma wouldn't hear of my marrying him. She said he wasn't good enough, being only a younger son and an officer in a Line regiment—not even the Guards! She wouldn't let me receive any of his letters—indeed, I don't even know if he wrote any—or write to him, even to tell him what she'd said, and she forbade me ever to mention him again. When I said I loved him, she said I didn't know what I was talking about, and I'm too young, and he's too old, and she locked me in my room.'

'But you're almost twenty!' Tatya exclaimed. 'Most girls have been married for two or three years by that age, and what if Vladimir is—how many?—twelve years older! How dare she say he's not good enough for you? He's a fine brave man, and Colonel of one of the *best* Line regiments—your own brother served under him during the war! He isn't in the Guards because he chose not to be! Alexander Pavlovich has offered him a place in any Guard regiment he liked to choose—at least twice, to my knowledge!'

The rest of the company nodded agreement—even Mila, who did not know Vladimir Karachev but was convinced by the sincerity of Tatya's speech in his defence. Igor and Vassily looked at Tatya with some awe, for she was quite afire with indignation on her brother-in-law's behalf and looked magnificent, with her normally tranquil face animated and her eyes flashing.

'Olga,' said Vassily judicially. 'The trouble with your Mamma is that, if you'll forgive the expression, she's a selfish b— vixen! She doesn't object specifically to Volodya, but to any man who might take her slave away from her and put her to the inconvenience of training someone else! She's played the invalid for years to get her own way in everything, and treated you little better than a serf! What does your father say about all this?'

'She won't let me discuss it with him. She says my marriage won't be his business until she gives her consent, and then he can deal with the legal side of it—settlements and so on! I did try to beg his help, but he just said it was for Mamma to decide, and she'll choose me someone suitable when the time comes! I don't want someone Mamma thinks is suitable! He'll be about fifty and horrible! I want Vladimir! I love him, and I won't marry anyone else!'

'And that's what your Mamma is counting on,' Vassily observed. 'She doesn't want you to leave her for any husband—you're too useful fetching and carrying for her, soothing her headaches and trotting about with her pills and potions!'

'I know,' said Olga wretchedly. 'She let me out of my room as soon as she had the headache, and sent me back to it when she felt better. I spent the whole winter either locked up or running her errands, and I've not heard a word about Vladimir in all that time! I couldn't bear it any longer, so as soon as the spring thaw was over, I escaped!'

'Good for you!' said Varya approvingly. 'I'd have done the same!' She received a severe glare from her uncle and a frown and a shake of the head from Mila, but she tossed her head at them and said, 'I would!' in a defiant tone which made Igor put his hand to his mouth to hide a smile, while he scowled at her even more.

'How did you manage that?' asked Vassily with professional interest, for he himself had escaped from a locked room on several occasions during his curious career with the Foreign Ministry, and knew something of the difficulties involved.

'Mamma always sent her maid and one of the footmen to lock me in, and they left the key in the lock on the outside, so that whoever brought my food didn't have to bother anyone for it. I found a sheet of paper and slid it under the door late one night. Then I pushed the key out with a hairpin until it fell on the paper, and then all I had to do was pull the paper back with the key on it. It was quite easy! Then I crept downstairs and took some servants' clothes from the store-room, and I took some of my own clothes as well, of course, because I thought that would make them look for a lady, not a servant, but I dressed as a servant. I had some money, because I'd had half a year's allowance and hadn't had a chance to spend any of it. I wrote a letter from myself, giving permission for a servant to go to Petersburg on family business, so that I wouldn't have to get a passport. I climbed out of a window at the back of the house, and over a broken bit of the wall of the stableyard—it's the way Boris used to go in and out when he was a boy. Boris is my brother,' she added for the benefit of those who were not acquainted with her family.

'Where did you go then?' Varya asked, absolutely entranced by the story.

'I took a public stage-coach to Petersburg.' Olga shuddered. 'I don't think I could ever do it again, for it was quite dreadful! The coach was fearfully uncomfortable, and the other passengers smelt, and I caught fleas and lice from them! One of the men kept pinching me until I lost my temper and hit him!' She looked so frail, with her eyes huge in her pale, thin face, that Mila wondered how she had ever found the strength to make the journey under those conditions.

'The inns were dreadful, too—not at all like the ones we stay in,' Olga continued. 'I'd no idea how terrible it must be to be a poor freeman, let alone a serf! It seemed to take for ever to get to Petersburg, and I was worried all the time that someone would ask for my passport, because I wasn't sure that the letter would be enough, and, besides, the police might recognise my name on it . . . Oddly enough, though, I had to show it only at the gate at Petersburg, and they just glanced at it. I don't think the man even read it!'

'And you went to our house in Petersburg, and found no one there?' Tatya said, looking quite distressed.

'Not at first. I went to the Petropavlovsky Fortress to begin with, because Vladimir's regiment was on garrison duty there last year, but they said that the Volkhovskys were on their way to Austria in case they were needed to fight in Piedmont, and that Vladimir had taken six months' leave due to him and gone abroad somewhere. I was really in despair then, for I was afraid he'd given me up. I went to Lev's house because I couldn't think of anyone else who might be in Petersburg and who might help me. I thought either you or Lev would be there, but everyone was away. I sat down on the steps and cried, but then I remembered Pavel Kuzmich, and asked if I could see him. They kept me waiting a long time, of course, because I didn't say who I was, and no one recognised me—people tend to see only what they expect to see, don't they? I mean, I was dressed as a servant, so they didn't think to look twice . . .'

'True,' said Vassily encouragingly. 'I must say that I had to look twice myself before I recognised you! You're not as blooming as you were last summer, by any means! We'll have to feed you up and give you plenty of fresh air and exercise.'

'You won't send me back to Moscow, then?' Olga asked eagerly.

Vassily gave an odd secretive smile, very much like Igor's, and said, 'Finish your story, and then I'll tell you what we're going to do.'

'Well, they eventually took me to Pavel Kuzmich's "pantry", they called it—like a little office—and he stared at me a moment, and said, "Oh, my goodness!" and looked a little like a stranded codfish, but I explained what had happened, and he said straight away that I could stay in the house as a servant, and they would pretend I'd come from Lev's Ryazan estate if anyone asked—not that anyone did, because no one bothers much about servants. I was worried, though, because I was in Petersburg last year for quite a long time and I was afraid to go out in case someone recognised me.'

'Then Varya Denisovna came asking to borrow a lady's maid to go to Kherson with her, and Pavel thought of me. He knew I'd enough sense to play the part, and I've done most of the things like arranging hair and looking after fine silks and lace, and pressing and mending for Mamma, because she'll never trust a maid to do anything like that—and it would take me right away from Petersburg to where no one would know me. I didn't realise that we would go to Moscow first, but I managed there by staying indoors all the time. I must say, it seems to have worked, for I don't think anyone suspected until you saw me, and then, of course, the game was up!'

'Marfa noticed something,' said Mila. 'She told me there was something odd about you, but neither of us suspected what it was!'

'You've been most enterprising!' said Tatya. She appeared to approve of her young friend's unconventional behaviour. 'Now, Vasya! Put her out of her misery and tell her what Vladimir's been doing!'

Everyone looked at Vassily, who lounged back in his chair, one leg crossed over the other (and he even managed to do that gracefully), smiled mischievously at their expectant faces, and said, 'Well now, you see—it happens that Alexander Pavlovich owes my brother a few favours, not least because he once put himself in the way of a bullet intended for someone else, and thereby saved our Imperial Majesty considerable embarrassment! Volodya went to Austria to see the Emperor and ask for a small repayment.'

'But what could the Emperor do?' Olga had obviously expected from Vassily's manner that he was about to tell her of some miracle, and was consequently the more disappointed when it appeared to be something so ineffectual.

'You may not have noticed,' said Igor quietly, 'that we happen to live in an Autocracy. The Emperor can do virtually anything he pleases within his own Empire. Because Alexander's less despotic than his ancestors, one tends to forget that he has the power to order where he usually requests.'

'Precisely!' said Vassily, his lively face alight with merriment. 'He wrote a most charming letter to your Mamma, congratulating her on her perspicacity and good fortune in securing for her only daughter's husband one of the finest, bravest and most worthy officers in the Imperial Army, expressing the hope that it would be possible for him to attend the wedding in person. With the letter, he enclosed a gift for the bride of an elaborate diamond parure of great value, and, if Igor will forgive me, shocking bad taste! His gift to the groom was three large estates from the Imperial demesne!'

There was a thoughtful silence as his audience digested what he had told them and appreciated the sheer cunning of the Emperor's tactics. Then Valentin Kusminsky said, 'That's what they call a *fait accompli*, I suppose.'

'Clever, too,' commented Igor. 'He doesn't tell her she must let Olga marry Vladimir—he just appears to assume that she planned it and approves! He's as wily as a Greek sometimes!'

'But Mamma will be furious!' Olga said uncertainly, unable to accept that even the Emperor could overrule the tyrant of the Kalinsky household.

'She was, but only at first. A positive river of diamonds has a remarkably soothing effect on the female mind,' said Vassily. 'Volodya's staying in your house in the Tverskaya at this very moment, and helping your father and Boris to search for you. I had a letter from him only yesterday.'

'Oh dear! Is he very worried about me?' Olga asked.

'He said he expected you'd found a safe hiding-place with a friend they haven't yet thought of, but he wishes he could contact you because he wants to get the wedding over quickly before your mother can re-form and counter-attack. I'll send another courier off to Moscow to tell him you're here, shall I?'

'Oh, yes, please!' Olga cried, clasping her hands together in a very pretty gesture of pleading.

'I don't know what things are coming to!' Vassily went out mock-grumbling. 'We shall have to do the house-work ourselves before long, with the servants all galloping about throughout the length and breath of Russia on one errand or another.'

'What a delightfully interesting morning we're having,' exclaimed Tatya. She glanced at the pretty French clock which graced one of the consoles. 'Oh, heavens! I'd no idea it was so late. You must be quite starving, for I'm sure you left Tula at some extraordinary hour. You'll all wish to wash and change, and something more suitable must be found for Olga to wear.' She rang the little bell which stood on the table beside her, and it was immediately answered by Mischa, who must have been hovering outside the door. Tatya gave him a string of instructions about having the visitors shown to their rooms, her own maid sent to her at once, and luncheon to be served in three-quarters of an hour.

It appeared that the rooms in the central block of the house were hardly used at all, and, indeed, they must have been very dark as all their windows were behind the colonnades at the front and back. Most of them were filled by Vassily's vast collection of books, which had been his main interest in life until he met Tatya. The visitors were shown to rooms in the north-west wing,

which all looked out across a lawn to a flower garden,
with a great mass of fine trees beyond. The furniture in
Mila's room was all of Chinese manufacture, as were the
embroidered silk curtains and wall-hangings, and even
the canopy over the bed was shaped like a gilded
pagoda, with little bells hanging from the projecting
corners.

Marfa was already there, putting away the last of
Mila's possessions, and she immediately gave her mistress a guided tour of the wonders of the room, for she
had never before seen anything like it. Eventually Mila
had to interrupt her raptures to remind her that she now
had only half an hour to change and be ready for
luncheon, but Marfa managed to babble on enthusiastically all the time she was pouring water, helping Mila out
of her travelling dress and into one of her muslin frocks,
and arranging her hair.

Olga appeared at luncheon in a silk frock of Tatya's
which was too large for her, for she was, as Valentin
Kusminsky pointed out, thinner than she should have
been. Both Mila and Varya exclaimed that they could
not understand how they had ever taken her for a
peasant, now that they saw her dressed according to her
proper rank, and it soon became clear that Varya and
her former maid had struck up a warm friendship.

After luncheon, as it was a beautifully sunny day, the
men went to inspect the partly built south-east wing, and
the ladies went out to the lawn, where some pretty
cast-iron tables and chairs from Tula were grouped
about. As an archery target had been set up there,
before long a footman was sent to fetch bows and arrows
so that Tatya and Olga could give Varya some instruc-
tion in the art of toxophily, for both ladies had some
ability—especially Tatya, who, although of necessity
seated in a basket-work chair on wheels, could still draw
a bow and shoot her clout.

Mila watched for a little while and then, as Tatya had invited her to explore the garden if she preferred, wandered away and strolled among the flowers in the warm sunshine, enjoying the scent of the roses and the quiet of the country, broken only by the sounds of bees and birds, the thud of arrow striking mark and the voices of the ladies, which receded as she wandered round to the front of the house, where the flowers grew in beds bordered by little box hedges.

She was watching a butterfly, and thinking that she could not recall when she had last seen one, when Igor's voice suddenly said behind her, 'What on earth are you doing here?'

Startled, she swung round with a gasp and stammered, 'Oh! I—er—I was just—I mean, Tatya Petrovna said I might look at the garden.' She was mortified to feel a wave of heat travel over her face, which she knew meant that she was blushing.

'I'd have thought it was far too hot to walk about in the sun,' Igor said bluntly. 'You should carry a parasol. Come among the trees, where it's cooler. I wish to speak to you.'

There was nothing to indicate that he thought her flushed cheeks were due to anything other than the June sun, and Mila hastily agreed that it was rather warm, and, seeing no way to avoid going with him other than a direct refusal, gingerly took his arm and walked with him between the flower-beds, across a strip of grass, and along a path which meandered among the trees.

'If we had to break an axle, it was a stroke of good fortune that it happened at Vassily Sergeivich's gate!' Igor commented. 'I've known his brother on and off for years, but Vassily's spent much of his time abroad, and seems to prefer to be here when he's in Russia, rather than in Petersburg, so I've never actually met him before. I've known Tatya for a very long time. Am I right in thinking that this is the first time you've met her?'

'I've heard of her, of course, but not met her.'

'Strange. I'd have thought you'd have been bound to run across her at some time. Surely, when you were first married, you lived in Petersburg—wasn't Étienne seconded to the cadets' riding-school? Didn't you meet her then?'

Mila hesitated much too long, seeking a suitably evasive reply which would not involve an actual untruth, and eventually said, 'I didn't go into Society.'

They had been walking very slowly, and Igor now stopped and turned to face her, so she, perforce, also stopped. He looked at her with a puzzled frown and she glanced away, pretending to be interested in the trees.

'It's very pleasant here,' she said.

'Yes.'

As he said nothing more, there was an awkward silence, and then Mila said rather desperately, 'Tatya Petrovna is very lovely.'

Igor smiled, and Mila, looking sidelong at him, saw that the smile was gentle and tender. 'She is indeed!' he said. 'In every way. I think she's the loveliest female I've ever known—in face, in form, and above all, in character. It's a particular delight to me to see her so happy, for there's always been a little touch of sadness about her as long as I've known her.'

'Has there?' Mila asked absently, feeling wretchedly sad herself, for it was clear that Igor loved Tatya so much that he could even bear to see her married to another man, as long as that man made her happy.

'Yes. Her first husband was a brute. He left her with a real fear of marriage. Added to that, she was crippled in a dreadful accident . . . She seems quite radiantly happy now, though. Thank God.'

He crossed himself, and Mila, automatically doing the

same, wondered what he would say if he knew the truth about her own marriage. Perhaps he would feel sorry for her, but that was small comfort. She sighed, and then, to her horror, her eyes filled with tears.

'Mila?' His voice was suddenly sharp. 'Why are you crying? Oh, I suppose it's Olga's story—it must have reminded you of . . . of your own past. I should have realised.' He paused for a moment, and then went on, 'Perhaps it's not the best of times to say this, but I may not have another opportunity. I think you might make an effort to be a little more sociable. I've hardly heard you speak since we arrived here, and it's hardly polite to your host and hostess to mope about and go off by yourself like this.'

'I don't mope about!' Mila protested indignantly, scrubbing her eyes with a small handkerchief. 'And, if I've not said much, it's for lack of opportunity. You and your—your friends have been talking incessantly, and, in any case, had there been a chance for me to speak, I've nothing to contribute, as I don't know any of the people you've been mentioning.'

'I can't imagine what you've been doing in Petersburg all these years not to know at least some of them,' Igor replied, frowning. 'I suppose we were talking a great deal at luncheon, but you could have stayed with Tatya while we went to see the new wing. I'd have thought you'd welcome an opportunity to get to know her better. I was most surprised, when we returned, that you'd gone off by yourself and were moping about in the garden.'

'I was not moping!'

'You're always moping!' he retorted. 'Most of the time you've a long face and an air of tragedy, which is quite unnecessary. Étienne has been dead these eight years—more than time enough for you to have recovered your spirits and be taking some interest in life again! You're still young, and should be married again by now. I know a husband is a great loss, and should be properly mourned for a decent period, but there's no necessity for you still to be going about in half-mourning, nursing your grief.'

'I am not in half-mourning!' Mila was stung to reply. 'Not that it's any of your business,' she added, biting her lip, for tears were blurring her vision again at the injustice of his accusations.

'It is my business while you're in my charge,' he replied. 'If you intend to remain an inconsolable widow for the rest of your life, you should go into a convent. Otherwise, try to accept that the past is over, that life goes on, and you must live in the present and look to the future! It's no use constantly mourning the loss of what you once had. So set it behind you, before it's too late!'

For a moment Mila's lips trembled, beginning to form the words which would tell him the truth, but instead she came out bitterly with, 'Then why do you not take your own advice? Tatya Petrovna is married, so why do you not accept it and stop basking in her presence like a love-sick boy!'

Igor seized her by the shoulders and swung her round to face him. He looked furious, his eyes wide open and blazing, his air of ironic detachment conspicuously absent.

'Tatya is my friend—my very dear friend!' he said in a cold, level voice, at odds with the look in his eyes. 'If your little romantic schoolgirl mind can't imagine such a friendship between a man and a woman, the fault is in you, not in the friendship! I thought the silly girl I once knew had grown into a sensible woman, but it seems I'm mistaken!'

'I—I thought . . .' Mila stammered. 'I mean, it appeared to me . . .'

'Then you'd best try to remember that appearances can be misinterpreted by those who don't trouble to look beyond them,' he replied curtly, still glowering, but he released her and turned as if to walk on.

'You might do well to remember that yourself!' Mila came back at him with some spirit.

He stopped and turned towards her again, studying her face intently. Suddenly the anger died from his own expression, his lids drooped over his eyes, and his normal calmness returned. 'And what precisely do you mean by that?' he asked.

'Simply that you mistake me quite as much as I mistake you,' she replied, seizing the chance to set one small thing right amid so much that was wrong. 'I don't wear dark clothes from choice, but because they're more suited to my position in life, and because they last longer than light colours. I'm quite poor, you know, and must live as economically as I can.'

'But I thought you said that you received a pension?'

'Yes, but it's a very small one. I couldn't live on it.'

Igor, his face at its most shuttered, was silent for a few moments—so silent and still, in fact, that a squirrel ran down a near-by tree and scampered across his feet without apparently seeing him, and neither did Igor appear to see the squirrel.

'I'm sorry,' he said at last, very stiffly. 'You're quite right. I made an incorrect assumption. My apologies.' He stretched out one hand and gently touched her cheek where the skin was still moist from her tears. 'My deepest apologies,' he added in a different, much softer, tone.

For a few more moments his fingers lingered against her face, so close to her lips that she need only have turned her head a fraction to kiss them, but she was unable to make that tiny movement, and his hand dropped to his side.

'And mine,' Mila replied quietly. Yet in her heart she remained unconvinced by his statement about his feelings for Tatya, although she did him the honour to believe that he was sincere in what he said, but mistaken or self-deluded about it, which she knew from her own experience was quite possible.

Silence descended again, and Mila, casting around for something to say, eventually volunteered brightly. 'How strange that none of us realised that Olga Mikhailovna wasn't really a servant at all!'

'Yes. But, as she said, no one ever really takes much notice of servants.'

'It's—it's very pleasant that everything is going to go well for her after all, don't you think? She was very brave to run away like that.'

'Very foolish, you mean,' Igor replied prosaically. 'She might easily have been robbed and murdered, or worse, and if she'd fallen foul of the police, she might have been flogged! I'll admit she showed considerable enterprise for a female of her birth and upbringing, and proved to be less bird-witted than I've always thought her, but it was all quite unnecessary. Had she remained comfortably locked up in her room, Vladimir Sergeivich would have been saved a great deal of worry, and the result would have been the same.'

'But she didn't know he could enlist the Emperor's support!' Mila was stung to retort, for it seemed clear that he was dismissing her support for Olga as a farrago of romantic nonsense.

'She should have had the sense to realise that he's a man of great courage and resource. Good heavens!— he's outwitted and outfought some very clever generals in his time. You don't imagine he'd let Olga's invalid mother defeat him, do you? On second thoughts,' with his twisted little smile, 'perhaps she could! Even Bonaparte might have been no match for a scheming female whose personal convenience is at stake.'

At that point, the path gave a twist and emerged from

the trees, and Mila was surprised to find that they had come out opposite the place where the archers had been shooting. They had now been joined by Vassily, Valentin and Maxim, and were sitting about being served with tea by a couple of footmen in country livery.

'Remarkably good timing!' Igor commented, and quickened his pace in the direction of the samovar, with Mila perforce accompanying him.

'Ah, there you are!' exclaimed Vassily. 'I was about to despatch another messenger to find you. Come and sit down and take some refreshment. You'll be pleased to hear that your *jäger* has been recovered from limbo, and is in conference with the wheelwright and the carpenter.'

'Many thanks,' replied Igor. 'I hope they don't effect the repairs too rapidly, although we've still a long way to go. However, I'm sure the prospect of your most delightful company is not something from which we would wish to rush away.'

Mila noticed that he particularly looked at Tatya as he spoke, and she responded by saying, 'We hope you'll stay for more than a day or two.'

'You wouldn't let me stay even one more day in Moscow!' Varya whispered a little too audibly to her uncle, and Maxim said something regretful about reporting to his ship, but he was obviously only mentioning it out of a sense of duty, for he was looking at Tatya as though he were mesmerised.

'Don't be pert, miss!' Igor murmured sharply to Varya, who flounced a little in her chair, and then whispered a gruff apology. She seemed to be a little out of humour, and Mila, observing the irritable glances she kept casting on both Maxim and Tatya, could guess the reason.

'How are you?' Mila asked Maxim, who looked rather pale under his tan, and was sporting a fine bruise and bump just below the hairline above his left eye.

'Quite well, thank you,' he replied politely. Then, more honestly, 'Well, I had the headache, but it's gone now, and I did feel a little dizzy, but it passed, and I'm not one for lying about in bed, you know. The surgeon said I might get up.'

He nodded towards Valentin, who twitched his nose and said warningly, 'Only if you keep quiet and don't rush about, mind!'

Mila was flattered to find that both Maxim and Valentin had somehow shifted their chairs nearer to the one she had taken, and were now one on either side of her, vying in the small attentions of offering cakes or fresh cups of tea, slices of lemon, jam, or whatever else occurred to them, and making conversation, although, as they chose different topics, she was hard put to it to reply equally to each without becoming confused.

After tea, the gentlemen went off again, this time to the stables, while Olga and Varya wandered into the flower garden, chattering away nineteen to the dozen. Mila remained with Tatya, partly because she did not like to leave her alone, and partly because she very much wished to discover whether she was indeed the paragon Igor obviously believed her to be.

They chatted about nothing in particular for a while, and then Tatya said, 'Varya tells me that you're a widow.'

'Yes.'

'And she says your husband was French?' Tatya sounded a little hesitant about pursuing the subject.

'Yes, but serving in the Russian Army.'

Tatya made a smiling little gesture, and said, 'Well, at that time there must have been nearly as many Frenchmen in the Russian Army as there were in Bonaparte's.'

'Not quite,' Mila replied rather stiffly.

'Do you miss him very much?' The sympathy shining in Tatya's clear grey eyes was unmistakable, and Mila decided that Igor was probably right about her.

'Not at all,' she replied honestly. 'In fact, I should never have married him. However, he was killed at Dresden, and it's all past and done with now.'

'Have you thought of marrying again?'

Mila was tempted for a moment to tell Tatya to mind her own business, but found herself responding to the other's obviously genuine interest. 'There's little use in thinking of it. I've no money and no prospects. My family disowned me for marrying against my father's wishes. I'm growing older and losing my looks. Who'd want me?'

'A year ago I thought the same about myself, but now look at me!' Tatya said encouragingly. 'Varya also told me that you've known Igor for some considerable time.'

Mila looked at her suspiciously, wondering if she was making a connection or starting a new topic of conversation. She decided it was the former, and said abruptly, 'I knew him a little, a long time ago. I think he's in love with you.'

Tatya laughed, but not at all unkindly, and said, 'Oh, no! Igor was never one of my Beaux! We've been good friends for years, but he looks on me as a sister, I assure you.'

Mila murmured something non-committal, but she thought to herself that a female is not always aware that a particular man loves her, and it was difficult to imagine that any man could fail to be attracted in a most un-brotherly fashion to someone like Tatya.

The conversation turned to other things, and before long it was time to dress for dinner, and after the meal there was music and conversation in another beautifully furnished room with a fine pianoforte, on which Olga played the accompaniment to various songs which everyone except Valentin volunteered to contribute to the entertainment. The doctor declined to sing, claiming

that he had the voice of a corncrake, but he recited a
stirring passage from *Ruslan i Lyudmila*, apparently as a
compliment to Mila, as he bowed most particularly to
her at the end of it.

'Er—isn't that by—er—Alexander Pushkin?' Maxim
enquired after the applause had died down. 'Yes, I
thought it was, but isn't he—er . . . ?'

'In exile,' Vassily finished for him, as he seemed
reluctant actually to mention a subject better avoided.
'Although he seems to be making the best of it. The last I
heard, he was travelling in the Crimea and the Caucasus
with General Raevsky and his family, which is an odd
thing for a disgraced poet to do. Personally, I think poets
should stay well clear of politics, for they do so much
damage, and it certainly doesn't improve their poetry!'

'Damage?' queried Maxim. 'What damage can a poet
do?'

'To give but one example,' replied Vassily, his hair
seeming to glow more brightly in the candlelight, and
fairly curl with animation. 'If Rouget de Lisle hadn't
written the words of *La Marseillaise*, I'd wager at
long odds that the French Revolutionary Armies, and
Bonaparte's after them, wouldn't have been half so
successful!'

'But that was his music as well!' Igor pointed out, and
everyone plunged into a lively discussion on the influence of poetry (or rather, perhaps, verse) and music
on peoples and events, as Vassily had probably
intended.

When Mila eventually went to bed, she thought about
Tatya's hint concerning the possibility of her marrying
Igor, and wished most desperately that it could have
been right; but after what he had said in Moscow, and
the way he had spoken about Tatya, it was only too clear
to Mila that it was wrong. If only . . .

In the morning, the *jäger* reported that a new axle had

been made, and also a new wheel, but the iron tyre for the latter had still to be made and fitted, and the new parts fastened into their places. He expected, he said, that this would be done during the day, and the other damage to the coach repaired, and the travellers might expect to continue their journey the next day.

Vassily and Tatya expressed genuine regret that their visitors would be leaving so soon, but quite understood that, with more than 1,600 *versty* still to go and an impatient captain awaiting Maxim's arrival, they must press on.

The morning was occupied with walking about the park behind the house, with Tatya accompanying the walkers in a small carriage drawn by a stout donkey, which she drove herself. There was a lake to be viewed, and a number of quaint little follies and summer-houses, and it was very pleasant to stroll about in the sunshine.

After luncheon, Vassily brought out to the lawn a number of wooden pegs, some mallets and some wooden balls and attempted to teach the younger ladies and the other gentlemen a somewhat complicated game which he had learned in England. His pupils became interested as they began to master the principles, and were all quite engrossed, as were Tatya and Mila in watching, when they were interrupted by the sound of horses approaching up the drive from the road, and they saw three riders come cantering out of the trees. The leader, a tall man with a black moustache, wearing the dark green uniform and black *kiver* of an army officer, caught sight of them, turned his horse, jumped the stone balustrade across the end of the lawn, and rode towards them over the grass.

'Oh!' cried Olga. 'It's Vladimir!' and she dropped her mallet and ran to meet him.

# CHAPTER
# SEVEN

THE OFFICER dismounted while his horse was still moving, and the animal slowed to a gentle amble and
eventually came to rest nose-down in a flower-bed where
it made a hearty luncheon of pansies, double daisies and
nepeta, unnoticed by its rider, who removed his *kiver*,
which he dropped on the grass, and gathered Olga into
his arms without a word, for he was a somewhat taciturn
man at the best of times.

His companion had dismounted in the drive, handed
his reins to the third man, who was the groom Vassily
had sent to Moscow, and came over to join the others in
a more sedate fashion. He was a tall young man with
smooth black hair and expressive brown eyes, who bore
so strong a resemblance to Olga that those who did
not already know him guessed that he was her
brother, before he was introduced by Vassily as Boris
Mikhailovich Kalinsky.

He made his bow to the ladies, kissing hands all
round, and causing Varya to blush quite becomingly by
giving her a glance with those expressive eyes which
obviously set her in a flutter. He then engaged in polite
conversation, casting a deprecating glance or two at his
sister and his friend, who remained a little apart from
everyone else with their arms round each other,
apparently in silent communication.

'Volodya,' said Vassily presently to his brother. 'Do
you mind if I have your horse removed to the stables

before he eats *all* the flowers?'

'She,' replied Vladimir without taking his eyes off Olga's face. 'You must have been a great deal of use to the Life Guard Hussars if you can't tell a mare from a gelding. And don't call me Volodya!'

'Well, I wasn't exactly *in* the Hussars,' Vassily said defensively. 'I just wore their uniform because it happened to be the only one at the depôt which fitted! Come along, horse!'

The last sentence was addressed to Vladimir's mount, which pulled away when Vassily caught hold of her reins and tried to remove her from the flower-bed; but he resorted to bribery in the form of a handful of grass now and shamelessly extravagant promises of oats and hay later, and succeeded in coaxing the beast back on to the lawn. When Vladimir said 'Stable' in Russian, she trotted off in that direction on her own, pursued by a footman who was supposed to be leading her.

The interruption appeared to restore Vladimir to a sense of his social duties, and he came over to the group sitting near or standing round the wreckage of Vassily's game, propelling Olga along with him with a hand on her elbow, which he removed long enough to shake hands with the men and bow over the ladies' hands. Then, after cuffing his brother in passing, he returned to Olga and informed her that she looked downright peaky, and enquired what she had been doing to become so thin and washed-out.

Olga gave him a brief résumé of her adventures, at the end of which he said lovingly, 'Silly goose!', bringing a radiant smile to her already happy face.

'Is it really true that Mamma will let us be married?' she asked breathlessly.

'Yes, but not until January,' he replied. 'It's to be a double wedding with Boris and Marisha. In Petersburg,' he added, which caused a stir among those present who were acquainted with Olga's mother.

'Petersburg!' exclaimed Vassily. 'But she hasn't been there for years!' It was not necessary for him to specify whom he meant by 'she'.

'Eighteen years,' said Boris gloomily. 'She made Father sell our house there six months ago to the fellow who's been renting it, and now, of course, we have to find and buy another! Come to think of it, I don't believe she's been out of the house these past ten years, except to get into the coach to go to one or other of our estates for the summer, or back to Moscow for the winter, yet she went out yesterday and bought a new bonnet, and was quite ready to come with us to fetch Olga!'

'Is she really resigned to losing Olga?' Tatya asked anxiously. 'She won't change her mind at the last moment?'

'I think not,' Boris replied, still sounding depressed. 'She's been busy writing to all her old friends and relations, boasting about her brave and handsome prospective son-in-law, who is Colonel of one of the finest regiments in the Army and holds the medal of St George, and is so friendly with the Emperor that HIM is to attend the wedding. That's why it's to be in Petersburg—Alexander Pavlovich might balk at travelling to Moscow for it!'

'You don't sound very pleased!' commented Varya, cheerfully coming out with the thought which had occurred to all the others, but which no one else had liked to express.

'Oh, I'm pleased about Olga marrying Vladimir, of course—delighted, in fact—but it's Mamma's insincerity that I can't swallow. One minute she was calling him a worthless scoundrel, insisting that he'd run off with Olga and would refuse to marry her until Father agreed to a huge dowry, and saying he wanted her only for her money, and the next she was enthusing over the kindness and condescension of the Emperor in sending such a wonderful letter, and going into raptures over his magnificent gift to Olga!' He shuddered slightly. 'It's the ugliest diamond parure I've ever seen, and Mamma insists that she must wear it for the wedding!'

'She can't,' said Igor decisively. 'It's Not Done! Nothing sparkling for young brides! It doesn't matter what it looks like, for Alexander Pavlovich bought it only for the quality of the stones—I know the one you mean, and I negotiated his purchase of it! He'll expect Olga to have them reset in a more suitable style of her own choice.'

Everyone concerned begged Igor to assure them that this was really true, and looked vastly relieved when he gave that assurance. Vladimir said laconically that he had been considering arranging for the parure to be stolen, but resetting would be easier. Noticing his singularly expressionless face, Mila could not decide whether he was joking or serious, and never did succeed in coming to any firm conclusion about it.

Vassily, looking in a puzzled fashion towards the now deserted drive, said, 'No valets or baggage, Volodya?'

'Following,' replied Vladimir briefly. 'And don't.' He did not bother to finish the sentence, as he had said it in full so often in the past that there was no need.

'Good heavens, yes!' exclaimed Boris, who was something of a dandy. 'Couldn't travel without a valet! They're coming in a coach with our bags, and they've strict instructions to be here in good time for dinner.'

'Meanwhile,' said Tatya, smiling to herself, perhaps remembering when Boris had been in the Army, and had sometimes not had a change of clothes for weeks on end. 'Shall we take tea?'

Under cover of the business of serving tea, Vladimir

somehow managed to separate himself from Olga, and approached Mila.

'Étienne de Romarin?' he enquired in a low voice.

'Yes. My late husband,' Mila replied nervously, wondering what was to come, for the tall officer was frowning and his dark eyes looked puzzled.

'Mm,' he said. 'Knew him slightly. Didn't know he was married, but the subject wouldn't necessarily have come up. Hussars and infantry don't mix much, except on battlefields.' He bit the edge of his moustache while he hesitated, and then added, 'Didn't like him, I'm afraid.'

Mila looked straight up into his face and said 'No', in a remarkably flat voice.

Vladimir contemplated her thoughtfully, then nodded and said, 'Well, you're free of him now. Don't let one mistake spoil your life.' Then Tatya called to him for a first-hand account of what the Emperor had said. He gave Mila a surprisingly expressive smile, and went to do as he was commanded.

Dinner that evening was very lively, for Boris, once he had thrown off his earlier air of gloom, proved to be very good company, and Vassily and Igor seemed to enjoy sharpening their wits on one another. The gentlemen did not linger over their wine after the meal, but followed the ladies to the salon with the pianoforte when Tatya, in her wheelchair, led them out.

Mila took a seat a little out of the centre of the gathering, and observed the others, content to watch and listen. She noticed that, apart from the doctor, every man in the room was taller than Igor by several inches, although only Vladimir actually topped six feet, and she wondered if he still felt self-conscious about his lack of height, although he showed no sign of being so at present.

She was surprised to find, however, that, despite her

withdrawn position, she was not to be left on the edge of the gathering after all, for, within a few minutes, she had her own little circle, consisting not only of Valentin and Maxim, but also of Boris. He had quite deliberately considered Tatya, laughingly chaffing her husband and Igor about their lack of horse-oriented knowledge, which had become obvious during dinner, and Varya, who was in animated discussion with Olga about bridegowns and Petersburg fashions, watched tolerantly by Vladimir, and then strolled over to Mila, pulled up a chair, neatly insinuated himself between her and Maxim, and proceeded to cut out both her cavaliers with the skill of long practice. His effective use of his expressive dark eyes made Mila remind herself more than once that he was shortly to be married, and was, according to his sister, a shocking flirt!

The various conversations continued, with much laughter and good humour, and the evening was marred only by one small contretemps, which arose when Boris said to Varya, 'And so you are travelling south to visit your father, I collect? Where does he live?'

'He's the senior Naval Captain at Kherson,' Varya replied proudly. 'And that's our most important naval port on the Black Sea!'

'Oh, hardly!' objected Maxim, from his professional expertise. 'It was the first to be built, I grant you, but it's only a backwater now. Nikolaev and Sevastopol are far more important, and even Odessa, although that's more for merchant shipping these days.'

Mila, who was listening to a rambling tale from Valentin, heard what had been said and looked sharply at Varya. She caught the girl's eye just as her lips parted to make what would probably have been a sharp rejoinder and shook her head, pressing her own lips firmly together in a deliberate and meaningful fashion. Varya faltered for a moment, and then said, a little too sweetly, 'Ah, but you must allow an ignorant schoolgirl to believe that place where her own father is to be the most important in Russia, let alone on the Black Sea!'

Maxim looked disconcerted, finding himself to have been put neatly into the wrong, despite his statement having been perfectly correct, and he subsided into a puzzled silence, not recovering sufficiently to speak again for quite ten minutes.

It was a little after nine when a footman came to enquire if the *jäger* might have a word with Count Charodyev, and, with Tatya's smiling consent, he was allowed to come in and murmur discreetly to Igor that the large coach was now ready for the road, and the smaller one had also been inspected and given a few minor repairs. 'You may leave whenever you wish,' he concluded, and waited expectantly for orders.

Igor thanked him and said to Tatya, 'Our coach is repaired and ready, so I'm afraid we must be on our way in the morning. I, for one, will be most sorry to go, but we still have a long journey before us . . .'

Varya, of course, pleaded for one more day, but Igor and Maxim were determined, and Mila did not consider it her place to say anything at all, so it was decided that they would set off after breakfast, taking Dorya, one of Tatya's maids, who had been looking after Varya, as a substitute for Olga.

Because of the need for an early start if they were to cover the 150 or so *versty* to Orel the next day, the travellers retired soon after a light supper had been served at ten. Mila made the mistake, once she was in bed, of indulging in a little day-dream in which Tatya's implied suggestion that she might marry Igor came true, but she knew that there was no hope of that, and consequently she made herself so miserable that she was quite unable to sleep for going over and over all the sensible things she should have done twelve years ago, when she was too young and inexperienced to have thought of any of them.

She eventually fell into an uneasy doze out of sheer emotional exhaustion, but it was already daylight by then, and soon Marfa arrived to wake her again and tell her it was time to be up and getting ready to leave, and she went down to breakfast trying to smother her yawns, to find that, despite the early hour, everyone had come down to join them for the meal.

Mila had been a little uncertain of her own position while she was staying in the house, for she was, after all, no more than a paid servant—a superior one, perhaps, but nevertheless no more than a sort of governess—and, although she had been treated in every respect as a guest at the same level as her companions, she had been careful not to presume on Tatya's and Vassily's kindness, and she had felt a sense of strain during her stay. Consequently, when, after the customary silent gathering of all the guests and their hosts, and prayers for those who were leaving, Tatya held out her arms to her and embraced her, even before she did the same to Varya, and begged her to come again and stay longer, perhaps on her way 'home' from Kherson, she was quite overcome and shed a few tears. Because of this, she failed to notice that Tatya whispered something to Igor as he bent to kiss her cheek in farewell, and they both glanced in her direction. Perhaps it was as well that she did not see, as Igor then shrugged and shook his head.

Valentin also bade her a very friendly farewell, holding her hand and assuring her that he looked forward to seeing her again in Petersburg, if Tatya and Vassily ever allowed him to leave Ash Glade; and Boris, dark eyes fixed admiringly on her face, said with every appearance of sincerity that the whole of Tula Province would be as a desert without her gracious presence. This fine sentiment caused Igor to break into a fit of coughing, much to Mila's mortification, for she was enjoying the un-accustomed pleasure of being flattered, without for one moment being taken in by it.

After the exchange of farewells and good wishes, everyone followed the coaches down the drive to the road, Tatya driving her little donkey-cart, and then stood in a group around her under the Doric temple to wave the travellers out of sight until they, leaning out of the coach windows, could no longer see for dust.

As they resumed their seats and pulled up the win-dows, Igor flicked dust from his dark clothes and new grey beaver with his handkerchief, and said, 'How lucky that Vassily's head is the same size as mine, for I'd not thought to bring a second hat with me.'

'Is your own one quite ruined?' Varya asked sym-pathetically. 'Well, never mind, for I think Vassily Sergeivich's grey one suits you much better than that old black thing. Uncle Igor, why do you always wear black?'

'Habit,' he replied briskly. 'Mourning for lost youth and so forth, I expect.'

'Why shouldn't he?' Maxim enquired. 'I always wear dark blue, even when I'm not in uniform.'

'But it's so dull!' Varya objected. 'I shall *never* wear dark clothes, even when I'm quite old. Not even if I'm . . .' She broke off suddenly and looked at Mila, her face a picture of contrition.

'I wear dark clothes for practical reasons,' Mila said quietly. 'Dark clothes last longer than pale-coloured ones.' She was wearing a dark blue muslin, for the weather was now too warm for the sensible travelling-dress and pelisse.

'I thought perhaps—half-mourning?' Varya said un-certainly, looking at her speculatively.

Mila shook her head, then looked out of the window at the passing scenery without saying anything more, and presently fell into an uneasy doze.

The day's journey was uneventful, very long, and rather dull. The road ran through a country of low, rolling hills, and they passed through only two small towns and eight or nine tiny villages, all of which looked the same, the whole way. The inns were poor, and the *jäger* seemed to greet them at every relay station with an apology, so they were bored, stiff and hungry by the time they reached Orel late at night, and stopped at an inn with a view over the river, for the town stood on a cliff above the Oka.

Varya said she was too tired to eat dinner, but Igor pointed out that she had hardly taken anything since breakfast, and would feel better with something in her stomach.

'We'll not try to reach Kursk tomorrow,' he went on. 'There's no point in killing ourselves in our efforts to reach Kherson as quickly as possible. There's a decent inn where the road to Kiev branches off from this one, and we'll stay there tomorrow night. It's not much about sixty *versty* from here, so you may sleep late in the morning.'

Compared with Tula and its hammering iron-smiths, Orel was a quiet town, and Mila went to her room after a good dinner feeling that at least she was tired enough to ensure that she would sleep soundly. She found that Marfa had already unpacked the things she would need for the night, but was now investigating the contents of a second valise.

'Why, what's that?' Mila asked. 'It's not mine!'

'Well, madame,' Marfa replied, straightening up with a very pretty pale green frock held up before her. 'Dorya says her mistress—Countess Karacheva, that is—told her to pack the things and bring them for you, but not to tell you or me until we got to Orel, and here we are! There's a note, look!'

She held out a folded and sealed sheet of paper, which proved to be a short letter from Tatya.

My dear Mila Levovna,
I do hope you will not be offended by my little gift. It is only a few frocks which I haven't worn, for I always seem to have more than I need, and, as we are much the same size and colouring, I thought you might like to have them. Please don't feel under any obligation to me, and don't bother to write to me about them— just wear them and enjoy them! I'm sure you will be more comfortable in the south in lighter colours, and, if you'll forgive me mentioning it, your dark clothes make people think you are still in mourning!

In friendship,
Tatya

Mila had long ago learned not to be offended if someone was kind enough to give her a wearable garment, and she felt only gratitude to Tatya for her thoughtfulness. Despite the request not to write, she resolved to send a letter of thanks as soon as she had an opportunity, and she felt almost light-hearted as she sat on the edge of the couch which was to serve her as a bed and watched Marfa unpack the valise, which proved to contain six pretty light-coloured muslins, some plain, some embroidered, and each with its own undershift. It was not until she touched them that she discovered that they were not muslin at all, but barège silk! At the bottom of the case were half a dozen pairs of white silk stockings, and a shawl dyed in pastel shades of rainbow colours.

'Oh, it's too generous!' Mila exclaimed, overwhelmed.

'Well, she's like that, is Countess Karacheva, so I'm told!' said Marfa, starting to fold the clothes with loving care and packing them again in their tissue paper, for Mila had decided to save them for Kherson, thinking that travelling on the dusty roads would spoil their fresh, light colours. 'And so I know, for that matter! She sent gifts for everyone—they'll all be looking at them now, I expect! I had an embroidered blouse and apron and a string of glass beads. First time I ever had a gift like that from anyone but our own Family, and it's not even New Year or my name-day! And talk about kind while we were there! Sent every day, she did, to ask if we were well, and if we needed anything, me and the valets, just as if we were gentry. A lovely lady, she is. Do you know, Mila Levovna, there's not one of her people, nor the Count's, is a serf. All of them free, every last one! Hers have been for years, but he freed all his to please her! I think that's the most Christian and loving thing I ever heard! Any other lady'd have asked for a diamond necklace, but not the Countess. Free souls are more to her than jewels, and that's something I never heard of before!'

Mila agreed, of course, that Tatya Petrovna was, indeed, a 'lovely lady', remembering only too clearly what Igor had said about her. She felt ashamed of herself for begrudging anything to someone so kind and generous, yet, now she knew that her own long-ago ambivalence towards Igor had veiled the love which she had never found with Étienne, but now grown stronger and easily recognisable, she could not help but envy the beautiful object of Igor's own affections. It was only later, during a brief period of wakefulness near dawn, that she realised that twice, the day before, someone had linked her dark-coloured clothing to the idea of mourning, and she thought ironically that it was now, when she had both found and lost her love, that she should indeed be wearing black, which she had worn before only because convention demanded it.

Orel was a pleasant town, and the travellers strolled about for a while after breakfast, which they had taken at a more reasonable hour than usual, and made a morning call at the house of an old acquaintance of Igor's—a retired cavalry officer called Turgenev— but the family were away at their country estate at Spasskoye for the summer. Igor admitted afterwards that this was a relief, as he could not stand the man's wife!

After an early luncheon, they set out again to travel a mere sixty *versty* to the inn that Igor had mentioned. It was still only late afternoon, and both Varya and Maxim seemed a little restive at the thought of stopping so soon. Varya suggested that they might as well go on for at least another three or four hours, and Maxim, as if under some compulsion to differ from her, said, 'We could take the Kiev road and go as far as Dmitriev–Ligovsky,' and then scowled as he realised that to go to Kiev now would take them well out of their way.

'You may feel able to travel twenty-four hours a day, my children,' said Igor in a sardonically paternal manner. 'But your elders find that their old bones begin to ache after a few hours on these infernal roads, and this inn is the best we are likely to find for many *versty*, so we'll stay here in comfort. With your kind permission, of course.'

The opposition subsided, and there they stopped, taking a leisurely dinner at a civilised hour, retiring reasonably early after (in the ladies' case, at least) taking a hip-bath and washing their hair, and the next day they pressed on to Kursk, where they stayed for two nights, the intervening day being Sunday, when they attended church in the morning. In the afternoon, Maxim proposed taking the party out on the River Seim in a hired sailing-boat, but Igor vetoed the suggestion very firmly, without giving a reason, and said that a ride on horseback would be better, thereby stopping Varya's protest before she was fairly started on it, for she had to agree that sitting in a boat would be less of a change from sitting in a coach than riding a horse.

Mila was not very happy with the idea, but, as usual, thought it not her place to protest, but she approached her hired horse nervously, thinking he looked remarkably tall and had an unpleasant way of rolling his eyes back at her. It was a very long time since she had been on a horse, but she reminded herself firmly that she had enjoyed riding in her youth—in fact, it was one of the pleasures she had shared with Étienne, for he had taught her a great deal of his cavalryman's skill.

'I recall that you were particularly fond of riding in former days,' Igor remarked, echoing her thoughts, as he stepped in front of Maxim, who had come to assist her, without apparently seeing him, and offered his linked hands as a mounting-block.

'I'm rather out of practice,' she replied as she mounted, wriggling into a comfortable position on the side-saddle and attempting to exercise some control over the horse, which backed slowly in a circle, scattering the other three animals and stepping on the foot of the groom who had led him out. The groom said something of a personal and derogatory nature to him, and he then stood meekly, head hanging, as if he had just ridden all the way from Moscow non-stop and was ready to drop from exhaustion.

Igor led the way out of the town at a brisk trot, and they were soon in the country, which was open grassland and remarkably hot and shadeless. Varya quickened the pace of her mount, saying that a gallop was the only way to raise a breeze, and then went tearing off, uttering an unladylike Cossack yell as she went.

Maxim, naturally enough, followed suit and set off in pursuit, obviously intending to make a race of it. Igor, clamping his new hat more firmly on his head, spurred his mount to a canter, but he glanced back, and, realising that Mila was not following, circled round and returned to her.

'Is something wrong?' he enquired, looking, she thought, rather more annoyed than concerned.

'Pray, go on if you wish,' she replied. 'I don't altogether trust this horse, and I'm very much out of practice.'

He turned to look after his niece and Maxim, then glanced around the rolling landscape and spied what appeared to be a grove of trees on the top of a near-by rise.

'I think I'd better go after Varya,' he said dubiously. 'Perhaps you'd care to wait in the shade of those trees over there until we return?'

'By all means,' Mila replied with some relief, for she was finding the sun too hot in the open, and her back was aching from the unaccustomed twisted postion necessary in riding side-saddle. Igor nodded, wheeled his horse in an accomplished fashion, and rode off at a gallop after the others, who had now disappeared over a ridge.

Mila jogged slowly along towards the trees, having a little difficulty in persuading her mount not to follow his stable-mates. In the shade of the trees she slid to the ground, tied the reins to a bush and looked around her. The trees were not, after all, a grove, but the edge of a much larger tract of woodland, and, in the distance among the mixture of oak, birch and rowan, she could hear the *plunk* of a woodman's axe. It was pleasantly shady under a large oak near the bush where the horse was now browsing, so she sat down on a convenient root and looked out towards the direction in which the others had disappeared, sighing a little and wishing that she did not seem to irritate Igor by everything she did.

It seemed odd, looking back over the past few days,

that she had, without even trying, attracted three of the six men she had met, which was a flattering proportion, considering that, of the other three, one was recently married to a particularly lovely woman and another had just recovered his lost fiancée, and it seemed extraordinarily ironic that the sixth man should be the one for whom she cared, yet he seemed to have developed an antipathy towards her which, she supposed, was entirely her own fault for having treated him so badly in the past.

She sat thinking for some time, failing to notice that the sound of the axe had ceased, and she was taken completely by surprise when a wood-pigeon suddenly flew out of the wood behind her with a great whirr of wings, speeding low directly over the head of her horse, which uttered a startled neigh, reared up, pulling the insecurely tied reins free, and bolted across country, rapidly disappearing over the next ridge as Mila scrambled to her feet with a cry of alarm.

'Lost your horse, have you, lady?' asked a voice from behind her in Russian with an odd-sounding accent. 'Should have tied him up proper, shouldn't you? What you doing here, all by yourself, so far from the town?'

The speaker was a tall, broad-shouldered peasant in a rough linen blouse and dirty Cossack trousers, who might have been any age, for his face was hidden by a remarkably shaggy, grizzled beard which met his fur cap and intermingled with it so that she could not see where one ended and the other began.

'I'm just waiting for my friends,' she replied firmly, hoping she did not sound as nervous as she felt.

'Oh, yes?' The woodman's beard split to reveal a row of jagged and discoloured teeth, and he casually hefted his axe from one hand to the other, then leaned it, head downwards, against the oak. 'Funny thing, but I didn't hear anyone else come with you, and I can't see no signs of these friends of yours! How're you proposing to get back to town, then? Walking?'

'My friends will be here soon,' Mila replied, looking out across the grassland hopefully, but there was no sign of anything except a lark, which mounted quickly into the cloudless sky and became a disembodied trill high above.

'Well, now,' said the man, grinning more broadly. 'If you were particularly good to me, I might feel inclined to help you! I just happen to have a horse and cart back there, in the trees, and I might be persuaded to drive you back to town. Maybe.'

Mila was suddenly struck by the unpleasant memory that the revolt led by Pugachev against the landowners thirty-eight years before had drawn much of its support from this part of the Empire, and from men like this woodman—men who had raped and murdered females like herself without mercy. She looked about her desperately, but there was nowhere to run to, nowhere to hide.

'Come on, now, I haven't got all day!' said the man, seizing her by the elbow. 'You come with me, and I'll see you're all right, if you see that I don't lose by it, if you see what I mean!'

'Very kind of you,' said Igor's crisp, dry voice from behind him, 'But not necessary, thank you.'

Mila turned and ran to him, clinging to his free arm, for his other hand was holding the reins of his horse.

'Oh, thank God!' she said in a broken whisper, which was all she could manage.

'Where's your mount?' Igor asked, looking about him.

'A bird startled him and he ran off,' she replied.

'Didn't tie him properly,' the woodman put in, scratching his beard and still grinning. 'Women never can tie knots, can they?'

'True,' Igor replied lightly, disengaging himself from Mila and walking towards the man. 'I'd no idea this wood was so large—I thought it only a grove! I've been working my way through it, trying to find my friend. You work here, I take it?'

Mila suddenly realised that Igor was speaking Russian with the same accent as the man, and supposed that it must be Ukrainian. She also realised that the man was not cringing or speaking in the grovelling fashion usual in a peasant—he had not even called Igor 'Sir', but spoke as to an equal.

'I'm working here at the moment,' the man said. 'I travel about as I like. There's always work for a skilled woodman.'

'You're Cossack, I think?' Igor went on, which explained the attitude which Mila had just noticed. 'I'm part Cossack myself.' He reeled off a pedigree of about a dozen generations, to which the woodman replied with an even longer one, and the two men shook hands.

'Well, thank you for offering to help my friend,' Igor said. 'Perhaps you'd like to drink her health next time you find yourself near an alehouse,' and he slipped a number of coins into the man's large hand. Mila saw the glint of silver in the sunlight, and was amazed.

'Very kind of you, brother,' said the woodman, slipping the money into his pocket without even looking at it. 'I'll drink to you, and the free brotherhood too, while I'm about it!'

He picked up his axe, nodded in a friendly fashion to Mila, and plodded off back among the trees with a casual '*Da svidanye*' called back over his shoulder before he disappeared.

Mila, feeling very foolish, waited for Igor's acid tongue to pronounce his opinion of a bird-witted female who let her horse run off and was frightened of a respectable free peasant, but he only said mildly, 'I'm sorry I was so long. It took me a while to come up with the others, and then Varya fell off her horse. Oh, she's not hurt,' he responded to Mila's cry of alarm. 'She'll always fall on her feet! When I came back for you, I struck the edge of the wood at the wrong place, and tried to come through it instead of following the edge. I suppose you were thinking of the Pugachev affair after that fellow turned up? I thought so!' He had noticed Mila's flushed cheeks. 'Quite right; for two of the names he mentioned were familiar from that tale! I doubt if he'd have harmed you, though, for he'd lose his freedom, if not his life, and it's too precious to risk. Well, I suppose we'll have to ride double—did you happen to notice which way your horse went?'

Mila pointed dumbly, and he said, 'In that case, he'll be making for his stable if he has any sense. Unless some more of my Cossack relations steal him on the way!'

Mila was at once alarmed that this might have happened, and said, 'If he has been stolen, I can't pay for him until . . . I mean . . . !'

'Until my brother pays you? Oh, don't worry! It's as much my fault as yours for leaving you alone like that. I'm a rich man nowadays, you know, and the expense of an odd horse or so is a bagatelle! Come, let's be on our way, or Maxim will be back with a search party as soon as he's delivered Varya in Kursk.'

He apparently thought that Mila would be safer sitting sideways in front of him, trapped between his arms so that she could not fall off, which was certainly more comfortable than bouncing about on his horse's rump, but it meant that she spent the next half-hour virtually in his arms. Her emotions were set into such chaos that she could hardly reply to his attempts at conversation, and so they rode most of the way in silence, broken only by sundry snorts from the horse, which obviously resented the double burden and refused to progress at anything more than a slow walk.

As Igor had suspected, Mila's mount had gone home at an easy canter once his fright had worn off, and he was snug in his own stable. Varya, far from being hurt or shaken by her fall, was trying to persuade Maxim to take her for a sail on the river as soon as Mila should return to chaperon them, but Igor soon quelled that idea by saying that she would undoubtedly overturn the boat and disrupt all the traffic on the river. In any case, Mila had suffered a fright and was to be left in peace.

This news, of course, led Maxim to exclaim and demand particulars, and make a great deal of unnecessary fuss, to Mila's way of thinking, from which Igor rescued her with unexpected kindness by sending her off to bed and ordering that her dinner be served to her in her room, and forbidding the others to go near her.

The next three days somehow combined themselves in Mila's memory as a most unpleasant and apparently continuous nightmare of heat, dust and jolting over corduroy roads (and not in good repair either), greasy, unappetising food, and bug-ridden inns, although in fact only the first of these, some twenty *versty* north of Belgorod, had bugs, and the second, a little short of Kharkov, was clean, but the food was inedible.

South of Kharkov, the landscape changed dramatically as they entered the Black Earth region. There were still trees, but they no longer formed forests, only small copses and windbreaks amid great rolling grasslands, cut by the tributaries of the Don. Villages were even further apart than they had been in the north, but now the wooden cabins stood among fruit trees, and the fields were vast, the growing crops already high.

They reached Novomoskovsk (New Moscow) in the afternoon of the fourth day from Kursk, which, considering the state of the roads, was what Maxim described in nautical terms as a fast passage. It was a fine town with well-designed buildings, and the rest-house (which was more than an inn, but not quite a hotel) was comfortable in a manner more reminiscent of St Petersburg than Old Russia.

Mila descended from the coach feeling as if every joint in her body had rusted solid, despite the hot, dry weather, and hobbled indoors, more than thankful to realise that another day's travel would bring them to Alexandrovsk and the possibility of taking ship for the rest of the journey. She felt depressed as well, for Igor, since they left Ash Glade, had seemed more interested in a book he was reading than in his companions; while they were in the coach, he had hardly so much as glanced at her, let alone spoken. Even during their day's rest at Kursk he had been quiet and abstracted, and Mila supposed he had been thinking of Tatya.

'Kindly have the bath-house prepared,' he said to the innkeeper, who came out with the *jäger* to greet them. 'The ladies will use it first, then Lieutenant Korovelsky and myself, then our valets, then the maids, and finally the grooms and drivers. You may join the valets, if you wish.'

This last was addressed to the *jäger*, whose tired and rather anxious face lit up at the invitation. None of the inns in which they had stayed since they left Moscow had boasted a private bath-house, and the discovery that there was one here had at least a temporarily lightening effect on Mila's spirits.

It was most pleasant to sit on the wooden bench, wrapped in clean, thick towels, feeling the dense, hot steam drawing the stiffness out of her limbs. From time to time the attendant shovelled more glowing charcoal under the walls into the trough which ran round inside them, and poured water on it to raise yet more and hotter steam, and there were freshly-cut birch twigs to stir up the circulation. After about twenty minutes both Mila and Varya felt pleasantly clean and relaxed, and close to suffocation. They finished their bath with a most enjoyable plunge into a marble-lined pool of cold water, which was just large enough for two, and deep enough to sit in immersed up to their necks, although the marble ensured that it was too cold to linger for more than a few seconds.

Mila's bedroom was at the side of the building, and when she was dry and had dressed as far as her under-shift, she sent Marfa away with instructions to return half an hour before dinner, and sat on the wide window-sill to be quiet, to think, and to look at the view.

Immediately below was a single-storeyed extension jutting out from the main building, and the river, which, she supposed correctly, was a small tributary of the Dnepr. There were pollarded willows, thick with leaves, on the opposite bank, and beyond those the steppes stretched away to the far horizon. The area near the town was under cultivation, the soil showing black be-tween plants which were far advanced in growth. Beyond were great areas of pasture, where cattle stood about in groups and seemed to be the only living things in sight. The monotony of the flat plain was broken by a road which ran eastwards, as straight as if it had been drawn across the land with a ruler, and looked as if it might go on in the same way until it reached the borders of China or the Pacific Ocean, and a few groups of trees, acting as windbreaks, for the bitter north winds howled across these plains in the winter.

The sound of voices caught her attention, and she looked down in time to see two naked figures run from the low building, which she now realised was the bath-house, across the few yards of grass to the river, where they both plunged in, the taller but clumsier figure of

Maxim a poor second to Igor's lithe, fast-moving form.

Mila, naturally, drew back from the window and averted her eyes, but she was not a prude and had no prejudices against the human body which, from what she had seen of nude statues, she thought could be very beautiful, and she was soon looking out again, standing back from the window so that she could see without being seen, hoping to catch another glimpse of Igor—not for any prurient reason, but simply because she loved him.

He was swimming vigorously up the river with a neat overarm stroke, his kicking feet just breaking the surface behind him, while Maxim was bobbing up and down like an elderly seal quite close to where he had jumped in. After a few moments, he called out that the water was cold, heaved himself out on to the bank, and disappeared back into the bath-house.

Mila moved closer to the window, and eventually pressed her face against the glass, for Igor had gone almost out of her field of view to her right, but presently he stopped, bobbed up and down a few times, then swam back, more slowly. When he reached the place where he had entered the water, he pulled himself out on to the bank and proceeded to rub himself briskly with a towel which he had dropped there during his dash across the grass. As he did so, he looked up suddenly, apparently straight at Mila's window, and she was caught, leaning forward, her weight on her hands, which were on the window-sill, unable to dodge back in time to avoid being seen.

For a few moments she was quite frozen with horror, conscious that she was only half-dressed, with her hair loose about her shoulders, that Igor was naked but for the towel, which he was holding somewhat negligently in one hand, that if she could clearly see his face, he must equally clearly be able to recognise hers and see that she was spying on him.

The colour rushed to her face, and then Igor gravely raised one hand in an airy wave, breaking the spell, and she shot away from the window to the far side of the room, her hands to her burning cheeks, feeling that she would never be able to face him again without dying of shame.

She managed to do so, of course, without anything so drastic happening. Marfa reappeared at the appointed hour, by which time her mistress had recovered her composure and almost convinced herself that the light on the window-glass would have prevented Igor from recognising her, and she put on one of her dark cotton frocks, had her hair brushed and arranged, and went down to dinner with considerable trepidation.

Igor behaved as any gentleman should—that is, as if nothing untoward or unusual had occurred. Baths, swimming, rivers, towels or windows did not figure in the conversation at any time during dinner, which was the best they had been served since they left Ash Glade, and which they took in a small private parlour that was theirs for as long as they stayed in Novomoskovsk.

After dinner Igor proposed that, for a change from reading or talking, they might play a few hands of whist, a card-game which had recently been introduced from England and was now very popular in Russia. Maxim agreed at once, and Varya admitted unashamedly that the game was not unknown (albeit clandestinely) in the rarified atmosphere of the Smolny, and Igor informed Mila quite kindly that a female of her good sense would soon pick it up.

Maxim produced a handful of coins and clinked them hopefully, but Igor said firmly that they would play for spills, as he considered that gambling destroyed the real pleasure of playing a game and had set far too many men on the road to ruin. Varya, unfortunately, spoiled the fine sentiment of this speech by adding in her usual tactless fashion, 'And Mila can't afford to wager, in any case.' Then she clapped her hand over her mouth, her fine eyes conveying a heartfelt apology to Mila for putting her to the blush.

For some time Mila was too busy learning the game to look much at Igor, and, in any case, had drawn Maxim for a partner, but there came a time eventually when she was sitting opposite Igor and had gained enough confidence in her play to be able to raise her eyes from the cards. She glanced up, met those dark unfathomable eyes which regarded her steadily for a few moments as she felt her colour rising, and then one heavy lid drooped in an unmistakable wink. She then played all the rest of the cards in her hand at random and succeeded in losing every remaining trick, which caused Maxim to take her back through each one so that he could explain where she had gone wrong, while Igor sat back in his chair looking quite amused.

## CHAPTER
## EIGHT

WHEN MAXIM's lecture had reached its conclusion, Mila thanked him in a rather dry fashion, but he gravely acknowledged her gratitude and then turned his attention to Varya, who was attempting to build a card-house with little success, and kindly began to give her expert tuition on that subject, while Mila drifted away to one of the windows of the parlour which looked out on the road, and stood there watching the passing traffic. It was considerable, with wagons and coaches, herds of cattle and marching companies of soldiers passing on their way to or from the Crimean peninsula to the south, or Ekaterinoslav, Nikolaev or Odessa to the south-west.

'I gather that war with the Ottomans is still considered a strong possibility,' said Igor, speaking in Russian, almost in her ear and making her start, for she had not heard him come up behind her. 'I still doubt it myself. Of course, this is always a busy place, but the volume of traffic seems much higher than usual. You'll notice that almost all the civilian coaches are going north, but the military forces and supplies are going towards the coast. If anything does happen, I shall, of course, take you and Varya back to Moscow at once. Or Petersburg, if you prefer.'

'Thank you,' Mila replied nervously, and there was an awkward silence, broken only by the voices of Varya and Maxim wrangling enjoyably over their card structure, which had just collapsed again, and the sounds of the passing traffic, which were muffled by the double window and the wide forecourt between the rest-house and the road. She glanced shyly at Igor, but he was watching the traffic with apparent interest.

'You—you must think me quite . . .' she began, also in Russian, her voice sounding quite raw with embarrassment, but she could not think of the right word to say next, and so the sentence tailed off.

'Anyone may look out of a window,' said Igor calmly, still doing so. 'And cannot be held responsible for what may be seen outside it. As for what I may think . . .' giving Mila one of his sidelong, inscrutable looks, '. . . I think I may claim to know you well enough to be aware that I should do you an injustice if I thought ill of any of your actions. Do you feel able to travel on to Alexandrovsk tomorrow, or shall we stay here another day?' He had reverted to French with the change of subject, and Mila realised that he had used Russian before so that Varya, if she happened to overhear, would not understand.

'It's not for me to say,' Mila replied, grateful that he had asked her. 'Varya is in something of a hurry to see her father again, and Maxim has a ship waiting for him . . .'

'The young are always impatient,' Igor said dismissively. 'We've taken a reasonably short time to come so far, despite our unexpected stay at Ash Glade. I'm aware, of course, that Potemkin habitually made the journey from Petersburg to Kherson in eight days, but I've no wish to emulate His Serenissimus and die of exhaustion at fifty-two!'

Mila looked at him when he mentioned Ash Glade, wondering if there might be some betraying glimmer of expression in his face, but she could discern nothing except a mild interest in the passing traffic, which he was still watching. She observed his profile, which was clean-

cut, and noted how smoothly his skin seemed to fit over
the bones of his face, without any slack lines or pouches
of fat. In fact, his face was as lean and taut as the rest of
him . . . and she felt her cheeks burn at the thought.

'So what do you wish to do?' he asked, suddenly
turning his head to look at her, catching her gazing at
him with flushed cheeks, but he showed no sign that he
noticed anything untoward.

'How are we to go from Alexandrovsk to Kherson?'
she asked.

'We could cross the Dnepr just below the last cataract.
There's a ferry which is quite reliable, despite the force
of the current. Once across, there's a road of sorts which
we could take down the west bank to Kherson. Alterna-
tively, we might continue on the Crimea Highway to
Melitopol, and go west from there, which is a longer
route, but a better road. Then again, we could go from
here to Ekaterinoslav, cross the river above the cataracts
and travel by way of Nikolayev, but that's an even longer
route.'

'I believe Varya had thought of taking a ship on the
river,' Mila ventured.

'Not from Ekaterinoslav!' Igor replied decisively.
'Not even our Varangian ancestors ventured willingly
down the six cataracts! *My* Varangian ancestors, I
should say!' he added, alluding to his Ukrainian descent
from the Viking lords of Kiev. 'From Alexandrovsk to
Kherson by river is a reasonable proposition, however.
It would certainly be more comfortable for you than the
coach, if we can find a ship of fair size. Would you be
willing to do that?'

'Yes,' Mila replied. 'In fact, I think it might be
pleasant. The river waters are sheltered and not likely to
be rough, I think?'

'Positively sluggish among the islands, provided the
wind blows downstream.' His dark eyes had been watch-

ing Mila's face ever since he turned away from the window, but in a cool, impersonal way which she found a little irritating. In fact, her feelings were quite confused, for she was afraid that, if he looked too closely, he might read in her face the feelings which she would rather keep hidden; yet she disliked the way his eyes seemed to slide over her as if she were a piece of furniture or a cabbage.

'That's settled, then. We'll go to Alexandrovsk tomorrow, and I'll instruct the *jäger* to make enquiries about a passage from there for the four of us and the maids and valets. The coaches can continue by road. It's only ninety-odd *versty* to Alexandrovsk, and we can wait a few days there, if need be, for a suitable ship. I'd like Varya to see Khortitsa Island while we're there, for it was the home of our Cossack ancestors before Catherine the Great had them turned out of it!'

'Why did she do that?' Mila asked, surprised. 'I thought she tried to bring more people into the Southern Provinces, not drive them out.'

Igor gave a twisted smile and a shrug, and explained the outlines of Catherine's policy for the Ukraine, especially the moves taken in reprisal for the Cossack support for the Pugachev rebellion.

'I see,' Mila said, thinking how successful the military part of the policy had been, for the Cossack regiments had won high regard among Russia's friends and enemies.

'Are you talking about those dreadful Cossacks again, Uncle Igor?' demanded Varya. 'All my friends say that they're no better than savages, and I have to be very quiet about my Zaporozhyan great-grandmamma!'

'Then you should be ashamed of yourself!' Igor retorted. 'They're a fine, brave people; honourable, honest and straightforward; and those qualities count for more than your precious Petersburg culture and your ladylike accomplishments! Never let me hear you speak like that of your great-grandmother's people again, you hear me?'

Varya and Maxim looked considerably surprised at the anger in his voice and the air of command which he had suddenly assumed, and both were obviously deeply impressed. Varya hung her head and murmured, 'I'm sorry,' in a very subdued manner, and Maxim said, 'Quite right, sir!' with as much respect as he would have shown an admiral. Mila said *'Pravilno!'* (Hear, hear!) in Russian, adding 'Bravo!' for good measure, and then remembered that she was not entitled to express an opinion. Igor looked at her gravely, as if reminded of that fact, and then to her surprise he smiled, put his hand on his heart, made her a little bow and said, 'Thank you.'

He then rang the bell for the waiter to bring supper. 'Bed after this, my children! We go to Alexandrovsk tomorrow!' he said crisply.

'And then on the river?' asked Varya, her face, which had been rather woebegone after her uncle's set-down, lighting up at the thought.

'Possibly,' was all the reply she received, but Igor relented next morning, and, soon after the coach had left the paved streets of Novomoskovsk for the corduroy highway, he admitted that he had told the *jäger* to make enquiries in Alexandrovsk about passenger shipping on the river.

In the early afternoon they stopped for half an hour at the inn of a village called, appropriately enough, Var-varovka, and Varya had little difficulty in persuading Mila to take a short walk with her to stretch their legs in a band of trees which protected the village from the north winds. Igor warned them not to go too far, as he said he had no intention of waiting beyond the half-hour, but otherwise made no objection.

'It's very decent of him to say we may go on the river from Alexandrovsk,' Varya said pensively, skipping over the gnarled roots of an oak. 'He was in a great wax last night, you know, for he's very particular about being not Great Russian, if you follow me. I mean—in Petersburg, it's not at all the thing to admit to being anything but Great Russian—apart from Polish, that is—which is quite fashionable—or Greek—that's in fashion, too! I keep very quiet about being half-Ukrainian and the Cossack connection, for the other girls would rib me something shocking if they knew, but Uncle Igor is really proud about both! Mind you, I think that when he was a boy in the Corps of Pages he had a great deal to put up with over it, and that seems to have made him very quick to take offence if anyone says anything slighting about being Kievan, or calls Cossacks savages, or anything like that. It was so silly of me to speak as I did. But, you know, it's so long since I've seen Uncle Igor that I'd quite forgotten! Do you think that odd? To know something so important about a person, I mean, and yet to forget about it? Does it show that I'm truly as bird-witted as Maxim says I am?'

'Maxim has no business to call you bird-witted!' replied Mila. 'It's very rude of him. That is the sort of remark that only a close relative is allowed to make! Besides, I don't believe you are, really. After all, your uncle has been away for—what did you say?—a year?—with your friends' prejudices ever present about you, shaping your own attitudes . . . I think, however, that your uncle is quite right. Your ancestry is something to be proud of, for both Ukrainians and Cossacks have a fine history and the people of Kiev were the founders of the Russian nation.'

Varya nodded thoughtfully. 'Yes, you're right, of course. I'll have to remember that, and stand up for my own people more, when I go back to the Smolny—if I go back, that is! Some of those girls talk as if nothing in Russia outside Petersburg is of any importance at all,

and even Moscow to them is a funny little backwater. Do
you know, they don't let us speak Russian there! Most of
the girls have talked in French all their silly little narrow
lives, and know only a few words of their own language—just enough to give orders to their serfs! I say, if
we turned back now, we should just have time for a glass
of tea before we have to get into the coach.'

Mila smilingly agreed, for the weather was far hotter
and drier here than she had been used to in Petersburg,
and she was thirsty. The land was so flat and open, and
the sun seemed to have burned all the greenness and
moisture out of it. Even the small watercourses were
dry, and the leaves of the trees under which they had
been walking was sparse and dusty. She wondered why
the country was considered to be fertile, and, as she had
heard some people say, beautiful. Presumably it was
green in the spring, after the thaw, and perhaps there
were wild flowers then, before the sun had grown hot
enough to scorch everything, but now, in late June, she
thought it little better than a desert.

At night, however, she discovered that it did become
beautiful. As they did not reach Alexandrovsk until late,
they were on the road after a splendid sunset had turned
the dry grassland to gold and the far horizon to flame.
When darkness fell, the sky seemed limitless—black
velvet with the faintest tinge of blue, and set with stars
such as she had never seen before, glowing like silver
lamps, undimmed by mist or cloud, and seeming near
enough to touch.

'I had no idea there were so many stars in the sky!'
Varya exclaimed, leaning out of the coach window to see
more of them. 'Or that the sky stretched so far! In
Petersburg it looks more like the inside of a black
parasol with a few little holes in it. The stars here are so
huge!'

'Bring your head inside, or you'll be up there among

them next time we meet another coach,' Igor said calmly. 'I don't think your father would appreciate receiving
a decapitated daughter!'

Varya obediently resumed her seat without arguing,
which surprised both Mila and Maxim. Mila could see
Igor's head silhouetted against the window, and, as he
turned it a little to continue looking out on his own side
almost as he was speaking, she supposed that he had
assumed Varya's obedience.

'It's certainly—er—very beautiful,' Maxim observed
in a slightly embarrassed fashion, as if he considered
aesthetic appreciation of stars unsuitable in a man who
normally regarded them as a convenient means of
finding one's way about.

'*In such a night*,' Igor said conversationally in English,
'*Did Jessica steal from the wealthy Jew, and with an
unthrift love did run from Venice, as far as Belmont.*'

'*In such a night*,' Mila continued without thinking
what she was saying, '*Did young Lorenzo swear he lov'd
her well, stealing her soul with many vows of faith, and
ne'er a true one.*' Her voice acquired a note of bitterness
as she realised what she was quoting and spoke the last
five words, but it appeared to pass unnoticed, for Varya
exclaimed in tones of enlightenment, 'Oh, you're *quoting*!' Maxim said, 'I beg your pardon?' sounding utterly
mystified, and Igor said, 'Yes, precisely. However, the
lines I *intended* to say were, "*There's not the smallest orb
which thou behold'st but in his motion like an angel sings,
still quiring to the young-eyed cherubims.*" My memory
must have played a trick on me. My apologies.'

Mila was silent, wondering what he meant, refusing to
admit even to herself that the first lines he had quoted,
and her own continuation of them, were in any way
appropriate to her own elopement, and, as he did not
know the truth about it, his quick intelligence must have
sensed something from her tone as she spoke the words.

'I don't understand English well enough to know what all that meant,' said Varya regretfully. 'Was it Poetry? You said it more like ordinary speaking.'

'It's a speech from a play by William Shakespeare,' replied Igor, sounding a little bored with the subject. 'Presumably his name has penetrated even the fastnesses of the Smolny?'

'Yes.' Varya sounded doubtful. 'I think so. Didn't he write something called *Hameau* (*village*)?'

'*Hamlet!*' corrected Igor. 'Good heavens!'

He made no further comment on his niece's educational attainments, but lapsed into silence, and the two younger members of the party apparently assumed that he was asleep. Mila, however, had an uneasy feeling that those watchful, unfathomable eyes were fixed on her, although she knew that, as the lamps inside the coach had not been lighted, it was too dark for him to be able to see her. She felt an almost irresistible urge to put her hand over her face.

When they stopped to change horses, one of the grooms asked Igor if he wished the internal lamps to be lit, but he declined without asking the others, saying that the stars were more interesting than the upholstery, and the journey was completed in darkness.

The moon had risen by the time they reached Alexandrovsk, and the pale stone of the fortress gleamed faintly beside the broad silver expanse of the great river, with the dark mass of Khortitsa lying in mid-stream like a sleeping monster. Between the town and the island, a line of sailing-ships lay at anchor, which roused Varya from her fatigued silence to talk with animation of the prospects for a voyage on one of them to Kherson.

'That can wait until tomorrow,' Igor said. 'The subject will not be mentioned again until we have eaten, slept, and eaten again.'

'Oh, but . . . !' Varya began, then broke off and substituted a meek, 'Yes, Uncle.'

Alexandrovsk was a small town, having grown up almost as an afterthought by the fortress to house the workers and administrators of the ship-building yard across the river, but it was an important staging-post on the Crimea Highway, boasting several good rest-houses, and the *jäger* had arranged accommodation in the best of them. Once more there was a private parlour for the travellers' use, and a late dinner was ready to be served to them within half an hour of their arrival.

Varya, who had slept in the coach for a couple of hours, seemed particularly lively during the meal, and, no doubt seeking to put her uncle in a good mood, said flatteringly, 'I've been thinking about that poetry that you said, Uncle Igor, and I do think you were clever to come out with it so neatly! It fitted Mila perfectly, from what I could understand of it, didn't it? Well—not the bit about stealing from a wealthy Jew, of course, but running off, you know . . .' Her voice tailed off uncertainly as she realised that her remarks were not having the desired effect, for Mila had turned quite pale, and Igor was scowling.

'Varya, you have the tact of a brigade of heavy cavalry!' he said bitingly. 'Be silent and finish your dinner! It's past time for such a child to be in bed!'

'I—I'm sorry . . .' she faltered.

'I said silent!'

Varya, looking troubled and almost frightened, finished her meal in silence as instructed, and seemed to have less appetite than usual. Maxim, who had looked quite blank during the exchange, glanced at Mila's pale face and Igor's now inscrutable one, and manfully plunged into a monologue about the navigation of the Dnepr and how inconvenient it was that the six great cataracts between Ekaterinoslav and Alexandrovsk prevented the passage of ships all the way to Kiev. This evoked a brief 'Yes' from Igor and no response from the ladies, so he went on to talk about the possibility that one day it might be practicable to cut a canal round the barrier and perhaps run a steam-boat on it, which was a proof of his good intentions, as only in the most desperate of situations would a naval officer admit the feasibility of steam-boats ever amounting to anything.

Eventually he exhausted the subject, excused himself, and went up to bed. Varya, hastily getting to her feet, said rapidly, 'I'm sorry, Mila. I'm sorry, Uncle Igor. Good night,' and almost ran from the room in his wake.

Igor silently poured another glass of wine for Mila and for himself, and said, 'I should like to assure you that what I said about it not being the quotation I intended was the truth, and I can't apologise enough for coming out with the wrong one. It must have seemed to you that I was deliberately trying to put you to the blush by alluding to elopement, but I give you my word that it was entirely accidental. If I could have recalled the words . . .'

'It doesn't matter,' Mila said dully, thinking how much more appropriate the quotation has been than he realised.

'The odd thing is,' he continued, 'that both quotations came into my mind, the—er—unfortunate one first, and that particular part of it, despite it being, as you may recall, the end of the exchange between Jessica and Lorenzo, not the beginning. I realised that it would be too . . .' He seemed uncharacteristically to be groping for words, '. . . too easily open to misconstruction, yet somehow, when I thought to speak the other, it was the first which emerged. I honestly can't account for it.'

Mila was silent, toying with the stem of her wine-glass. After a moment, he continued, 'The words don't really fit particularly well, I suppose. After all, your father

wasn't robbed, and your Lorenzo's vows were true
enough. It was cruel to remind you, though. I'm truly
sorry.'

Mila looked at him, wondering what his reaction
would be if she told him the full story. Because she was
afraid to open her lips for fear that the truth would
emerge from them, she still said nothing, and Igor,
misinterpreting her silence, said, 'Do you think so ill of
me that you can't believe it was an accident? My dear
girl! I wish with all my heart that things had gone well
with you, that your father had relented, that your
Étienne could still be with you! I would never wish to
cause you one moment's unhappiness. Oh, for heaven's
sake say something before I plunge any further into the
mire!'

'I know,' she said. 'It truly doesn't matter. It's one of
the penalties of being well-read, I suppose. A suitable
quotation slips into one's head, and one naturally says it
without thinking of what follows. After all, I picked up
where you left off, and went on with it without realising
. . . I didn't suspect you of any ill intent.'

Igor looked her straight in the eyes across the table for
a moment, then raised his glass to her in a silent toast.
She inclined her head in acknowledgment, and said,
'Don't be angry with Varya. She's at an age when
elopement is still something romantic, and she didn't
mean any harm. I think I'll go up, if you'll excuse me. It's
very late.'

Igor rose and opened the door for her, and as she
passed him, touched her arm lightly and said, 'Good
night, my dear,' in a voice quite unlike his normal dry
ironic tone. Mila caught her breath, replied 'Good
night,' in a whisper, and went slowly upstairs, feeling as
if every fibre of her body had turned to quivering jelly at
the unexpected tenderness she thought she had heard in
those few words.

By the time she reached her room, she had told herself that she was mistaken, and when Marfa had left her, she climbed wearily into the narrow, rather hard, bed after saying her prayers, and thought to herself that he perhaps pitied her, knowing what she had risked and a part of what she had lost. That conclusion made her cry herself to sleep, with the result that she went downstairs next morning feeling depressed and listless, despite the continuing bright sunshine which made the pale stone buildings of the town and the fortress gleam like a fairy city, and the wide waters of the river shine like an immense sapphire between the creamy sand and emerald verdure on its shores.

The *jäger* arrived while they were still at breakfast to say that he had secured cabin accommodation for the party on a well-appointed ship of comfortable size that was due to sail on Monday (it then being Saturday) to Sevastopol with cargo, calling at Kherson on the way.

'Good,' said Igor. 'That gives us a little time to visit Khortitsa and do the inevitable shopping.'

'What is there to see on Khortitsa?' asked Varya a trifle rebelliously when the *jäger* had gone.

'Not a great deal,' Igor replied equably. 'In the earliest days of the Kievan Rus, it was the place where the Varangian and Slav traders to Constantinople stopped to repair their ships after shooting the cataracts, and to get them ready for the portages on the way back. There's an extremely ancient oak beneath which they are thought to have offered sacrifices to their gods, but after Kiev became Christian, the island was dedicated to St Grigor—though I doubt if that stopped the sacrifices! Sailors, if you'll forgive me, Maxim, tend to be a superstitious breed!'

'Oh, I quite agree!' replied Maxim, who was well into his second helping of *bliny* and soured cream. 'I never set sail on a Friday myself, not even on land.'

'When did the Cossacks come here, then?' asked Varya, her interest caught in spite of herself.

'The island was a gathering-place for centuries, for it provided a safe base, easily defended, and roomy enough for a very large army. When the Cossack hordes began to form in the fifteenth century, the Ukrainian groups collected here, and that's how they got their name—Zaporozhye means "Below the cataracts". It's said that Bogdan Khmelnitsky . . . You *do* know who he was?'

'Oh . . . er—Yes, I think so.' Varya sounded disconcerted and a trifle guilty, because she was not sure. 'He was the *Hetman* of the Zaporozhye Cossacks who drove the Poles out of Kiev and freed the Eastern Ukraine, and then made the alliance with Russia in . . .'

'So they do teach you something other than useless accomplishments at the Smolny!' Igor commented.

'Oh, no!' Varya replied blithely. 'I learned that from one of the books you gave me!'

Igor's odd little smile appeared, but he went on gravely, 'Bogdan Khmelnitsky is said to have decided to drive the Poles out of Kiev while he was sitting under the famous oak, and he called the Cossacks together and they swore an oath to be as loyal to their homeland as the roots of the tree were linked with its soil.'

'And the tree is still there?' asked Varya. 'Well, I should like to see that, for it must be very large and fine by now, but what else is worth a visit?'

'To the discerning, *tongues in trees, books in the running brooks, sermons in stones, and good in everything,*' Igor replied in English, and as Varya obviously found that hard to grapple with, he translated it into French for her, then added, 'I really must stop this habit of quoting. Vassily Sergeivich seems to have infected me with it, for I believe he was quite infamous for it at one time! It's a pleasant place to walk about and take the air after being cooped up in a coach for best part of two weeks. Shall we go?'

'It sounds quite interesting,' Varya admitted cautiously, and both Mila and Maxim said that the thought of walking about amid trees on an island after dusty roads and a jolting coach was most attractive. After breakfast they set out in an open landau which the *jäger* had hired for them, and drove down to the riverside.

Mila was amazed to find how busy the quays were, for ships of all sizes were tied up alongside them, or moored out in the river, and swarms of boats and lighters moved among them, loading or unloading goods, which lay in casks, cases and bundles on the wooden quays, or were piled in warehouses beyond them.

The carriage drove slowly along the quayside, the passengers looking about them with great interest, for this seemed an even busier port than Petersburg, where navigation had to cease for the six winter months of every year. Eventually they came to the end of the port area, and here the well-constructed quays gave way to odd piers and jetties, with stretches of grass and sand between them. Here the boatmen plied for hire, ferrying carts and coaches across the river, which was about a *verst* in width, poling them over on rafts, so that, once they were well out from the bank, the vehicles appeared to be driving slowly over the surface of the water.

Igor stopped the carriage, and the passengers alighted and went down to the water's edge, where Igor and Maxim walked to and fro, looking at the dozen or so boats plying for hire, and entered into the usual protracted bargaining with their owners.

Mila stood watching the craft on the river and looking across to the island, which was much larger than she had realised. It was a beautiful scene, and would make an interesting painting—not the ladylike sketch in pencil or water-colour, which was all she could manage herself, but a fine large landscape in oils. There was colour, with the almost cloudless sky reflected in the deeper blue of the river, which was broken by little waves, the white stone of the island rocks and the cliffs of the far bank, and the dark green of the trees which covered the island.

On the water were the boats and a couple of ships slipping down-river, deep-laden with cargo, and in the foreground there was a most dilapidated-looking jetty sticking out some twenty feet over the river to her left . . .

As she turned her head to look at the jetty, she realised, to her horror, that Varya was on it and had, indeed, gone out to the end, where a tall post reared up out of the water. A shaky-looking handrail, more or less supported by half a dozen uprights, ran along the left side of the jetty, but it was easy to see that the whole structure was far from safe and appeared to be on the point of collapse.

'Varya!' she called urgently. 'Come back at once. It's not safe!'

'It's only a little rickety,' the girl called back. 'I'm being very careful to try each plank before I step on it, and this post that I'm holding on to is perfectly secure. Don't fuss, Mila! Come here and see the fish. I've never seen so many!'

Mila took a few steps on to the jetty, which shook alarmingly, even under her light weight, and said, 'Please come back, Varya!' in tones which were more pleading than commanding.

'Come and see the fish, and then I will,' Varya replied. 'It's quite safe, truly!'

'I'd rather you came back now,' Mila said, biting her lip and feeling herself to be in a most difficult position, for, as little more than a paid servant, she had no right to give Varya orders, yet the girl was obviously not about to comply with a simple request.

'No, you come here first!' Varya said imperiously. 'I want you to see the fish. It won't take a moment.'

Mila hesitated again, then gingerly crept out on the jetty, one step at a time. The boards creaked and moved a little under her feet, but they were indeed more firmly fixed than they appeared to be, and she reached Varya's side without mishap.

The girl had one arm round the solid post, and was leaning forward a little to point out the fish. Mila went as near the railed edge of the jetty as she dared to look down, one hand on the rail, and saw a shoal of small fish which were feeding on something below the surface of the river, which was deep here, but very clear. Whatever it was which had attracted the fish—carrion, Mila suspected—was caught in long trails of weed which grew on the timbers, and it moved and tugged at its bonds as the current dragged on it, so that the mass of silver fish was in continual movement.

'Come back here at once!' came a roar of command from Igor, who had just looked up from his chaffering and seen the two females on the jetty. They both jumped, for the sudden shout had startled them, and Mila swung round, inadvertently stepping on a plank at the very edge of the jetty. It gave way, throwing her against the rail, which simply fell away and dropped with her down into the river.

## CHAPTER
## NINE

MILA FELT the sudden icy shock of the water, and then she seemed to plunge on, down and down, for an age. The current was pulling at her, and her reaching hands felt nothing to grasp. There was a tug at her neck, and then her bonnet-strings parted and the neat straw bonnet she had worn each summer for the past three years was gone, and still she was plunging downwards.

Far above she could see light, but it was fading in a red mist, and there was a sound like the roaring of a cataract in her ears. She thought, 'I must be drowning!'

Somehow, the clarity of the thought seemed to spur her into an effort to survive, and she began to try to force her way upwards, kicking with her legs, which were hampered by her long, clinging skirts, and then, just as she realised that her lungs were about to burst and she was not going to reach the surface, she was seized about the waist from behind in a tight grip, and felt herself being hauled up towards the light. Her head burst out suddenly into air and sunshine, and she took a great gasping breath. Then Igor's voice said breathlessly in her ear, 'For God's sake, don't struggle! Keep still! I've got you safely.'

'Yes,' she sobbed, turning her head in an effort to see him, for he was behind her.

'Now, listen,' he said. 'Can you understand me?'

'Y-yes.'

'Good. I'm going to swim on my back, with you lying

164

on top of me. Just lie still, as if you're floating, and don't move a muscle. Try not to hold yourself stiffly—the more relaxed you are, the better you'll float. You understand?'

'Yes,' she replied, more collected now, and his body pushed up beneath her until she was almost lying on the fairly calm surface, with his arms still about her waist. She made a deliberate effort to let herself float limply on the water, and then she felt him kicking strongly as they began to move through the little wavelets. She cautiously looked about her, moving only her eyes, and saw that they were going away from the bank, heading diagonally out downstream into the river. She could see the jetty and the little boats, now far behind them, receding with every kick of Igor's legs.

'We're going the wrong way!' she said, trying not to sound panicky.

'I know, but we have to go with the stream,' he replied. 'We can't go back against the current. It sets across to the island, so we shall fetch up there eventually. All we have to do is keep our heads above water, and I'll help us along as best I can. Don't be afraid. We shall get ashore safely if you keep calm.'

'Yes,' she replied meekly, and fell to praying silently as there was nothing else she could do to help. Somewhere in the back of her mind, the words 'the River of Time' echoed, and after a while, she recalled that Igor had said something about it that evening in Moscow, during the storm. She thought confusedly about rivers and currents, and how impossible it was to go back, and then how easy it would be to go forward if Igor was there to help her.

After what seemed to her a long time, but was probably only about ten minutes, the current swept them almost on to one of the beaches of the island. Igor scrambled to his feet, hauling Mila up with him, and staggered ashore with her, and they fell together on to the pale sand, Igor's arms still tightly around her body, and lay there panting for a few minutes.

'Are you all right?' Igor asked eventually, releasing her and propping himself on one elbow to look down into her face.

'Yes, thank you,' she replied. 'I—I never learned to swim.'

'It's as well that I did, then!' he replied crisply. 'I gather that Maxim can't, or no doubt he'd have come in with me. I didn't stop to ask him, of course.'

He got up with an effort and went to the edge of the water, shading his eyes and looking upstream and across towards the shore. He must have thrown off his coat and kicked off his shoes before he dived in, for he was in his shirt-sleeves, the white cambric clinging wetly to his body and frosted with sand, and he was unconsciously wriggling his stockinged feet in the soft sand. Mila was surprised to see that his hair, which was normally brushed smooth, curled when it was wet.

She was sitting up now, her arms clasped about her bent-up knees, shivering and miserably aware that a lawn shift and a muslin frock were not only uncomfortably clinging when wet, but also revealingly so.

'Cold?' Igor asked, coming to stand over her.

'Not really,' she said, for they were in a miniature cove, sheltered by rocks and trees, and the sun was very warm. 'I'm just shocked, I think.'

He sat down beside her and put an arm comfortingly round her shoulders, and she was feeling so wretched that she leaned against him and let her head rest on his shoulder.

He shifted a little, but only to move closer, and he turned so that he could put his other arm round her waist.

'Don't ever do such a thing again!' he said unsteadily.

'I thought I'd—we'd lost you! One moment you were there, and the next there was nothing but Varya screeching and a disturbance in the water! I've never taken such an age in my life to kick off my shoes and throw off my coat—they seemed to be stuck to me— running down the bank was like wading through treacle!'

'I'm sorry,' Mila replied in a muffled voice against his shoulder, and she trembled as she realised how near she had been to death.

'Oh, my dear girl!' he exclaimed, but whether in amusement, exasperation, or something else, she could not tell. She only knew that he was holding her comfortingly closely, that he was stroking her wet hair, and his lips were moving gently about in the region of her left ear in a series of little kisses. For once his physical nearness did not paralyse her, and she shifted her head a fraction so that he could kiss her cheek as well, and for a few minutes she was happy.

'The boat will be here in a few moments,' he said. 'I could see it heading in this direction. Can you breathe properly? It doesn't hurt when you breathe in, or feel difficult to get enough air into your lungs?'

'No,' she replied, puzzled, after trying a few breaths.

'I don't expect you've taken any water into your lungs, then, but we'll get a doctor to have a look at you when we get back to the rest-house. What happened to your bonnet?'

'It came off,' she said with a little sob. 'And it's the only one I have with me.'

'Well, you still have your reticule,' he pointed out reassuringly, for that article, which contained most of her small store of money, still had its chain twisted about her wrist.

It was very quiet on the island. The light breeze whispered in the trees, the little waves lapped gently on the beach, and the sounds of the port came faintly over the water. The sun poured warmth down into their little cove, drying their wet clothing. Gradually Mila stopped shivering and began to feel a strange contentment stealing over her, an enjoyment of being here, alone with Igor, her head on his shoulder, his arms firmly about her, and the warmth of his body stirring her senses. If only she could have married him—it might always have been like this!

A voice gave a command in Russian, and there was a grating sound as a rowing-boat grounded on the sand, and one of the men in it jumped out and pulled it up further on to the beach. Mila opened her eyes, raised her head almost sleepily, and automatically drew away from Igor, who gently released her and got up to greet Maxim, who leaped agilely out of the boat and crunched over the sand towards them.

'She's all right,' Igor told him. 'But I think we should take her back to the rest-house quickly, before she catches a chill.'

Maxim nodded, looking at Mila, who struggled to her feet, hampered by her still-wet clothes, and said, 'You'd better carry her,' in a doubtful tone.

'I can manage,' she began, but Igor picked her up as easily as if she were a child and carried her down to the boat, where he settled her well down in the bottom in the bows, and wriggled in beside her, so that they were very close together. Then he said in a matter-of-fact manner to Maxim, 'I'll try to keep her warm, for I don't suppose you thought to bring the rug from the carriage?'

Maxim admitted shamefacedly that he had not thought of anything but getting the boat into the water and coming after them. He helped the boatman to push off, both of them wading into the water and vaulting into the moving boat, one on either side. Then, to Mila's surprise, Maxim took a pair of oars and set to work to row behind the boatman, and the boat began to crawl back diagonally across the current to where it had come from.

Both men had their backs to the passengers, so Mila was not embarrassed when Igor took her in his arms again, although he was very impersonal about it, and, as she did not wish to betray her feelings to him, she tried to be cool and unresponsive herself. But it was very hard to be so close to him, his cheek within an inch of her lips, and not kiss or caress him, as her whole body seemed to be willing her to do. He seemed to be shivering, and she wondered anxiously if he were taking a chill himself.

By the time the boat reached the shore, she was tense almost to the point of screaming with the strain of keeping still and not giving way to her love and longing for him, but her trembling hand as he helped her ashore, and the tears which would keep filling her eyes, were easily ascribed to reaction after her near-drowning. She could even allow herself to cry a little when Varya, who had been left to pray on the shore, flung her arms round her and burst into noisy sobs, crying that it was all her fault, and she would never forgive herself for being so selfish and thoughtless.

'I should think so, too!' Maxim said sharply. 'Of all the bird-witted scrapes—going out on a jetty that any fool could see wasn't safe. You must be loose in the attic! Your trouble, my girl, is that you're a spoiled brat, and too fond of your own way. Just because you have the whip-hand over Mila Levovna and me, you think you can order us about as you please! Well, perhaps this will teach you that you're not as infallible and important as you think.'

This outburst snapped Varya out of her tears, remorse and self-pity, and she looked at Maxim in open-mouthed astonishment.

'What do you mean?' she demanded. 'How have I the whip-hand over you both?'

'You know very well!' Maxim replied, his tanned face brick-red with emotion, but whether it was anger or embarrassment was unclear. 'To put it crudely, you employ Mila Levovna as your companion, so she must do as you say or you may well dismiss her and leave her stranded, unable to return home. As for me—you know very well that any adverse remark you may choose to make about me to your father could put my career in the Navy in jeopardy! Don't tell me that you haven't realised that—or perhaps you haven't.' He suddenly sounded uncertain and sheepish.

'Oh, I wouldn't do anything so mean and unkind!' Varya exclaimed indignantly. 'How could you think so badly of me? Why, I'm cut to the quick!' She did, indeed, look so deeply hurt and upset that Maxim, suddenly plunged from the heights of righteous anger to the depths of being in the wrong, stammered an apology and did his best to assure her that he did not really think badly of her at all.

'Very touching,' commented Igor, who had occupied himself meanwhile by fetching the rug from the carriage and wrapping it round Mila, and then helping her to her place in the vehicle. 'We're going back to the rest-house to change our clothes, and you'd better come too, unless you propose to walk.'

Varya and Maxim hastened to get in the carriage, which then rattled off back towards the centre of the town and the rest-house. No one said anything for a while, and then Varya stammered, 'Uncle Igor, are—aren't you going to s-scold me?'

'For what?' he asked off-handedly, without looking at her.

'For going out on the jetty and not coming back when Mila told me to, and then saying I wouldn't unless she came first to look at the fish, so it was my fault she fell in.'

'Ah, so that's what happened,' he said with mild

interest. 'In fact, if I hadn't shouted, she probably wouldn't have fallen in, so it's as much my fault as yours. What's the point of scolding you? You know what you did, and I trust you have the sense not to do it again.'

There was the faintest hint of a question about the last sentence, and Varya hastily assured him that she would *never* do such a silly thing again.

'That's the end of it, then,' he replied, and nothing further was said until they reached the rest-house, where Mila was sent up to bed, despite her protests, and a doctor was summoned, who sounded her chest and said that she did not appear to have inhaled any water, but she should rest for twenty-four hours to allow her body to recover from the shock.

After luncheon, which was served to Mila in bed, the other three, having first enquired through Varya's maid if she minded, left her to rest and went to make their belated visit to Khortitsa, and Mila, after lying on her bed for a while, got up and tried on the frocks which Tatya had given her. They fitted well, but were a little too long, for Tatya was taller than she, so she set to work with needle and thread to take up the hems, enjoying the feel of the soft fabric and the pretty, light colours.

Presently Marfa, who had taken her wet clothes away to be laundered, brought her a tray of tea, so Mila sent her back for a second cup and dish, and they spent a couple of enjoyable hours, drinking tea and stitching hems, while they talked in Russian, for Mila, after years of living in the Haymarket area, spoke the language fluently.

It was, of course, Marfa who did most of the talking. She had belonged to the Charodyev family all her life, as had her parents and grandparents before her, and had worked for many years in their Kiev house, where Igor's grandfather had resided until his death a couple of years before, and where Igor's father, now retired from the

Imperial Navy, now lived. She had many tales to tell of Igor's childhood before he entered the Corps of Pages in Petersburg, and of his doings during his rare holidays.

Mila had not been sure whether Marfa knew that Igor had once been her suitor, but she now discovered that Marfa knew about that, and about her elopement with Étienne de Romarin. In fact, she knew more than Igor did, for there seemed to be some sort of underground network for information among the serfs employed in the households of the Moscow nobility, and Marfa informed her that the serfs in her father's house had been quite sure that she had not really intended to 'run off with that Frenchy Hussar captain' at all!

'It's all a long time ago now,' Mila said, thinking that she had better change the subject as Marfa's gossiping was coming too near home. 'Perhaps I'll wear one of these frocks for dinner tonight. It will make a change from my dark-coloured ones.'

Marfa expressed enthusiasm for the idea, and presently took all the frocks away to press them.

A little while later there was a perfunctory knock at the door, and Varya rushed in, clutching a band-box in either hand, and exclaimed, 'Oh, good! You're not asleep—I was afraid you might be! Why are you out of bed? You're supposed to be resting. Well, I suppose you can rest just as well sitting up as lying down. Just look at what I've brought you!'

She flung the band-boxes down on the bed, unwound her shawl, which seemed to have looped itself round her arms in a restricting manner, and then began to unfasten the boxes, chattering all the while about how they had been to Khortitsa and seen the monstrous great old, old, *old* oak-tree, but Uncle Igor said his legs ached from swimming, and, after walking about the island a little, they had returned to the town to look at the shops.

'Only Maxim wouldn't come, and he went to look up a friend of his on—in—one of the Navy ships across the river, so just Uncle Igor and I went, and he said you'd lost your bonnet this morning, and we should buy you a new one as it was both our faults. So we chose two— Well, Uncle Igor chose them—and here they are!'

She produced the two bonnets, one balanced on each hand, with a flourish and rather a flat imitation of a trumpet-call. Mila, a little bewildered by the rapid and lengthy speech which preceded the unveiling, looked at the two creations in amazement, recognising at once that they were probably imported from Paris and must have cost more than her whole year's pension from the War Ministry. Both were made of natural-coloured straw, and one was trimmed with ostrich-feathers dyed the same creamy-gold, and the other with silk flowers which were so well made that they looked like pink and cream roses.

'Don't you like them?' Varya asked, her face falling. 'I thought them rather dull myself—I'd have chosen something more colourful, but Uncle Igor said that not every lady wishes to appear in public with a parrot and a bunch of grapes on her head!'

'I like them very much,' Mila replied when Varya paused for breath. 'But they're really far too good for me!'

'Oh, what stuff!' Varya exclaimed indignantly. 'I don't see why being a widow and poor has to stop you wearing something pretty, and if Uncle Igor says they're right for you, then they are, because he knows about things like that! Do try them on.'

Mila did so, and could not help but smile at her reflection in the mirror, for both bonnets were immensely becoming, framing her face in a most flattering manner. She managed to catch a glimpse of the labels inside them as she changed from one to the other, and

found that her suspicions about their origin were correct
—both labels bore the coveted word 'Paris'.

'We can change them if you're not sure,' Varya said
anxiously. 'But I think they're perfect! Uncle Igor was
right—the green feathers would have been too bright,
and I don't think purple would have suited you at all.'

'I think they're perfect, too,' Mila assured her, and
tried to thank her, but she was not allowed to do so, and
the girl went off like a whirlwind to change. Dinner was
to be at the more convenient hour of six instead of the
ten o'clock or later to which they had become used while
travelling.

Mila dressed in one of the barège frocks—one in its
natural honey colours, trimmed with gold-coloured
lace—and went down to dinner a little early. As she
descended the last flight of stairs, Igor emerged from one
of the rooms opening off the hall, heading for their
private parlour, but he glanced up, saw her, and stopped
in his tracks, staring for a full second before he pulled
himself together and went to wait for her at the foot of
the stairs.

'I thought you were supposed to be resting,' he said
with that unusual note of uncertainty in his voice which
she had heard once before.

'I am rested,' she replied. 'There's nothing at all
wrong with me.'

'No.' He smiled slightly, and his eyes travelled over
her face and figure in a look which turned the single word
into a compliment. 'I'm glad to see that you do own a
light-coloured garment, and very attractive you look in
it!'

'Tatya Petrovna gave me some barège frocks, for
she said I would need something light in the south,' Mila
replied, watching to see if his face showed any reaction
to the name of his 'lovely lady', but there was nothing
more than interest to be seen there.

'She seems to have given all of us presents,' he said. 'Mine was a new hat and an old Chinese snuff-bottle.'

'But you don't use snuff!'

'It's not for use—just for admiring! It's a particularly fine one, in carved lacquer. I wouldn't dream of using it, for fear of damaging the carving!'

Mila then tried to thank him for the bonnets, but he brushed her careful little speech aside with a brief, 'Not at all,' and offered his arm as he was speaking, then conducted her to their parlour, where Maxim and Varya were already sipping a glass of wine apiece and conducting polite conversation.

'Oh, Mila!' Varya exclaimed when she caught sight of her. 'You look tremendous! Why do you wear dark things when you look so pretty in light ones? I thought you hadn't any . . .' As usual, her tongue was carrying her away, and she put her hand over her mouth and looked guilty.

'It was a gift from Countess Karacheva,' Mila replied self-consciously, for, although she was glad to have been given some pretty clothes, she did not much enjoy proclaiming the fact.

'Tatya Petrovna's so clever!' Varya said with enthusiasm. 'She gave us all something—even the servants. I had a lovely necklace of little pearls, and Uncle Igor had a funny old bottle, and . . . Oh, Maxim! Do show her your telescopic thingummy.'

Maxim obediently produced a small telescope from his coat pocket. It was no longer than his hand, but it opened out to twice that length, and was quite powerful. He allowed Mila to look through it, taking her to the window and pointing out several objects which she might view through it, although she found it difficult to point the thing precisely at whatever she wished to see, as she had never used such a device before.

'Isn't it fine?' Varya said in a proprietary fashion.

'Maxim let me look at some ships through it, and I could even see the faces of the men on the decks! It will be tremendously useful to Maxim, to see what all the other ships are doing.'

'A good perspective glass is always a desirable acquisition,' Maxim agreed rather portentously, retrieving the article before Varya could make off with it. He gave it a loving polish on his thigh before closing it and putting it in his pocket.

'I do think it most kind of Tatya Petrovna!' Varya continued as they sat down to dinner. 'I mean . . . She didn't know any of the servants, and you'd never met her before, had you, Maxim?'

'Unfortunately, no,' Maxim replied, his face reddening slightly and a note of regret in his voice.

'I suppose you must have known her slightly,' Varya continued, turning to Mila with those wide, innocent eyes. 'When you were first living in Petersburg, at least. Of course, after her accident she was in the country for simply ages, but everyone in Society knew her before, didn't they, Uncle Igor? She was just about the most popular lady in Petersburg, I should think!'

'Don't exaggerate, Varya.' Igor said repressively. 'There's no reason at all why Mila should have known her, and, as a matter of fact, she didn't. Are you not wearing the pearls she gave you?'

'I thought I'd save them for a Special Occasion,' Varya replied, neatly side-tracked from her former line of enquiry. 'My father might give a ball in my honour, and I'd like to have something quite new to put on for it. I haven't any other real jewels, only little trinkets. Didn't Mamma have any jewellery?'

'Yes,' said Igor.

'What happened to it?'

'It's in a safe place, waiting for you to be old enough to wear it. You're not Out yet, you know.'

'I'm almost seventeen,' Varya said coaxingly. 'I expect I shall have my Come-out in Kherson, don't you think? I dare say there will be all sorts of functions where I shall need some jewels to wear.'

'Even when you are *quite* seventeen,' Igor replied in firm tones, 'you are not gallivanting about in full fig like a Dowager Empress! Your mother's jewels were made for *her* mother, and are old-fashioned and much too elaborate for a young girl. When you are older, we'll see about having them refashioned into something more suitable, and that will be done in Petersburg.'

'By the way,' Maxim said, as that conversation seemed to have reached its conclusion. 'We can send our gear aboard *Chaika* in the early afternoon, and the captain would like us to embark for dinner in the evening. He wants to sail at first light on Monday.'

'*Chaika*?' queried Varya. 'Is that the boat we're going to sail on . . . in. What does the name mean?'

'*Seagull*, my ignorant niece! Good heavens, don't you even know in your own language the name of those white birds that flap about over Petersburg?' exclaimed Igor, followed immediately by an outraged 'Ship, not boat!' from Maxim, who did not even give the poor girl credit for remembering, if belatedly, to say 'in' and not 'on'. Even Varya quailed before the double attack, and said nothing for quite five minutes.

She had recovered, however, by the time dinner ended, and persuaded Maxim to allow her to stand at the window and look through his telescope at whatever was to be seen, which appeared to afford both the young people amusement in differing degrees. While they were absorbed in this pursuit, Igor somehow manoeuvred Mila to some chairs at the opposite end of the room, and, after a few general remarks, fixed her with an unusually straight and open gaze for a few moments in silence, so that she wondered uneasily what he was about to say.

At length he gave a quick glance towards the pair at the window and said quietly in Russian, 'Mila, there's something I should very much like to say to you, and I hope you'll not be offended, for it's kindly meant, even if it sounds hard. I know that it's difficult to set things behind one, to accept that something is over and gone and can never be recalled. I know that one is always regretting that one didn't perhaps value what one had as much as one now wishes . . . Oh, damn these impersonal "ones"! What I'm trying to say is this—the River of Time flows on; you can't go back, so it's best to strike out boldly for the future. You're still young and beautiful—don't waste yourself in vain regrets for something that you can never have again! Stop looking back, and see what lies around and ahead of you.'

'He knows!' she thought. 'I must have given myself away this morning, I suppose, or perhaps even before! He's right, of course—he loved me once, and he thinks I didn't value his love, and now when I want it more than anything else in the world, it's too late! It's dead and gone. I can't wonder at it—I treated him shamefully, hurt and humiliated him, so no wonder he stopped loving me.'

Aloud, and also in Russian, she said, 'Please don't go on. I know what you mean, and I accept that you're right. I expect one day I might be able to—to do as you say. May we please leave the subject?'

'As you wish. I've offended you. I'm sorry.'

His voice sounded so odd, so flat and expressionless, that Mila gave him a puzzled look as she said, 'No, indeed I'm not offended.' His heavy lids had drooped over his eyes again, and his face had assumed its usual unreadable mask. There was an awkward silence, suddenly made worse for Mila, reminded by his use of the expression 'River of Time', that she was guilty of a breach of good manners amounting to a show of base ingratitude.

'I—I haven't thanked you!' she blurted, reverting to French and unconsciously wringing her hands together.

'For what?' he asked, looking startled.

'For saving my life!'

'Oh,' he said blankly. 'Oh, yes—that. There was nothing particular about it. I could hardly let you drift down to Kherson in a drowned condition! Any idiot who can swim can hold someone's head above calm water, if they have the sense to keep still, until the current carries them somewhere.'

Mila gave him a pathetic look, her lips trembling, unreasonably upset at the way he had taken her romantic vision of him throwing off his coat and diving into the fast-flowing river to find her in the depths, raise her to the surface, and then fight his way across the current to carry her to safety, and turned it into a prosaic matter of keeping something like an inanimate log afloat on the surface until it was cast ashore like so much flotsam. Or jetsam? Which was it? Her mind, having taken one unpleasant shock of considerable magnitude, found the lesser shock of his reduction of his noble rescue to something trivial too much to cope with, and diverted itself into a mild consideration of semantics as a form of escape.

'Is something the matter?' Igor enquired when she had been silent for a few moments, puzzling in a vague manner about the two words, which had come into her mind in English and for which she could think of no equivalents in French.

'Oh!' she started. 'I was just trying to think of the difference between flotsam and jetsam. That's what they're called in English. Do you know what I mean?'

Igor smiled a little. 'Yes, but I'd not class you as either! As I remember, flotsam is lost by accident, and jetsam is thrown away on purpose. Does that solve your puzzle?'

'Yes. Thank you. I don't know what they're called in French.'

'Neither do I. Something long-winded, no doubt. In Russian, flotsam is *oblomki*, but jetsam is "things thrown from ships", which is not very enterprising! They used to say that "the Greeks have a word for it", but I think we may substitute "the English" nowadays.'

'You wouldn't let me thank you for the bonnets, either,' Mila said despondently, trying vainly to comfort herself with the thought that he had chosen them, but guessing correctly what he would say.

'They were from Varya. She was very anxious to show you how sorry she is for what happened, which was largely her fault, of course, and had set her heart on some sort of magnificent presentation. All I did was to persuade her that a new bonnet would be more use to you than a solid silver toilet-set, and guide her away from the more vivid colours and *outré* styles. Did you like them?'

'Very much!' Mila found a crumb of comfort in the knowledge that he had taken an interest in seeing that Varya's gift was something she would like to have. 'Varya said you chose them.'

'Well, as you've already said that you like them. I'll admit to that.' His twisted little smile appeared. 'Varya's taste tends to the bizarre at times. Maxim!'

The Lieutenant turned at the sound of his name, rescued his telescope from Varya with a remarkably deft movement of his right hand, and crossed the room with the air of a man who has just been shown the way out of a tedious situation.

'Yes, sir?' he said smartly.

'Oh, for heaven's sake stop calling me "sir"!' Igor

protested. 'What's the French for "things that fall off ships"?'

'Things that fall off ships,' Maxim replied, using exactly the same words as Igor had done, but as a statement instead of a question. He looked decidedly mystified as he spoke.

'Isn't there a special word?' Mila asked.

'I expect so, but we generally use the English word "flotsam". Come to think of it, we use English words for a lot of things. I suppose it's because English naval officers did so much to help to establish our Navy, as theirs was the best in the world.'

Varya bridled patriotically at that, and protested vehemently that *no* navy could possibly be better than the Imperial Navy, and gave it as her opinion that the best Fleet in the best Navy was the Black Sea Fleet, and the best squadron in the best Fleet that which was based at Kherson, at which Igor sat back looking vastly amused and let Maxim fight his way out of the action as well as he could.

Mila was a spectator to all this, but in a vague, half-aware fashion, sunk in a daze of misery as she tried to adjust to the knowledge that Igor had guessed her feelings for him and had warned her that, as far as he was concerned, the hope of any love between them was long past and done with, and she must look elsewhere for a husband. It was only what she had already told herself, but hearing it from Igor drove it home like a dagger to her heart, and she could hardly bear the pain of it.

# CHAPTER
## TEN

AT BREAKFAST the next morning, Igor appeared a little out of humour, and when Varya took to chattering excitedly about the voyage down the Dnepr to Kherson, he said rather dampeningly, 'I hope you realise, my girl, that there's a distinct division in our family between those, like your father and mine, who are good sailors, and those who are not, like me. Do you know to which category you belong?'

Varya looked disconcerted, but then recovered with her usual rapidity and said that she was sure that she was an excellent sailor and, in any case, sailing on a river must be less likely to cause unpleasant feelings than sailing on the sea, because it was calmer.

'Not necessarily,' Maxim put in his expert opinion. 'River estuaries can be very rough at times, and although Kherson is just above the estuary, it can be quite choppy there if the wind blows against the current.'

'Oh, I'm not in the least worried!' Varya dismissed the possibility airily. 'It can't be worse than jolting and jouncing about in a coach all day, with so little chance to stretch one's—er—limbs!' She had just recollected in time that at the Smolny one did not mention one's lower extremities, and she seemed also to recollect something else immediately after, for the excitement suddenly left her expressive face, and she said anxiously, 'Oh, but Uncle Igor! Did you say you were in the other category? You mean, you get seasick?'

'It's not an unknown occurrence,' Igor replied in his most ironic manner.

'Then, in that case, we can't go by ship after all,' Varya said positively. 'I didn't think of it upsetting anybody. I'm sorry.'

Igor regarded her in an unusually open-eyed and direct fashion, and said, 'Would you really give up your plan so easily? I thought you'd set your heart on taking ship.'

'Not if it will make you ill,' she replied seriously. 'I know you all think me silly and selfish, but it's only because I don't think—I wouldn't wish to do anything to upset anyone if I knew it would.'

'Of course we'll go by ship,' said Igor, quite warmly for him. 'As you say, it has certain advantages over road travel, and I dare say I shall do well enough on a large ship on a calm river—it's these little cockle-shells bouncing about on great waves which I find distressing, and I've always recovered fairly quickly before so I doubt if I'll ever actually succumb enough to require burial at sea. Unless anyone else is prone to seasickness, that is?'

'Good heavens, no!' Maxim sounded quite shocked, unaware of or ignoring the fact that many of the most illustrious seamen were sufferers.

'I don't know,' Mila replied honestly. 'I've never been on . . . in a ship.' (Varya's habit of correcting that particular solecism was catching.)

'Our luggage is to go aboard after luncheon,' Igor observed. 'Perhaps you will be kind enough to instruct your maid or valet accordingly. I assume we are going to church this morning? In that case, it's time we were off.'

The bells of the various churches in the town had been clanging and clashing in the usual unmelodious Russian fashion for some fifteen minutes, so they hastened to collect their hats and set off. Maxim had particularly requested that they might go to the church of St Nikolai, the patron saint of sailors as well as of the Russian people, and they found that a large number of other members of the sea-going fraternity of the town had had the same idea. The church was large, as one would expect in a port, but it was crowded with worshippers, most of them men, and nearly all either in uniform or wearing the sort of clothes that Mila associated with seamen. There were very few other females present, but the men seemed pleased to see ladies in what was clearly 'their' church, and Varya and Mila were enthusiastically waved and beckoned forward until they were right at the front (there are no seats in a Russian church). Mila found it a little embarrassing, but Varya thoroughly enjoyed the attention, and smiled prettily on bearded lower-deck men and handsome young officers with charming impartiality.

Luncheon was taken in the rest-house, and the final plans for the rest of the journey were made with the *jäger*, who was to see his charges safely aboard and settled in to *Chaika*, and then continue by road to Kherson with the two coaches, their drivers and the grooms, taking the route *via* Melitopol as the road was better that way, having been built for the convenience of Field-Marshal Potemkin and kept in repair ever since.

The baggage and servants went aboard during the early afternoon, and the four travellers followed a little later, driving down to the quay in the hired carriage with the *jäger* up behind with the groom. The ship, having already been loaded, was not alongside the quay, but anchored out in the river. The captain was on the lookout for his passengers, and sent what Maxim called the captain's barge to fetch them, although to Mila it looked like a large rowing-boat and not a barge at all. She stepped down into it very gingerly, thinking it already over-full with four oarsmen on the thwarts and a man with a boathook in the bows, and another in the stern steering. There was, in fact, plenty of room for five passengers, provided they sat still, and the few hundred yards out to the ship was accomplished at a cracking pace, the sailors obviously pleased to be able to show off before a real naval officer.

Once alongside the ship, even Varya was aghast at the wall of wood which seemed to rise to a great height above them, and the rope-ladder which was apparently the only way up, but the coxswain of the boat called up to some invisible confederate on high, and a stout chair came swinging down suspended in a cat's cradle of ropes, and first Mila and then Varya soared up to the deck in style, finding on arrival that the contraption was worked by three sailors with a block and tackle. Maxim, meanwhile, went up the ladder as if he had been doing it all his life, which he had, of course, at least from the age of seven. Igor followed without any apparent hesitation, and the *jäger* was in honour bound to do the same.

The Captain, a large square-rigged man with a mahogany face and hair bleached white by sun and salt, was on deck with his officers to greet them. This was a merchantmen, not a warship, but the officers wore dark blue Navy-style coats and trousers, and stiff-brimmed shallow crowned hats, and the crew were dressed in striped jerseys and canvas trousers, not unlike naval ratings. Even Maxim, who looked about him with exceptionally sharp eyes, could see nothing to find fault with in the men or the ship, which had holystoned decks, pipeclayed fancy ropes, polished brass and neatly tarpaulined hatch-covers, just like a man-of-war.

The Captain presented his First, Second and Third Officers and then conducted the passengers to their quarters, which consisted of three cabins on either side of the ship at the stern. On the port side there was one for the two maids and a larger one each for Mila and Varya, with a similar arrangement on the starboard side for the gentlemen and their valets. Between the two sets, right across the stern of the ship, was a large cabin furnished as a dining-room, with four comfortable armchairs fastened to the deck in a group by the wide transom window, which gave a fine view of whatever was behind the ship.

The *jäger* enquired if they approved of their accommodation, and having received an enthusiastic affirmative, even from Igor, he wished them a pleasant voyage, expressed a hope that they would all meet again safely in Kherson, and departed.

Mila went to her cabin to settle herself in, and took a liking to it at once. It had a square window instead of a porthole, and the bed was a box-like bunk along the side of the ship, which she found very comfortable when she tried it. Moreover, she could hear the river lapping against the timbers, and the sun on the water sent a dappled, rippling reflection through the window on to what Maxim later said was called the deckhead. There was a large cupboard with shelves against one wall ('bulkhead', again according to Maxim), with a washstand beside it, the jug, basin and other fitments each having a shaped compartment in the table-top to sit in so that they would not slide off when the ship heeled. On the opposite side was a table which could be used as a desk or a dressing-table, with a mirror above it and a fixed chair before it. The cabin was only about ten paces in length in either direction, and the fittings were very simple, but Mila thought it more comfortable and homely than any of the inns or rest-houses they had stayed in on the journey.

The passengers dined with the captain and his three officers that evening, in a cabin as large as their own dining-room ('saloon', Maxim said) and immediately above it, and it soon emerged that the Captain was the only officer with more than a dozen words of French, so the conversation was in Russian. This was quite convenient for all the passengers except Varya, who could manage only a few halting sentences full of mistakes, the speaking of Russian being discouraged at the Smolny.

As it happened, this was just as well, as the Captain expressed surprise that a non-military gentleman, let alone two ladies, should be going to the Black Sea coast now, when a great many other ladies and non-military gentlemen were hurrying away from it. 'What will you do,' he asked, 'when the war with Turkey starts and their Fleet arrives off Kherson?'

'I doubt very much if it will come to war,' said Igor. 'And if it does, the Sublime Porte would be well advised not to send any ships within a hundred *versty* of Kherson! I'd back my niece here against the Sultan and all his Janissaries—she'd soon have them all running back to their harems!'

The officers grinned and looked at Varya, whose expressive eyes had already had a devastating effect on the Third Officer, an impressionable young fellow. Maxim gravely nodded agreement with Igor, and said, 'She'd probably man a battery of guns herself and sink the lot,' and also looked at her.

'You're talking about me!' she said accusingly. 'What are you saying?'

'Only that if the Sultan arrives in Kherson, we'll give you to him to bribe him to go away,' Igor replied kindly in French.

'She'd be Sultan herself within a year, and open the Bosphorus to our warships!' Maxim said in Russian. 'Shall we write to the Emperor and suggest it?'

'We are taught at the Smolny,' Varya said primly, 'that it's very bad manners to talk about a person in that person's presence in a language which the person doesn't understand.'

'It serves you right for not bothering to learn your own language,' Igor replied good-humouredly.

'Oh, are you speaking Ukrainian, then?' she riposted. Igor's private little smile appeared briefly, and he bowed an acknowledgment of the hit, and turned the conversation to graver and more general subjects.

Mila found it a pleasant novelty to sleep in a ship, with the current chuckling along the timbers by her bed, which rocked gently in a soothing fashion. She slept well, and woke in the morning to find that the sound of the water had changed to a hissing, rushing noise, the timbers were creaking rhythmically, and everything was leaning to one side. The ship had sailed just after midnight, and when she had quickly washed and dressed and run up on deck, staggering at first until she adjusted to the sloping decks and the slight roll of the ship, she found that Alexandrovsk and Khortitsa had disappeared, and the ship was sailing amid islands of various sizes and shapes, all but the smallest clothed with a rich verdure of trees and shrubs, as were the river banks on either side, The vegetation looked almost tropical in its lushness after the sun-scorched aridity of the steppe-land which they had crossed between Novomoskovsk and Alexandrovsk.

Varya was already on deck, leaning over the side and watching the white water running along the ship's side. She turned as Mila stopped beside her, and exclaimed, 'Isn't this exciting? The sailors let me climb up the rope-laddery things that hold the masts up . . . Only a little way,' she added, seeing the look on Mila's face as she glanced up at the rigging. 'We're having to go from one side of the channel to the other in a zig-zag, because the wind is blowing up the river. Maxim says it's called "tacking". See, we're almost into shallow water, and we'll turn in a moment!'

There was a shout from the poop-deck at the stern of

the ship, and a rush of sailors to slacken ropes on one side, and to haul them tight on the other, and the ship came about neatly and headed back across the channel, making a little more distance downstream by following a slanting course on the new tack.

'Where is Maxim?' Mila asked after they had watched the manoeuvre with interest, if not much understanding, admiring the skill with which it had been carried out.

'Up there on the poop-thing with the Captain,' Varya replied. 'I thought the Navy and merchantmen didn't get on, but Maxim said some complimentary things about the ship and the crew, and now he and the Captain are great friends! A lot of naval officers look down on merchant ones and think they don't know anything, and I'm glad Maxim isn't like that. He told the Captain that he was looking forward to learning some useful things.'

'I thought you couldn't understand Russian?' Mila said suspiciously.

'Oh!' Varya looked disconcerted for a moment, then admitted, 'I can understand it fairly well, but I can't speak it properly, that's all. Don't tell Uncle Igor, will you?'

Mila thought of the occasions when Igor had spoken to her in Russian in case Varya might be able to hear what he was saying, and felt that she could not keep the information from him if such an occasion arose again, and said, 'I may find it necessary to tell him at some time, but I won't volunteer the information unnecessarily.'

'Good!' said Varya, smiling happily about her and dazzling a couple of impressionable sailors near by. 'Let's go down to breakfast—I'm quite famished!'

Despite the stiff breeze, the sun was powerful enough to make the open deck quite uncomfortably hot when the passengers went on deck after breakfast, but the Captain had arranged for an awning to be put up to give them some shade, and some chairs and a table were set out under it so that they could sit in comfort and watch the passing scenery and shipping, taking an occasional stroll about the deck for exercise. Maxim returned to the poop, where he was in earnest discussion with the Captain most of the time, and Igor sat reading a book in silence for a couple of hours, but then he said he thought he would go down to his cabin for a while.

Mila looked at his face as he stood up, and said, 'Are you not well? Can I get you anything?' For he had gone an odd greenish-white colour.

'Apart from a piece of firm dry land, I think not, thank you,' he replied with a wan imitation of his usual ironic tone. 'I'll go and lie down. Perhaps the wind will change, or drop before long, or the ship run aground. Don't be concerned—I shall be better before long.'

'Oh dear!' said Varya, showing a proper concern. 'Poor Uncle Igor! He looked quite peculiar, didn't you think, Mila? I expect Yevgeny will know what to do for him, but I feel quite guilty, making him come on the ship. I didn't realise that being seasick was like that—I thought one just—well—vomited a little, you know— but he looked really ill. I think I'll ask Maxim . . .' She got up and sped across the deck to the poop-ladder and called to Maxim from the foot of it, apparently knowing that she might not go up it uninvited without Giving Offence to a catastrophic degree.

Mila, who had a vague recollection of having heard of this taboo somewhere, thought abstractedly that Varya must have collected information about the Navy and the sea like a squirrel, shut up in the Smolny, so far away from the father she could hardly remember. She felt a great deal of pity and sympathy for her, realising a little of what she must have felt, abandoned by one parent and forbidden to communicate with the other, and she said a silent prayer that Varya might find all that she hoped for in her reunion with her father.

Maxim, meanwhile, had condescended to respond to Varya's call, and joined her for a few minutes at the foot of the ladder, inclining his head gravely to listen as she spoke earnestly, gesturing with her hands, her large, expressive eyes on his face. Then he said something which appeared to reassure her, and returned to the poop-deck.

Varya came back to her seat, and reported that Maxim said it sounded like a typical case of seasickness, and that her uncle would be better as soon as he got his sea-legs, whatever they were. 'Apparently there isn't anything one can do to help, and it's too late to change our minds and go by road. He said that Uncle Igor would have insisted on going overland if he'd been very concerned about being ill.'

'That's true,' Mila replied. 'After all, he's taken a firm line on several things since we left Moscow, and you did offer to give up the idea of the ship if he'd rather.'

'Yes, so I did.' Varya looked comforted. 'It's odd, isn't it—I feel quite well—Very well, in fact. I find it exhilarating, and I'm sure Maxim does too—he's quite lively and bright-eyed, as if he's only happy near water—like a frog! How are you?' She looked anxiously into Mila's face.

'Quite well, thank you,' Mila assured her. 'I know what you mean. It really is exciting, being on a ship—in, I mean!' Both ladies glanced up at Maxim, who had now taken the wheel and was steering the ship, with the Captain nodding approvingly at his elbow. 'I do hope your uncle soon recovers, though.'

'Perhaps, if he lies down quietly, it will go off,' Varya said hopefully. 'He'll probably be better by dinner-time.'

But he was not. In fact, Maxim reported that he was unable to sit up because of vertigo, but the Lieutenant seemed unconcerned and spoke as if the symptoms were all perfectly normal. He did, however, add a sympathetic, 'It must be a very distressing business, especially for anyone who must go to sea. I'm most thankful that I don't suffer!'

'Is there really nothing we can do?' Mila asked, feeling unhappy to think that Igor should be indisposed, and frustrated at being unable to help him.

'No, not really.' Maxim replied. 'Yevgeny seems to know the ropes. He's best left alone.'

By morning, however, Yevgeny was incapacitated as well, and, according to Maxim's valet, was lying on his bunk moaning and talking of death by turns, and Igor was no better. Mila sat under the awning on deck, watching islands, trees, boats and ships all morning, her frustration and anxiety bottled up inside her and building a dangerously high pressure until, not long after luncheon, she said to Varya, who was still entranced by the experience of being aboard ship, 'The sun is dazzling on the water and making my eyes ache. I think I'll go downstairs for a while.'

'Below,' Varya corrected knowledgeably. 'I say, you're not going to be ill, are you?' She looked anxious.

'No,' Mila reassured her. 'I feel very well. It's just that I'd like to be out of the glare for an hour or so. I'll come back presently.' And she went off, leaving Varya under the care of Marfa and Darya, who were sitting under a smaller awning near by, doing some sewing and talking to Maxim's valet, Mitya.

It was quiet in the passenger area, for there was rarely any reason for any of the crew to go there. Mila hesitated at the bottom of the companion-ladder and listened. The ship's timbers creaked, and there was the faint sound of a voice, which she identified as Yevgeny's, moaning and muttering in French—mostly swearing, as far as she could make out. Otherwise, there was not a sound, and

she knew that Varya, Maxim and the other servants
were on deck.

Swiftly she moved to the door of Igor's cabin and
knocked softly. A voice inside said something unin-
telligible, which she suspected was, 'Go away!', but
she opened the door and slipped inside, closing it
soundlessly behind her.

The cabin was a mirror-image of her own, except that
the clothes and other belongings hanging or lying around
were masculine. Igor was lying flat on his back on the
bunk, minus his coat, cravat and boots, but otherwise
fully dressed, with his eyes closed and his face still very
white, but no longer with the frightening greenish tinge.
It was beaded with sweat, and his hair, usually so
smooth, was wet-looking and curling.

'What do you want?' he asked in Russian, without
moving or opening his eyes.

'I—I wondered . . .' Mila began nervously. His eyes
opened and he turned his head to look at her, frowning,
then tried to sit up, but she said quickly, 'No—lie still! I
only wondered if you needed anything.'

He resumed his former position, looking up at the
deckhead, but a scrap of cobweb up there was swinging
with the roll of the ship, so he closed his eyes again. 'I
don't think so, thank you,' he said.

'I thought—as Yevgeny is ill too . . .'

'Yes. A fine pair, are we not?'

Mila looked round, desperate to do something for
him, and caught sight of the water-jug and a clean towel
on the wash-stand. She picked up the towel, dipped a
corner in the cool water, and gently bathed his face with
it.

'Thank you,' he said, sounding oddly detached. Then,
after a pause, 'It was kind of you to come.'

Mila felt utterly wretched and very near to dissolv-
ing into tears, for it had taken courage to break with

convention and risk giving away her feelings for him by coming to his cabin, and she had so much longed to do something to help him, but he was speaking to her as if he hardly knew her and was too busy thinking of something else to bother with her.

'You're sure there's nothing I can do, or fetch, for you?' she asked miserably, almost all her concentration fixed on the necessity to prevent herself from crying.

His lips twitched in a faint shadow of his little private smile, and he quoted a couple of lines from an old Russian soldiers' song,

'Kiss me goodbye,
Leave me to die.'

As if she were sleepwalking, Mila leaned forward to kiss his cheek, taking him literally in her fog of unhappiness. At that moment the ship came about on the other tack, pitching her forward slightly until the side of the bunk prevented her falling any further, and jerking her into consciousness of what she was doing, just as the kiss landed squarely on his mouth. She fled in total confusion, barely remembering to shut the door after her, and took refuge in her own cabin, her heart racing and her face crimson with horror to think that she had actually gone into a man's room and kissed him! She was unaware, of course, that Igor's eyes had opened abruptly as her lips touched his, and he was now sitting up on his bunk looking incredulous and puzzled by turns, his vertigo quite forgotten.

It was some time before Mila was calm enough to go back on deck, and, indeed, she would not have gone at all if she had not expected that Varya would come to look for her. As there was no possibility that anyone other than Igor could know what she had done, she was able to behave quite normally, and join with amusement in the Russian-speaking lesson which the two maids were giving Varya.

When she woke in the morning, she was almost immediately aware that something had changed, for the ship was no longer rolling or pitching, but riding smoothly and almost on an even keel. She looked out of the window and found that *Chaika* was no longer zig-zagging across the channel like a romping dog, but proceeding demurely along the right-hand side of the river, and it was the vessels going upstream which were having to tack, so she deduced that the wind had changed.

She was greatly relieved when Igor appeared at break-fast, looking quite his normal ironic self, but her immediate reaction on seeing him was one of confusion and embarrassment. He bade her 'Good morning', however, in his usual courteous fashion, and gave no hint that he had any recollection at all of her visit to his cabin. So, after a few uncertain minutes, she concluded that either he had been too ill to realise that she was there at all, or he was going to pretend that he had forgotten. Then her attention was distracted by Varya saying that she would like to climb up to the main-top to see the view.

Mila had no idea what the main-top might be, but Maxim, of course, knew very well, and said flatly, 'You'll do no such thing!'

'I don't see why not!' Varya argued. 'Even the youngest sailors positively run up there several times a day, with the greatest ease!'

'They know what they're about,' Maxim replied, unimpressed. 'If you try it you'll frighten half the crew into a fit, and give the Captain a seizure! Besides, when you fall, you'll make such a mess on the deck that I doubt if they'll be able to holystone it clean before the ship reaches Sevastopol!'

'Oh, is that where's she's going?' Varya was diverted for a moment. 'I hadn't realised—I thought she was only bound for Kherson. What cargo is she carrying?'

Maxim looked surprisingly put out, and said sharply, 'You've been in the ship two and a half days without finding out where she's bound or what she's carrying? Good heavens!'

'What is she carrying?' Mila asked, sensing that he was trying to avoid answering the question.

Maxim looked even more put out, but, after a brief hesitation, he said, 'Cannon and shot.'

'And?' Igor enquired, his attention caught by Maxim's manner.

'Powder,' he admitted, but added hastily, 'Only a little—not as much as a man-of-war usually carries.' He obviously expected some reaction from the others, but Igor merely nodded and Mila said, 'Of course. The guns wouldn't be much use without.' But Varya returned to the attack and said, 'I don't see why you think I might fall. I've a very good head for heights!'

'Where precisely does my scapegrace niece propose to intrude herself now?' Igor enquired in his most sardonic manner.

'The main-top, sir,' Maxim replied, then seeing that Igor was unenlightened, 'It's the platform half-way up the main-mast.'

'*Angels and ministers of grace defend us!*' Igor quoted in English, with feeling, and added decisively in French, 'No!'

'But Uncle Igor . . .'

'No. *Non, nyet, nein, no!*' Igor replied. He did not raise his voice, or look otherwise than perfectly calm.

Varya scowled rebelliously for a moment, then shrugged and said, 'Oh, well—I'll walk twenty times round the deck instead, then', which she did during the morning, wreaking devastation in the hearts of a number of sailors who encountered the full charm of her eyes and smile.

Mila walked with her for a few turns, and then went

with some trepidation to sit under the awning, for Igor was there, again reading a book, as he had done before his attack of seasickness. He looked up as she took her seat and said, 'Are you enjoying the voyage?'

'Yes, very much. It's far more pleasant than travelling by coach, for there are so many things to see, and one can walk about.'

'And there's no dust,' he added, looking up at a gull which was hovering over the ship's rail. 'They're much bigger birds close to than one realises.'

'I'm sorry you were ill,' Mila felt obliged to say, feeling she must mention the subject for politeness' sake, although she would rather have avoided it. 'Are you really better now?' She glanced covertly at his face, but it was as unrevealing as ever.

'Yes, thank you. I suppose it takes the body some time to adjust to the movement. I felt fairly well last night, and the wind changing completed the cure. Yevgeny's on his feet again, too. We seem to be making good time—the Captain tells me we should reach Kherson in the morning.'

Mila was sorry to think that this pleasant mode of progress would soon end, and, after two and a half weeks of travelling, the idea of being in one place for an indefinite period seemed strange and unsettling. After dinner that evening she went back to the deck and stood for a while by the bulwark, looking out over the dark water which shone white in the bow-wave of *Chaika* and of the other vessels plying on the river.

The sky was still the wide, remote heaven of the steppe-land, which spread beyond the irrigated lushness of the river-valley to the infinite distance, and the stars burned in the velvet darkness, shaming the little yellow points of man-made light on the ships and the occasional clusters of cabins on the shores and the islands. The night was full of the swish of water and the warm air smelt of tar and water, green growing things, and, very faintly, of salt.

'When I was a child,' Igor said softly, materialising beside her. 'My old nurse said that the stars were the lamps of Heaven, and each one had an angel to tend it. The first time I saw a shooting star, I thought its angel must have dropped it, and I was very worried that he might get into trouble! Thank you for visiting the sick yesterday. It was a kind thought, and much appreciated, although I doubt if I sounded very appreciative at the time!'

Mila, caught unawares by his silent arrival and the way he had switched from one subject to another without any change of tone, blushed in the darkness and murmured something incoherent.

'By this time tomorrow we'll have delivered our charge to her father,' Igor continued. 'I can only pray that neither of them will be disappointed.'

'You think they might be?' Mila asked, wondering why the possibility had not occurred to her.

'They were very fond of one another before, and Varya's mother wrenched them apart very abruptly, without giving either a chance to speak to the other. I fear that they've each built up an idealised picture of the other, and they may find the reality not . . . You know how these things happen.'

'They've not communicated at all?'

'No. Denis respected his wife's wishes—he loved her very dearly and would have done anything to heal the breach, but he was given no opportunity. It's nearly twelve years since he and Varya saw one another, and I doubt if she really remembers him at all, although she's always been anxious to hear about him, as he has been about her. I've had to be something of an agent for them both, passing on odd tidbits of news. I'll admit that I'm nervous about tomorrow.'

'He does know that she's coming?'

'Yes. She wrote to him as soon as she heard that her mother had died, and he wrote to me to say what she intended to do.'

'That's why you were in Moscow when we arrived!' exclaimed Mila, suddenly enlightened. 'You weren't there just to sort out her mother's affairs at all!'

'No. I thought it best to be with her, unobtrusively, just in case . . . I've been responsible for her for a long time, and old habits die hard.'

Some of the crew had gathered on the foredeck after their supper, and fell to entertaining themselves with singing. Varya and Maxim came to join their friends to listen as the sailors sang choruses and solos, most of which seemed to Mila to dwell poignantly on the sorrows of lost or unrequited love, which sent her to bed feeling depressed, as well as anxious about Varya's coming meeting with her father, and her own uncertain future now that the task for which she had been employed was almost done. She tossed restlessly in her bunk, which now seemed hard and lumpy, listening to the eternal sounds of water and timber, and praying for Varya, for Denis Charodyev, for Igor, and most earnestly for some lightening of the dark loneliness to which she would soon have to return.

# CHAPTER
# ELEVEN

At Kherson, on the west bank of the Dnepr just above the point where the estuary opens out to meet the Black Sea, the river was still comparatively narrow. The port and dockyard were protected by an island, which was used as a fort and a quarantine station. The moorings and quays were thick with ships of all sizes, many of them merchantmen unable to sail for the southern shores of the Black Sea or through the Bosphorus to the Mediterranean because the Turkish Fleet was known to be attacking Russian shipping.

The four travellers stood together at the starboard side of the ship, watching with fascinated interest as *Chaika* threaded her way between cutters, pinnaces and numerous other small boats that scurried about from ship to ship, or from ship to shore, making for her berth against the commercial quay, beyond which could be seen the masts of a dozen men-of-war moored in splendid aloofness off the naval dockyard. 'Their yards are across,' commented Maxim, looking at them through his telescope, for they were far more important to him than all the portly merchantmen and small coasters lying between.

'That means they're not ready to sail,' Varya informed them. 'They take the yards down when they're going to stay in harbour. The yards are the cross-pieces of wood that hold the sails up,' she added for the benefit of the less well informed. Maxim lowered his telescope, smiled

quite kindly upon her, and offered to let her look
through it, which Mila felt was either very noble of him
or a symbolic sign that his somewhat dour attitude
towards her was softening a little.

'There's my father!' Varya exclaimed in the hushed
tones of one beholding something long dreamed of and
at last attained.

At first, the other three could not see where she was
looking, but she pointed, still gazing through the telescope, and they made out a group of three or four men in
dark clothes standing together on the commercial quay.

'Are you sure?' asked Igor, shading his eyes and
peering.

Varya did not answer, but pressed close against the
bulwark, staring across the narrowing gap of water until
*Chaika* was close enough for them to see with the
unaided eye that the dark clothes were naval uniforms,
and that one of the men was staring towards them,
holding his cocked hat instead of wearing it, and making
jerky movements as if he might be about to throw
decorum to the winds and wave it violently above his
head.

The ship came neatly alongside the quay, and for one
dreadful moment Mila thought that Varya was about to
leap over the side, but she only leaned over, staring at
the bare-headed naval captain, who stared back at her.
Then Igor touched her elbow and said, 'The gang-plank
is across. You can go to him,' and Varya turned and ran
like a deer, her feet hardly seeming to touch the deck or
the railed gang-plank, and within seconds she was down
on the quay and in her father's arms.

The others followed more sedately, Maxim carefully
handing Mila down the sloping plank as if she were made
of porcelain, and then he unobtrusively abstracted his
telescope from Varya and quietly faded into the background, finding himself outranked by all five of the

reception committee, who were some of Denis
Charodyev's fellow-captains. There was a great deal of
saluting and hand-kissing for Mila and Varya once the
latter's father had collected his scattered wits enough to
perform the presentations, and he even let go of Varya's
hand long enough to embrace his brother and to look
about for Maxim, lurking in the middle distance, to
shake him by the hand and thank him for escorting his
daughter safely to Kherson.

Knowing that Kherson had existed as a town for only a
little over forty years, Mila was amazed to find that it was
not the rather primitive collection of wooden houses that
she had expected but a fine modern city, bearing a strong
resemblance to Petersburg. The streets were broad and
straight, lined with shady trees (very necessary, for the
sun was uncomfortably hot here) and thronged with
people of all kinds, swashbuckling Cossacks, Kalmuks,
Tatars, Ukrainian peasants, soldiers and sailors. Smart
carriages carried not only army and naval officers about
their occasions, but also ladies dressed in the height of
fashion.

There were shops, too, with signs which proclaimed
that imports from France and Italy, as well as Persia and
the silk cities of the east, could be obtained within. The
houses, built of a fine creamy-white stone, were palatial,
and the churches and public buildings, especially the
Naval Academy, would not have looked out of place in
Petersburg or Moscow.

'We've a fine city here,' Denis Charodyev remarked
as they drove along a broad avenue to his official residence, seeing that Mila was gazing about her with
interest. 'Plenty of social life as well. I'm giving a ball
tomorrow night, to let all Kherson see my lovely
daughter!'

'But how did you know we'd be here in time?' asked
Varya, her face alight as she gazed at him.

'Your uncle sent a courier from Alexandrovsk to say which ship you were in, and the semaphore reported your progress down-river,' he replied, smiling.

He was very much like Igor in appearance, with dark eyes, and hair which was not smoothed as firmly as his brother's and so curled as it wished, the same thin-lipped mouth and curved nose, but a far more open expression. His eyes looked directly at other people, and had a bright guilelessness which Mila found attractive, and his smiles were broad and open, not secretive or sardonic. He was taller than Igor as well, and more heavily-built, and, although he was a few years the elder, his fresh-complexioned face looked younger than Igor's. Mila had taken an immediate liking to him, which he seemed to reciprocate, for he chatted away to her in the carriage as though they were old friends, although he was looking at his daughter most of the time as if he could hardly take his eyes off her.

There was the usual formal reception by the house-serfs when they arrived at the house, which was an austerely neo-classical building set back from the street behind railings adorned with anchors and tridents and a carefully groomed shrubbery of flowering bushes. Inside, the decorations also tended to the nautical, with pale tinted walls befriezed by tritons and mermaids, shells and seaweed, and the balustrades of the main staircase and first-floor gallery were formed by twisted ropes upheld on the tails of dolphins, balanced uncomfortably on their chins, all carved in a lustrous pinkish-white marble.

Mila's room, one of the principal guest-rooms on the second floor, had sea-green walls adorned with white plaster nymphs trailing shells and seaweed instead of the more usual flowers, and her windows looked over a terraced garden to a dark mass of trees, above which rose the gilded domes of a church and a veritable forest of ships' masts. The salty tang of the air coming in through the windows reminded her sharply of Petersburg, and the difference between her surroundings there and the luxury, albeit temporary, of her present situation.

Luncheon was served as soon as the new arrivals had been given time to wash and change their clothes, and Mila was conducted to the dining-room by a servant dressed in a close imitation of a naval uniform instead of the usual livery. It was only when she sat down at table with the Charodyev brothers and Varya that she realised that Maxim was no longer with them, having gone to report aboard his ship.

'He'll be here for the ball tomorrow,' Denis assured her. 'Varya's been telling me how lucky she was with her travelling companions, and I must say that I'm extremely grateful to you for coming all this way with her. I gather that you had no particular reason to come to Kherson otherwise?'

'No,' Mila replied, then, feeling that so bald an answer sounded rude, hesitated a moment, then volunteered, 'In fact, Varya employed me to come. Perhaps she forgot to tell you?'

'Employed?' Denis looked taken aback. 'You mean, she's paying you?'

'No,' Igor put in smoothly. 'You are, actually! Varya was, to begin with, but I thought the arrangement unsuitable, so I changed it. I trust you've no objection?'

'No—No, of course not,' Denis replied absently. He continued to look puzzled, and there were obviously a number of questions hovering on his lips which he did not quite like to ask, but, after an awkward pause, Igor put everyone out of their apprehension.

'Mila is in the unfortunate position of having married against her father's wishes, for which he disowned her.'

At this point Denis looked in amazement first at Igor and then at Mila, with dawning comprehension written all over his face, and then nodded once; but Mila knew that he had jumped to the right conclusion and was grateful to him for his silence.

'And then,' Igor continued without the slightest sign to show that he had seen this small pantomime, 'her husband, who was in the Army, was killed in battle, leaving her with only a small pension. I think that clarifies the situation?'

'Yes. Of course. Quite so,' Denis said, obviously casting around for some tactful way of continuing the conversation. 'Er—which regiment was—er—your husband in?' He actually managed to sound as if that was the only question he wished to ask.

'The Akhtirsky Hussars,' Mila replied.

'Ah, a Ukrainian regiment! Was he one of us?'

'No. He was French.'

'Is Akhtirsky in the Ukraine, then?' Varya asked. 'Well, that makes him an honorary Ukrainian, and Mila too, doesn't it?' This was so clearly intended as a compliment that Mila acknowledged it as such with a smiling little bow, and the conversation, steered smoothly by Igor, moved on to less dangerous ground.

Igor's fears about this longed-for meeting between Varya and her father proved to be groundless. It was clear from the start that father and daughter were in accord about everything. They laughed at the same jokes, agreed about the same things, and generally behaved like old and close friends.

That evening a number of Denis's closer friends and their wives dined with him to meet Varya, and Mila, who had expected at least a subtle change in her own treatment now that he knew her true position, was pleasantly surprised to find that it did not appear to make the slightest difference. She was introduced to the guests (who were all naval officers, apart from the commander of the garrison and the Military Governor) as a family friend who had accompanied Varya on her journey, and would be staying 'for some time'.

Later, when Mila had just climbed into bed, Varya arrived, perched herself on the end of the bed, and said, 'It's all just like a fairytale, isn't it? I was a little afraid that it might not be, because it's such an age since I saw Father, and I wasn't sure if I really remembered him, or only thought I did. But he's exactly as I thought he would be, and he seems to like me quite as much as I like him, so it's all completely marvellous! Did you notice, though, that all his friends seem to be married?'

Mila cautiously admitted that this appeared so, and Varya plunged on happily, 'I rather thought he might have married again, you know, although I suppose Uncle Igor would have told me if he had. He could have done, of course, as soon as Mamma took her final vows, and I'm quite surprised that he hasn't. I shall have to see what I can do about it!'

The idea of Varya doing something about the matter gave Mila a sharp twinge of concern for poor Denis, who had still to discover his daughter's juggernaut proclivities, and the concern turned to alarm when Varya, with one of those sidelong glances so reminiscent of her uncle, said consideringly, 'I rather think you would suit me very well as a stepmother!'

'Varya!' Mila expostulated. 'It's not twelve hours since I met your father for the first time, and—and—Oh, really!'

'Well, if you don't care for the idea . . .' Varya sounded quite soothing. 'I just thought that if I'm to have a stepmother, it would be pleasant to have one I can get along with . . . or an aunt, for that matter . . .' Her lashes dropped demurely as her lips curved in that same little private smile, and Mila looked at her with a hollow feeling in her stomach, wondering how much the girl had guessed.

'I'm only teasing,' Varya said blithely. 'Except, of course, that if either idea appeals to you, I'm completely with you! Now, you've almost made me forget what I came for! About tomorrow night—have you something to wear?'

'Yes, thank you,' Mila replied, touched that the girl should have thought about the matter in the midst of all her excitement. 'One of the frocks Tatya Petrovna gave me is just the thing, I think.'

'That's all right, then. I don't expect you've much jewellery, though . . .' It was a tactful way of expressing it, for she must have guessed that Mila had none, apart from a tiny pair of ear-studs and her marriage ring. 'Uncle Igor says I may give you this.'

She produced a flat leather case from the midst of her frills and furbelows and put it on the bed-cover close to Mila. 'That's what I'm supposed to say, actually, but really he bought it in Alexandrovsk, only don't tell him I told you. I suppose he expects you to think it was part of Mamma's jewels, although it would seem very odd that he should happen to be carrying it about with him, and in a brand-new case at that!'

Mila opened the case and found inside a very simple necklace of single diamonds mounted in gold, with an eight-pointed star of gold, pavé-set with diamonds, suspended from it.

'It's very beautiful,' she said. 'But I can't possibly accept it! I think he meant that you might lend it to me.'

'We won't argue about it,' Varya said dismissively. 'Borrow it if you prefer, but don't try to give it back, or I shall be Mortally Offended! Oh, I'm so sleepy! It's all the excitement, you know.' She gave a large, inelegant yawn, swooped over Mila to kiss her in a flurry of lace and ribbons, uttered the customary blessing and was gone. Mila was left with the blazing star on its stream of diamonds hanging from her fingers, reminding her vividly of the night sky over the steppes, and the lights twinkling on the surface of the river. How clever of Igor to find it, and how thoughtful of him to see that, should Varya wish to give her a present, there would be something available that she could not help but long to possess, although it was, of course, far too valuable to accept. She would wear it for the ball and then return it afterwards, perhaps to Igor rather than to Varya, who might not understand how impossible it was for her to keep it.

There was much exploring to do the next day, for Denis wished to take the new arrivals about the town to see the earth rampart of the early settlement, the grandiose tomb of Potemkin (empty now, since his body had been ejected from it by order of Paul I), the Art Gallery, the Naval Academy and, above all, the ships. That occupied the morning; in the afternoon Varya wished to inspect the shops, where she made several purchases but was by no means extravagant, and her father's own ship, to which they were rowed out in the captain's barge, and piped aboard with the ceremony due to an admiral, save that there were no saluting guns.

There followed an hour of climbing up and down companion ladders and peering into the innermost recesses of the ship, apart from the magazine, which Varya knew she might not enter, and then tea was served in the great cabin before the visitors returned ashore to rest before the ball. The whole crew turned out to line the bulwarks and man the rigging to cheer the Captain's daughter, which attention so overwhelmed her that she was actually silent for quite ten minutes.

Denis Charodyev had not invited any of the ball-guests to dine beforehand, so an early dinner was taken *en famille*, and the ladies retired to change after it. Mila's

choice of gown was the most elaborate of Tatya's gifts, a
charming leaf-green shantung over a lighter silk slip,
with a trail of cream roses embroidered diagonally
across its belled skirt. Its modest décolletage was just
sufficient to frame the diamond star, and she wore no
other ornaments—indeed, she had none. There was a
matching reticule on a silk cord with the frock, and a pair
of elbow-length gloves from the bundle given her in
Moscow by Varya completed her toilette. Marfa had
brushed and polished her hair and arranged it deftly *à la
Madonne*, and was just wishing aloud that she had some
feathers or a diamond comb to fasten above the upswept
back when a footman arrived with a box containing some
tiny cream rosebuds mounted on a real tortoiseshell
comb, and seemed woodenly incapable of understanding Mila's questions in French or Russian about their
provenance.

Varya came whisking in as the comb was being put in
place, radiant in a crêpe frock of elegant simplicity in the
delicate pale pink of a seashell, with Tatya's string of
little pearls about her neck. There was a wreath of pink
jasmine round her chignon, from which her hair fell in
ringlets, forming a happy compromise between being
Up and being not Up, suited to her situation of being not
exactly Out, but having a ball given in her honour.

'Oh, you look just the thing!' she exclaimed, darting
about to view Mila from all angles. 'Except that Uncle
Igor forgot the ear-rings—here they are!' And she produced another case—a small one this time, in which
nestled a pair of little stars to match the pendant, which
were put into Mila's ears despite her attempts to protest.

'Will I *do*?' Varya demanded, twirling round. 'Darya
said not a *colour*, exactly, but I didn't want *white*, so this
seemed a good compromise.' Mila inspected her and
gravely agreed that she would *do* very well, and they set
off together downstairs to the *piano nobile*, where Varya

joined her father to receive their guests, and Mila went into the ballroom to find a suitably unobtrusive place for herself among the chaperons.

It was not a vast apartment on Petersburg's scale, but it was ample enough for sixty or so couples, and was elegantly, though nautically, decorated with plain white walls divided by fluted pilasters, topped by gilded demi-ships like those on the Rostral Columns in Petersburg, instead of the more usual acanthus leaves or rams' horns. Between the pilasters were windows on to the garden on one side, facing long mirrors in gilded frames topped by sea-horses as a change from dolphins. These ubiquitous mammals, however, appeared in the eight chandeliers which hung from the coved ceiling, cast in crystal and forming the branches, twenty to each chandelier. The floor was inlaid with a selection of assorted fish, swimming quite naturally in the wood, and including a sinister-looking octopus cunningly fashioned in ebony.

'This is a remarkably fishy house!' Igor's voice said in her ear as she stood just inside the doorway, looking about her. 'May I claim a dance or two, Mila, before your programme is full?'

'Oh, but I'm here to chaperon Varya, not to dance!' she exclaimed, wondering if he was being sarcastic, but he twitched her pristine card from her fingers and said 'Nonsense!', so she continued to look about the room, wondering if anyone else would ask her to dance or if she would end the evening with only the one set of scribbled initials on her card.

The room was filling up with as elegant a company as one would expect to see in Petersburg, except that most of the men were in the sober dark blue of the Navy and only a few in the more colourful and varied plumage of the Army. The orchestra, protected by a barricade of flowers, was tuning itself at one end of the floor, and the wall at the opposite end was dominated by the only picture in the room—a vast portrait of the Emperor on horseback, quite life-size. Mila, who was observant, noticed that its elaborate frame bore the monogram of Catherine the Great, the present Emperor's grandmother, and she wondered what had happened to the original portrait which must have occupied the frame.

'As if Alexander Pavlovich isn't tall enough in the flesh, without putting him on a great horse!' Igor remarked, following the direction of her gaze and handing back her programme. She glanced down at it and found that his neat IGC monogram was written three times, one of them against the supper dance, and she felt this was very kind of him.

More guests were coming in, and Mila moved away from the entrance, thinking to find a place on one of the little gilt chairs by the windows, which were open, for it was already very warm in the ballroom. To her surprise Igor went with her, looking about him, nodding a greeting to an acquaintance here and there, and several times drawing Mila to a halt while he presented one or another of them to her. Gradually her programme began to collect a sprinkling of other initials, which made her wonder apprehensively if she would be able to remember how to dance, for the classes she had attended all those years ago seemed very remote.

'It's just occurred to me,' she suddenly heard herself saying quietly. 'This is my first ball!' Then, realising too late what she had said, she bit her lip and looked at Igor, wondering if he had heard.

He obviously had, for he was looking at her with unusual directness, and frowning, but before he could say anything, Maxim appeared before them, clearly in very good spirits, wished them 'Good evening', and relieved any anxiety they might have had on his behalf by telling them that he was actually to serve as fourth lieutenant in Captain Charodyev's own ship. He had found his brother-officers amenable and much impressed by his arrival in company with the Captain's daughter. He also begged the favour of Mila's hand for the first polonaise, which had just struck up, and she had the pleasant distinction of being the second lady, after Varya—who was dancing with her father—to take the floor.

The first hour or so of the ball passed away most enjoyably for her. She managed to remember the steps of the various dances, and had far more partners than she had expected, so that she did not have to sit among the wallflowers and chaperons at all. Even when she was not dancing there were several gentlemen whom she had already met who seemed happy to engage her in conversation, although they were too old or otherwise disinclined to dance.

Disaster arrived completely unexpectedly. Her first dance with Igor had just ended—an exhilarating waltz in which her feet hardly seemed to touch the floor at all, and the delight of being so close to him had banished for a few brief, spell-bound minutes the heartache of knowing that he was lost to her for ever. They were standing poised at the edge of the floor, just completing their respective bow and curtsy, when her eyes were somehow drawn beyond Igor's sober black-clad figure to someone coming purposefully towards her with Denis—a painfully familiar, colourful figure in the brown, yellow-collared dolman and vivid red pelisse of the Akhtirsky Hussars.

She caught her breath in a sobbing gasp, which made Igor look at her in surprise, then he swung round to see what had startled her as his brother and the Hussar came to a halt beside him.

Mila felt as if her whole body was about to break into a

violent trembling as she looked up at the Hussar's face. He was tall, fair-haired, handsome, and his blue eyes regarded her with interest, but also with some puzzlement, and she stared at him in mesmerised horror as Denis presented him—she did not take in his name at all—and then she heard the fateful words, 'And this is Countess Ludmilla Levovna de Romarin, whose husband served in your regiment.'

'De Romarin? Étienne de Romarin?' The young man had a pleasant voice, but it sounded like the knell of doom to Mila, and his expression became even more perplexed as she nodded speechlessly. 'But I knew him very well! He was your husband? I'd no idea that he was married!'

'Perhaps you knew him before his marriage,' Denis suggested. He had the look of a man who had intended to give someone a pleasant surprise, and suddenly found it showing signs of being a social gaffe of the most disastrous kind, but to Mila his voice sounded very distant and quite unidentifiable.

'Hardly!' the Hussar protested. 'Why, after he returned from his secondment—let me see, it was after we came back from when we were supposed to fight the Austrians, but nothing came of it because Bonaparte beat them at Wagram, and all we did was gallop about Galicia—yes, during the next spring—1810, it would be—and I remember he arrived just in time for Easter . . . From then on, we were in the same squadron. There were four of us, always inseparable—we shared a billet, rode together, messed together, got drunk together, fought together—you know how it is . . . until Dresden . . . That was three years we lived in each other's pockets, and I'll swear I never heard him mention that he had a wife. Isn't it extraordinary? Why, he came home with me a couple of times when we both had leave, because he said he hadn't anywhere to go, and I know he never received any letters, for I used to feel sorry for him when the mail arrived . . .'

At this point it seemed to occur to the Hussar that he was trampling heavily on some very unstable ground, and his puzzled recollections were hardly fitting for a meeting with his dead comrade's widow. He broke off suddenly, and there was an uncomfortable silence. Mila felt as if she had been turned to ice, unable to move or speak, unable to take her eyes from the Hussar's embarrassed and perplexed face. The orchestra was playing a lively mazurka in some infinitely remote place, and the dancers seemed to be spinning about dizzily in the distant background. She wondered vaguely if she might be about to faint.

'I think,' said Igor's calm voice, 'that this is my dance, if you'll excuse my interrupting you?'

'Oh—yes—of course.' The Hussar grasped this lifeline in a tight corner. 'I'm so sorry—I didn't realise! Pray carry on—perhaps we can—er—talk later . . . ?'

'Oh, indeed!' Denis also plunged in to the rescue. 'Plenty of time. I'd also like you to meet . . .' and he took the Hussar away without unseemly haste.

A warm hand pierced Mila's frozen state, clasping her arm just above the elbow, and she was gently propelled along the edge of the ballroom, gradually becoming aware of what was happening as her feet returned to her control and the frightening numbness began to wear off. Igor took her firmly through a door that she had not noticed before, and along a deserted corridor. They stopped at a door, which he opened, and he put his head inside for a quick glance round and murmured, 'This will do,' and pushed her inside.

She advanced into the middle of the room—a small salon, pleasantly furnished with a few upholstered chairs and a table—and turned to look at Igor in some surprise as her senses returned to normal and she realised that he was turning the key in the lock.

'I think a little conversation has become essential.' He spoke rather sternly, putting the key on the table as he walked towards her. 'I've locked the door to discourage interruption, not with any evil intent. The key's there if you wish to leave.'

Mila made no reply but simply waited, standing and looking at him, wondering what was coming next.

'Sit down,' he said, and put his hands on her shoulders, steered her to a chair and pushed her down into it, all quite gently, then took a seat facing her, crossed his legs, steepled his hands before his chin and contemplated her for a few moments.

At length he said, 'I should very much like to know how it is that a man could elope with a young lady in the summer of '09, then rejoin his regiment the following Easter, and thereafter make no mention of the fact that he has a wife, even to his closest friends, nor receive any letters, nor, apparently, go home to her for his leave. I don't ask out of idle curiosity, you understand. My interest is genuine.'

Mila bit her lip and stared unseeingly at the embroidered roses on her skirt.

Igor waited, and then continued, 'You may tell me to mind my business if you wish, but I can't help but speculate. You've said several things in the past three weeks which seemed odd enough, but this beats all!'

'It was all a terrible mistake,' Mila said wearily, giving up the struggle to go on pretending. 'He seemed so kind and understanding, so much in love with me, and he listened to everything I said, and treated me as if my opinions mattered. It was that more than anything, I suppose, for no one else ever listened.'

'I'd have been glad to do so,' Igor's voice was low. 'But I could rarely coax you into speaking to me at all.'

'I was afraid of you. What I might have said to you always seemed foolish, and I thought you'd be sarcastic.'

'Was I so great a fool?' he asked musingly. 'Yes, I suppose I was—so busy defending myself that I hardly noticed whom I was attacking. I'm sorry. In that case, I can understand why you fell in love with him—I've always thought it was just his good looks and the Gallic charm.'

'I wanted to love you,' Mila said, hesitating. 'There was something about you . . . But I was afraid too, in case you hurt me. I didn't understand you then, but now I think I do and I realise that I . . . Oh, but that's only what might have been. What really happened was that Étienne flattered me, and he *was* handsome, so it was easier to believe that I loved him.'

'So you ran off with him.'

'Yes. It was a romantic adventure, to slip out of the house in the middle of the night, and drive away in a carriage with him. He bribed the police at the barrier, and we drove all the rest of the night and part of the next day, and then we stopped at a little village church— Étienne had it all arranged—and the priest married us. We went to Petersburg, because Étienne had been seconded there as a riding instructor to the Cadet Corps. He had papers, of course, and he forged my name on them as his wife. He hadn't much money, so we found a cheap room in the Haymarket and lived there.'

'Where Varya found you?' Igor asked, and he winced when she replied 'Yes', as if the thought of her living in such a place was physically painful.

'He said I should write to Father,' Mila went on, 'and beg his forgiveness, tell him that we were happy but for that, which I thought we were! Father didn't reply, so I wrote again and again, and then Étienne wrote as well, but he wouldn't show me his letters and I wondered afterwards if he had made threats. Anyway, none of the letters did any good, for Father sent them back un-opened.

'We waited all through the winter, and it was very hard, for Étienne said he had to pay his share when he went out with his friends, and that left very little money for food or firing. We began to quarrel, and he changed so much that I hardly knew him. He drank, and stayed away from home for days at a time. I began to real-ise what a mistake I'd made, that it wasn't Étienne that I really loved, but . . .'

'But whom?' asked Igor when she hesitated.

'You,' she whispered.

He made no reply, and she dared not look at him. After a moment, she continued, 'One day, towards the middle of Lent, he came home to find another letter sent back, and it was as if his patience snapped! He said he was tired of waiting, and if the "old fool" wasn't going to pay up, he might as well cut his losses!

'It was horrible!' Mila was gazing unseeingly into space, reliving that dreadful day, and again did not see Igor's face, which was, for once, completely unmasked. 'He was a different person by then—arrogant, cold and cruel! He said I was no use to him without a dowry, and if there was to be no money, he didn't want me! Then he said he didn't even consider us to be properly married, for the ceremony was Orthodox, and he was Catholic! Then he packed his bags and left, ignoring me—well, I was terrified! I cried and begged him not to leave me alone. I could hardly understand what was happen-ing! He just knocked me aside, and cursed me for get-ting in his way, and then he left, and I never saw him again.'

Her voice had remained low and matter-of-fact throughout her narrative, and now she simply sat quite still and waited, not knowing what she might expect Igor to do or say.

'Why didn't you write to your father again and tell him the truth? Or even to me?'

'I was ashamed.' The whole tragedy was contained in those words.

'You still wear his ring.' Igor seemed to be groping after trivialities, as if his mind shied away from what he had heard.

'It's my badge of respectability,' she replied bitterly. 'Without it, I couldn't make an honest living. If I didn't have it, I might find myself being made to sweep the Nevsky Prospect—that's what they make the whores do in Petersburg, you know.'

Igor got up, took her right hand from her lap, pulled off the ring, none too gently, then went to the open window and hurled it with all his strength into the darkness of the garden.

'I'd noticed that it left a greenish mark on your finger,' he said grimly. 'I'll give you a true gold one, if you'll let me.'

'Why should you?' she asked dully, hardly taking in what he had said.

'You know damned well why!' He returned from the window and stood over her. 'I still don't understand. That evening in Alexandrovsk, after you fell in the river—I said something clumsy about your need to stop clinging to what was past and beyond recall . . . Do you remember?'

'Yes.'

'You said you couldn't—not yet . . . What did you think I was talking about?'

By now, Mila was beyond concealment. She felt as if she had been stripped bare of every evasion and subterfuge, and there was no difficulty at all in telling the simple truth. 'You were warning me that it was no use going on loving you and hoping, because for you it was over and done with.'

'That's not what I said, or what I meant!'

'But it was clear enough! You said in Moscow that you loved me when . . . then.' She could not be more specific. 'You spoke then of it being in the past, and what you said about Time being a River—that one can't go back—I knew what you meant. That you loved me once, but not any more. Besides, I know that it's Tatya now.'

'Tatya? What has she to do with it?'

'You love her,' Mila said patiently, too numb for the statement to hurt now.

At that moment someone outside tried the door, turning the handle to and fro and shaking it impatiently. Igor said something sharp in Russian and called out, 'Who is it? What do you want?'

'Uncle Igor! Is that you?' came Varya's voice.

Igor went over to the door and said quietly, 'What is it?'

'It's Mila!' the girl replied. 'Father says she was upset about something, and I can't find her anywhere! Have you seen her?'

'Yes. She's here.'

'Oh. Is she all right? Can I see her?'

'No.'

'Can I do anything, then?'

'Yes. Go away.'

'Oh.' Then, as if enlightenment had suddenly dawned, 'Oh, yes! Very well! Good luck!' and there was silence.

Whatever Igor may have made of this last he said nothing about it, but turned back to Mila and said, 'I do not love Tatya Petrovna. I admire and respect her, but I've loved only one female these past twelve years. What I made such a pig's nest of trying to say to you was that I wished you might stop mourning for Étienne and give me a second chance.'

Mila looked at him uncomprehendingly for a moment, and then gradually understanding began to dawn on her as if it emanated from the upright, black-clad figure standing looking at her with an unshuttered face and his whole heart in his dark eyes. For the first time she saw Igor with his defences completely down, and what she saw brought her to her feet, across the room and into his arms, with no clear idea of how she came there.

'Oh, my dear love!' he exclaimed, and his mouth came down on hers in a kiss which was healing, benediction, promise and fulfilment, all in one.

Some unknown time later, which might have been minutes or weeks, the door-handle rattled again, and Varya called urgently, 'I say—I'm sorry, but they've gone out to supper, and Father wants you to come!'

Igor lifted his head and said in a dazed voice, 'Oh, very well!' He pulled himself together with an effort, gave Mila a quick look over and adjusted a curl which had come loose, then straightened his cravat with one hand while he scooped the key from the table with the other, opened the door and ushered her out of the room.

Varya walked sedately along the corridor on his other side as they went towards the supper-room, smiling a little to herself. Then she gave a little skip, and said, 'You'll be married here, won't you? Then I can be bridesmaid, and Father and Maxim can hold the crowns for you, don't you think?'

Igor said nothing, but exchanged a look with Mila and took her hand in a tight clasp.

'It's no use not answering!' Varya said. 'You can't fool me, you know! It's written all over your faces!'

'Minx!' was all the reply her uncle vouchsafed her, but it was said quite affectionately.

As they entered the salon where supper was being served, they found the company seated at small tables, all talking nineteen to the dozen over the delectable food which the footmen had set before them. Denis was standing by a table near the door, the remains of his own meal sitting amid a number of filled wine-glasses, with another in his hand. He was clearly waiting for them, and as soon as they joined him he thumped on the table with the handle of a knife and let out a quarter-deck bellow which, naval discipline being excellent in Kherson, brought silence and attention from all the gentlemen present. Although there was a slower re-action from the ladies, in a few moments every head was turned towards him, and everyone waited to hear him propose the Emperor's health.

Into the expectant silence, Varya's voice dropped with the perfect clarity of a silver bell.

'I say, Father—isn't it capital? Uncle Igor's going to marry Mila!'

# MARCH 85 (UK) HARDBACK TITLES

## ——— ROMANCE ———

| | |
|---|---|
| SOUTHERN SUNSHINE Gloria Bevan | 0 263 10774 4 |
| CAPRICORN MAN Jacqueline Gilbert | 0 263 10775 2 |
| BUSHRANGER'S MOUNTAIN Victoria Gordon | 0 263 10776 0 |
| BIG SUR Elizabeth Graham | 0 263 10777 9 |
| THE OBJECT OF THE GAME Vanessa James | 0 263 10778 7 |
| TAKEN OVER Penny Jordan | 0 263 10779 5 |
| HOSTAGE Madeleine Ker | 0 263 10780 9 |
| ALMOST A BRIDE Maura McGiveny | 0 263 10781 7 |
| DARK OBSESSION Valerie Marsh | 0 263 10782 5 |
| A COMPELLING FORCE Margaret Mayo | 0 263 10783 3 |
| TRUST IN TOMORROW Carole Mortimer | 0 263 10784 1 |
| MODEL OF DECEPTION Margaret Pargeter | 0 263 10785 X |
| THE IRON HEART Edwina Shore | 0 263 10786 8 |
| DOUBLE DECEPTION Kay Thorpe | 0 263 10787 6 |
| EAGLE'S RIDGE Margaret Way | 0 263 10788 4 |
| A ROOTED SORROW Nicola West | 0 263 10789 2 |

##  HISTORICAL ROMANCE

| | |
|---|---|
| THE RIVER OF TIME Dinah Dean | 0 263 10814 7 |
| BEWARE THE CONQUEROR Anne Herries | 0 263 10815 5 |

## DOCTOR NURSE ROMANCE

| | |
|---|---|
| A SURGEON CALLS Hazel Fisher | 0 263 10796 5 |
| PATIENCE AND DR PRITCHARD Lilian Darcy | 0 263 10797 3 |

## LARGE PRINT

| | |
|---|---|
| AN ELUSIVE DESIRE Anne Mather | 0 263 10818 X |
| CLOUDED RAPTURE Margaret Pargeter | 0 263 10819 8 |
| JILTED Sally Wentworth | 0 263 10820 1 |

# Mills & Boon

# APRIL 85 (UK) HARDBACK TITLES

## ───── ROMANCE ─────

| | |
|---|---|
| **Time of Change**  *Rosalind Cowdray* | 0 263 10798 1 |
| **Don't Play Games**  *Emma Darcy* | 0 263 10799 X |
| **A World of Difference**  *Sandra Field* | 0 263 10800 7 |
| **Age of Consent**  *Victoria Gordon* | 0 263 10801 5 |
| **Outcast Lovers**  *Sarah Holland* | 0 263 10802 3 |
| **Time Fuse**  *Penny Jordan* | 0 263 10803 1 |
| **Man Hunt**  *Charlotte Lamb* | 0 263 10804 X |
| **Acapulco Moonlight**  *Marjorie Lewty* | 0 263 10805 8 |
| **Eclipse of the Heart**  *Mary Lyons* | 0 263 10806 6 |
| **Dreams to Keep**  *Leigh Michaels* | 0 263 10807 4 |
| **Lovers in the Afternoon**  *Carole Mortimer* | 0 263 10808 2 |
| **Dare to Trust**  *Anne McAllister* | 0 263 10809 0 |
| **Impasse**  *Margaret Pargeter* | 0 263 10810 4 |
| **Inherit the Storm**  *Valerie Parv* | 0 263 10811 2 |
| **Pelangi Haven**  *Karen van der Zee* | 0 263 10812 0 |
| **A Secret Pleasure**  *Flora Kidd* | 0 263 10813 9 |

## MASQUERADE HISTORICAL ROMANCE

| | |
|---|---|
| **Black Ravenswood**  *Valentina Luellen* | 0 263 10849 X |
| **Spaniard's Haven**  *Lynne Brooks* | 0 263 10850 3 |

## DOCTOR NURSE ROMANCE

| | |
|---|---|
| **Dr Delisle's Inheritance**  *Sarah Franklin* | 0 263 10816 3 |
| **Bachelor of Hearts**  *Leonie Craig* | 0 263 10817 1 |

## LARGE PRINT

| | |
|---|---|
| **Gallant Antagonist**  *Jessica Steele* | 0 263 10821 X |
| **Forbidden Wine**  *Lynsey Stevens* | 0 263 10822 8 |
| **No Alternative**  *Margaret Way* | 0 263 10823 6 |

# 4 Mills & Boon Paperbacks can be yours absolutely FREE.

### Enjoy a wonderful world of Romance....

Passionate and intriguing, sensual and exciting. A top quality selection of four Mills & Boon titles written by leading authors of Romantic Fiction can be delivered direct to your door absolutely **FREE**.

Try these Four Free books as your introduction to Mills & Boon Reader Service. You can be among the thousands of women who enjoy brand new Romances every month **PLUS** a whole range of special benefits.

### THE NEWEST PAPERBACK ROMANCES —
**reserved at the printers for you each month and delivered direct to you by Mills & Boon — POSTAGE & PACKING FREE.**

### FREE MONTHLY NEWSLETTER
**packed with exciting competitions, horoscopes, recipes and handicrafts PLUS information on top Mills & Boon authors.**

### SPECIAL OFFERS
**Specially selected books and bargain gifts created just for Mills & Boon subscribers.**

There is no commitment whatsoever, no hidden extra charges and your first parcel of four books is absolutely free.

Why not send for details now? Simply write to Mills & Boon Reader Service, Dept. HBEP, P.O. Box 236, Thornton Road, Croydon, Surrey CR9 3RU, or telephone our helpful, friendly girls at Mills & Boon on 01-684 2141 and we will send you details about the Mills & Boon Reader Service Subscription Scheme.

### You'll soon be able to join us in a wonderful world of Romance!

Please note: Readers in South Africa write to:-
**Mills & Boon Ltd.,
Postbag X3010, Randburg 2125, S. Africa.**

Readers in North America write to:-
**Harlequin Reader Service,
M.P.O. Box 707, Niagara Falls. NY 14302**